PEACHES AND DREAMS
GREEN VALLEY HEROES BOOK #4

JULIETTE CROSS

www.smartypantsromance.com

For my husband, my true north

CHAPTER 1
~MARLY~

"Holy mother in a manger. Would you look at that tall drink of water?"

I heaved another box closer to me. "Kayla, we don't have time to drool over customers. We've got three more boxes of Peppermint Patty to stack into pyramids."

Popping open the lid, I lifted out two jars of the newest moonshine flavor and set them on the floor next to me.

Though I complained, I actually enjoyed creating fun displays. I was currently contemplating how to get the Peppermint Patties into the shape of a Christmas tree, even though we just passed Halloween yesterday, when Kayla up and abandoned me.

"You've got this, Marly. I'm gonna go see if the red-headed mountain man needs my assistance."

In my peripheral vision, I caught her pushing up her boobs and fluffing her hair. Readying for battle. And while I huffed in exasperation that she was choosing to appease her hormones over helping her favorite co-worker, I waved her off and went back to work.

Normally, I'd be straightening my posture and poking my girls out too to flirt with the hottie who'd just disappeared into the back corner behind the Green Valley Shine merch. But today, I was focused—and distracted. Now that I think about it, that was pretty much my norm. There was just more on my mind today.

I wanted to lose myself in work and dream about my own project, not think about…my father.

I heard Kayla's lilting laughter across the store. After finishing another tier of my masterpiece, I glanced over my shoulder to where she stood among the sweatshirts, a behemoth of a man with his back to me. Not red-headed exactly, I'd call that shade auburn. I squinted, trying to figure out where I knew that vaguely familiar broad-shouldered shape from, when the crash of shattering glass sounded over by the back wall of shelves.

The distinct scent of spicy cinnamon hitting my nostrils told me someone had just broken a jar of Hot Mama Moonshine. After weaving around the shelves, I found a wide-eyed little boy standing over what looked like a murder crime scene. The pool of red was seeping under his left sneaker.

"Uh-oh," I said, shaking my head, my ponytail sliding against my bare neck.

The auburn-haired boy, brown eyes round as saucers somehow got even bigger. "Am I in trouble?"

"Marly!" came Kayla's voice from across the store. "Was that you?"

"Quick," I whisper-yelled and ducked down then reached out my hand to him. "Follow me."

The little boy didn't even think twice. He took my hand like the life-line it was and crept behind the displays and shelves, mimicking my hunched over position. Smart kid. I tugged him to the back where we had a square-shaped bar for visitors and tourists wanting taste-tests. After ducking inside first, he followed me. Then I sat on the wood floor and crisscrossed my legs. He did the same, facing me.

We stared at each other a minute. Then we heard. "Marly?"

I widened my eyes, put a finger to my lips, and gave him a sneaky smile.

"Jake?" came a deep male voice from farther in the store.

The boy sitting in front of me, about eight years old I'd guess, mimicked my expression, complete with devilish smile. Oh, yeah. This kid was definitely my kind of person.

"So, Jake," I whispered now that I knew his name. "Where do you go to school? Green Valley Elementary?"

"Second grade. How'd you know?"

"It's the only elementary school for twenty miles. You seem like a local."

He picked at a loose piece of rubber on the sole of his sneaker. "My cousin Winnie goes to another school in Merryville."

"She does?"

"Yeah. Their mascot is the raccoon. That's a dumb mascot, don't you think?"

"No way." I shook my head emphatically. "Raccoons aren't dumb. They're pretty dang smart, actually. My Granny Mae, that's what we used to call my grandmother, she had a passel of raccoons living in her shed that used to get in her garbage every night. She even tied the lids down but they still figured out how to untie the knots and get in there."

"Really?"

"Cross my heart." I crossed two fingers over my chest to prove to him I was being one hundred percent truthful on the matter.

"That kind of makes sense."

"What does?"

"Well, raccoons sorta look like bandits with the big stripe across their eyes. Like a mask bandits would wear. Makes them look sneaky. Like they were born to be good bandits."

"Huh. You're right, Jake."

We heard the distinct sound of glass being swept up across the store and murmuring voices. Jake's relaxed expression creased into a worried frown as he peered up. The bar was far too high for us to see over from our seated position, but I could tell he was expecting to be in trouble any minute.

"Do you like to read?" I asked him.

His attention came back to me. His frown now one of confusion instead of worry. "I love to read. My teacher Ms. Harley said I read really good." He thought a second then added, "No, she said I read really well. My favorite are dinosaur books."

"You like dinosaurs?"

"Yep. I'm going to be a paleontologist when I grow up."

"That will be a cool job," I added with a nod. "What other books do you like?"

"Funny ones."

I smiled wide. "Me too!" Then I clamped my hand over my mouth and glanced toward the bar counter above us.

He giggled, which is what I was after.

Then I whispered, "Do you like *Captain Underpants*?"

"You read *Captain Underpants*?" He blinked in disbelief, those sweet brown eyes growing impossibly bigger.

"My nephew in Knoxville loves that series. I buy him the new book every time one comes out. I'm considered pretty cool with the boys. The seven and eight-year-old variety, mostly."

"I'll be eight in January." He smiled even brighter, revealing the cutest dimples I've ever seen in my life.

"Wow, you sure are tall for almost-eight. I thought you were ten at least," I fibbed, but only a little. He really was tall.

"I love *Captain Underpants*, but Dad thinks they're silly."

"Your dad's right. They are silly. But that's what makes them so much fun." I poke him in the belly and he giggled again.

That's when a large shadow loomed over us, and I looked up into a very familiar face.

"I thought I knew those shoulders," I muttered.

The giant-sized, bearded version of Jake braced both hands on the bar and peered down at me, his brows denting into a deep scowl. Huh. Jake made that same expression a few minutes earlier. He looked a lot like his daddy. Except way cuter.

"Marly?"

"Hi, Wade."

"What are you doing down there with my son?"

"Talking about raccoons and *Captain Underpants*."

Unbeknownst to me, that scowl on his face could burrow even deeper. I stood and then helped Jake up.

Ignoring me, Wade turned his scowl on Jake. "Did you break that jar of moonshine?"

With fear bright on his adorable face, which was now turning pink, Jake opened his mouth to answer.

But I quickly butted in. "No, it was my fault." I walked out of the square bar, Jake following behind me.

"How's that?" asked Wade, planting his giant paws low on his hips.

Today, Wade was wearing faded jeans and a threadbare Nirvana t-shirt. I'd say he was going for a vintage look, but the truth was his clothes were probably old as dirt and he wasn't going for a look at all. He just didn't bother spending money on frivolous things like new clothes. He never bothered with his appearance much, it seemed. Same as in high school.

Except that night when we recreated Senior Prom in Jed's sister's barn so Lola could get her hot hunk of man Jed back. That night, Wade in a tuxedo looked good enough to lick. Right now—though the grizzled lumberjack look did have a certain appeal—he simply looked intimidating. And mean.

I glanced down at Jake, reading that he was getting the same vibes.

"I was talking to Jake when he told me this funny joke, then I laughed so hard, I swung out my arm and knocked the jar over." I mimicked the incident that never happened by flinging my arm.

Wade looked at me like I'd lost my mind. It was a common expression I was used to receiving. So I waited till his brain caught up.

"Then you decided to hide behind the bar?"

"Actually, I was putting myself in time-out for breaking the jar of moonshine. Jake was being a polite gentleman and decided to keep me company."

Jake straightened about two inches taller, lifting his chin with a smile.

"Uh-huh," grunted the big bear. His eyes narrowed. "What was the joke?"

"What?" I squeaked out, glancing nervously down at Jake.

"The joke. That made you laugh so hard you knocked over the merchandise of this store you apparently manage."

I looked down at my name tag with *manager* below my name. Then I tapped my chin, eyeing my partner in crime and hoping like hell he could help me out here. "What was it again, Jake?"

He gulped and stared down at his shuffling feet. "Um."

"That's what I thought," Wade murmured in a deep, gravelly voice that made my skin tingle.

"What do you call a cross between a turtle and a porcupine!" Jake suddenly shouted so loud that Kayla craned her neck from where she was still cleaning up the Hot Mama mess.

Wade blinked but didn't say a word.

"A slowpoke!" Jake yelled just as loudly.

I burst out laughing. First, the joke was pretty damn funny I had to admit. But also, the look of disbelief on Wade's face was priceless.

"Yep." I snickered and patted Jake on the back. "That was it."

While Jake and I basked in our brilliant cover story with wide smiles, his dad never cracked even the tiniest one. After heaving a loud sigh, he said, "Son, why don't you go on and wait in the truck."

"Yes, sir."

"Bye, Jake." I waved to my little minion who tossed that devilish smile back at me with a little wave.

After Jake was gone, I was left with the goliath curmudgeon still scowling down at me. "That's not what happened."

"Pardon?" I asked innocently.

He blinked. "Is it?"

Wade was obviously trying to decipher one of two things. Was I truly so clumsy that I'd break a jar in the store I'd been running for three years? Or, was I fibbing to get his son out of trouble?

The answer was neither really. I simply liked to have fun and tended to play the rebel most of the time. I also liked kids. True, I didn't like seeing Jake's sad little puppy-dog eyes when he broke that jar, but I could've told him it was all fine and that it happened at least once a month. We were used to it. But where would be the fun in that? Running and hiding from Daddy was way more exciting.

Realizing Wade responded best to normal, responsible adults, I put that mask on for him. "It's fine. It happens more often than you'd realize."

"You mean, you break their moonshine all the time? And they keep you employed?"

"Pfft. You're a hoot. Is there something else I could help you with?"

Yes, Wade Kelley, I just slyly steered that conversation and didn't answer your question.

"Um, no. I found what I was looking for."

I glanced in his hand to see him holding a jar of our 128 proof. And yes, he was holding it with one hand, his fingers touching at the top curve. Jeesh, he was a big'un.

"Need a little nightcap to take off the edge?"

"It's for my grandfather."

"He likes the good ole classic stuff, huh?"

"Mmhmm." His gaze roved over me quickly, seeming to be thinking about something though I have no idea what.

"Can I help you with anything else?"

He cleared his throat and glanced back toward the door. "No. This is it. I'd better go. Jake's in the truck."

"Yeah. I was standing right here when you told him to go wait in it two minutes ago."

He gave me that confused expression again, but I don't know why. He was the one stating the obvious.

"Right." He turned and marched for the door.

I followed him toward the exit. "Did you want to pay for that? Or were you planning on stealing it?"

"Huh?" he turned near the door.

I was used to flustering people, particularly men, so this didn't surprise me.

"You already paid Kayla?" I pointed to the jar in his hand.

"Oh, hell." He shook his head and met me at the register.

I glanced out the window to check on Jake. He was sitting in the passenger seat of a big Chevy next to my Ford-150. After ringing Wade up, I gave him his change then bagged his jar of moonshine.

"You sure you don't want me to pay for that broken jar?" he asked. "I don't know why, but I feel like you're covering for Jake. Kids gotta learn to pay when they make mistakes."

"I'm sure you're absolutely correct and know much more about parenting than I do, seeing as I am not a parent. But don't you worry your pretty little head about it. It's all good."

Again, he gave me that blank-faced, puzzled expression as I handed over his moonshine in a paper bag and beamed brightly up at him.

"You're a funny kind of woman, Marly."

"You better believe it. I put the fun in funny." I winked.

He shook his head and took the bag, but I swear I saw him actually crack a smile before he ducked his chin and strolled out to his truck.

Kayla joined me behind the counter while we both watched him walk across the parking lot. Though I was not a fan of Wade Kelley—the grouchy man hated country music, for Pete's sake—I had to admit he looked awfully good walking away.

"Why'd you make up a story for the kid?"

I shrugged. "Just wanted to. He's a cute kid who looked like he was about to cry. I wanted him to smile."

"His daddy is more than cute. Good gracious alive."

I watched Wade slide into the driver's seat and say something to his son. He didn't seem angry as he started the truck, braced his arm across the backseat and looked back as he reversed.

"You think so?"

"Hell, girl. Are you kidding me? That man is a full-on smoke-show."

"I don't see it." Not entirely.

As Wade's truck reversed, I could make out that deep frown of his through the window. His dark eyes caught mine for a split second. Or two. Then he turned around and drove out of the parking lot.

"Fine by me," added Kayla, heading toward the breakroom. "You let me tend to his every need next time he comes in."

Frowning, I headed back to the boxes of Peppermint Patty and the display I needed to finish, wondering why Kayla was annoying me so much today.

CHAPTER 2
~MARLY~

"Pass me the sour cream."

I took it off the shelf and handed it over to Lola, then she wheeled her grocery cart away from the dairy section. I followed with my little basket on my arm.

"So what else is going on?" she asked, stopping to grab a container of guacamole. "You're awfully quiet tonight."

I hadn't noticed, but I suppose that's because I'd been in my own head this afternoon. "I talked to my dad for a while the other night."

"Oh, Marly." She heaved one of those I'm-so-sorry sighs. "Let me guess. He asked when you're going to stop playing around and find a real career."

"I think you should start a side business as a psychic."

She snorted, veering down the chip aisle and grabbing a giant bag of Tostitos. "Doesn't take a psychic to know that your dad has had one agenda your entire adult life."

"I should've joined the circus when they came when they came to town our senior year. That would've really made his hair fall out."

She stopped her buggy and turned to look at me. Her dark curly hair was piled in a messy bun, the curls springing out everywhere. With no make-up and wearing her yoga pants/sweatshirt uniform as a work-from-home marketing guru, she didn't look much older than when we graduated. She also looked so happy. That's what I loved best about Lola's life now.

A few years ago, she almost left Green Valley for good, giving up Jed and me and her family, until she got some sense knocked into her. Since then, she's been steadily building her own marketing firm from home, including running her ever-popular podcast, Kiss-n-Tell, which I happen to co-host. She still picks up shifts at Bucky's from time to time, but her little business is taking off. I suppose that's what finally gave me the confidence to seriously consider my own little dream.

A sting pinched inside my chest. Not that I begrudged my best friend her every happiness, because she totally deserved it. But because I was usually the one riding cloud nine and loving life to the fullest. Until recently when my dad got a new burr up his butt about me approaching thirty and not yet having a "real" career.

Lola reached over and squeezed my shoulder. "Seriously, M. I'm super sorry. Just ignore him."

"I always do. But he's been more pesterly lately."

"I don't think pesterly is a word."

"That's what he is though." I grabbed a family size pack of Kraft Mac & Cheese and put it in the basket on my arm. "Good thing I'm a master at ignoring his texts and phone calls and life advice."

"You know what you want, so just stay on course." Lola steered us toward the meat aisle. "How's your new project going anyway?"

"I ordered the new copper still. Should be in any day now."

"And the recipe? You finally know what you want to do?"

Lola was right. I typically always knew what I wanted and had a fail-safe plan for success. But in this endeavor—my plan to win the annual Green Valley Shine Amateur Moonshine Contest—I honestly had no idea what recipe to use. I'd been researching for months and experimenting with flavor combinations in my kitchen, but nothing had shouted *I'm the winner* just yet.

The contest came with a five-thousand-dollar prize and name recognition with the locals as a top competitor in the moonshine industry. That was the dream I hadn't told my father about—to open my own moonshine distillery. Because I knew exactly what his reaction would be, and I just wasn't ready to climb that hill.

"Not yet," I finally answered her, watching her pick up a big pack of ground beef. "But I'm working on it. Is it taco night at your house?"

Lola flinched as she dropped it in her cart. "Uh, no. Nachos, actually."

"I have no idea why you're blushing about that."

"So, when is your next podcast date? Or is it Bekah's turn?"

She was changing the subject. I knew because I was the best at circumventing subjects I didn't want to talk about. But nachos? What's so embarrassing about nachos?

"It's my turn, but you know this. You have all of our schedules color-coded on your calendar."

Since Lola had gotten serious with Jed, she'd asked me to take over the dating routine for the podcast. Kiss-n-tell was founded on the idea of interviewing a date after the night out and ranking the night as a whole on the show. I'd accepted, but over the past year we'd made even more changes. We added Jed's sister, Bekah, into the mix as well. We also changed the routine of letting our dates know ahead of time that it was for the podcast.

While Lola thought that would skew the genuineness of the date itself, I told her it only made them try even harder and hopefully would make them come out a winner in the dating arena. In addition to the date interviews, Lola had added specials once a month like where to take your guy or girl on an anniversary or where to go for a romantic getaway. It meant that I only had to go on a podcast date about once a month.

"Who is it again? Arthur, that big, broody postman?"

"That's the one. Gwen said he was super nice, though not very talkative."

"And he was fine going on a date for the podcast?"

"Gwen said he was. I haven't actually talked to him in person. He took over her route last week, and I waved from the porch. He waved back but didn't even stop to say hi. Not very promising."

Lola put her things on the conveyer belt. "You probably scared him."

"Me? I'm not scary."

She barked out a laugh. "Newsflash, Marleen. You are *very* scary and kind of a lot. Especially to shy guys."

I preened and flipped my hair, liking that description. "I'm kind of a femme fatale, huh?"

"More like a femme frightfully flamboyant."

"That's too much alliteration. But I still like it." I placed my one box of Kraft macaroni on the conveyer behind her groceries. "Anyway, Gwen said not to let that bother me. He's a man of routine and wouldn't veer off his route unless a house was on fire or something."

Lola snorted. "This should be an interesting date."

"Why?"

"Because you don't like routine."

"Routine's boring. Maybe we'll have that opposites attract attraction," I added, waggling my eyebrows.

"It'll be entertaining for the podcast, that's all I can say."

After paying for our groceries, I carried out my nutritious dinner, thanks to Kraft, and followed Lola to her car to help her put her bags in the trunk. My brain kept side-winding like a snake on sand to one topic I hadn't brought up just yet. I wanted to, but also didn't for some reason. Then I finally gave in.

"I bumped into Wade this week. Well, his son bumped into our moonshine then that brought on an entertaining meeting with big Daddy Bear."

"Wade Kelley?"

"The one and only." I set another bag in her trunk.

"Poor Jake. Did Wade fuss at him for spilling the moonshine?"

"No." I grinned. "I connived a way out for him."

"I bet you did."

"What's wrong with him anyway? Why's he always so grouchy?" I bit my bottom lip, watching an older lady pushing her buggy to her car. "Probably needs to get laid," I muttered.

"You volunteering as tribute?" Lola nudged me to get my attention.

"Tribute for what?"

"To get Wade laid."

"Cute rhyme." I laughed. "And hell no! He'd probably growl and bite the whole way through."

"Nothing wrong with that," she winked. "Besides, that's just his personality. He's a growly kinda man."

A sudden shiver tumbled down my spine, leaving a pleasant buzz in its wake. *No ma'am. No sexy tingles in relation to Wade Kelley.*

"He's way too broody and frowny all the time. He's a total party pooper."

"Huh. You just described Arthur, the postman, the same way a few minutes ago and were pretty excited about a possible opposites attract attraction if I recall." She bumped me with her hip as she closed her trunk.

"That's different."

"How so?"

"Because Wade is" —I spread an arm out to the universe— "Wade."

"That makes no sense," she laughed.

"I'll see you next week," I told her, walking back toward my truck, not wanting to talk about growly Wade Kelley anymore.

"See you then," she called before getting into her car.

The older lady was putting her groceries away in her Buick right next to my truck. She dropped one of her bags, peaches rolling out onto the concrete.

"Here, let me help you," I called out, jogging over.

"Thank you, dear."

"No problem." The sweet smell of the peaches, now a little bruised wafted up to me. "I can't believe they had any peaches left in season."

"Oh, they only had the few at the register. Octoberfest Peaches. Chase sells them on consignment from his peach orchard."

"But it's November first. Thought they were all out of season."

"I thought so too. Probably the last of this season's harvest, for sure."

I helped her with the rest of her bags and wandered back to my truck, frowning and wondering.

"Peaches," I murmured to myself as I started my truck and veered out of the Piggly Wiggly parking lot, the sun lowering over the horizon of trees.

Without even thinking about it, I took a right and headed out to Chase's peach orchard. It was a beautiful sprawling property in the valley, dotted with rows and rows of peach trees and not too far away.

As I was aware when I pulled up the long drive, most of those trees didn't have any fruit on them since the harvest season was past waning. But as I hopped down out of my truck and peered against the setting sun, I could see a few trees on the distant hill with bright pops of color.

"Well, whatta you know?"

"Hey there, stranger." Chase walked toward me, his long legs eating up the distance between his front porch and my truck. "What are you doing out here, Marly?"

Chase was a delicious-looking man. Tall, dark hair, nice trim beard. He also had piercing hazel-gold eyes. Of course, that made me think of the burly bearded, hazel-eyed man I was trying not to think about.

I smiled brightly. "Came to see you and coerce or blackmail you into selling me some peaches that you won't sell to any other moonshiner."

He chuckled as he came to a stop, propping his hands low on his hips. "What do you have to blackmail me with?"

"Nothing at the moment. But I'll find something if it means I can coerce you into selling me a few bushels of those Octoberfest peaches and *not* sell them to any other moonshiner who comes sniffing around."

He looked out at his orchard then smirked back down at me. "I don't think you'll need to resort to crime just yet. The last of the Octoberfest are being harvested right now. And I've got buyers for all of them already. None of them moonshiners. But I *believe* I can spare a few bushels for you."

"See. I knew you weren't just a pretty face." I winked. Chase was a fine farmer/culinary genius who owned and was chef at his supper club The Noble Pig. I couldn't help but flirt a bit. "So how come you still have peaches in early November?"

"The Octoberfest is a special type." He walked toward the fence post where his first row of peach trees started. I followed.

"Special sounds perfect for what I need. Are they more on the sweet side or tart side?"

"Sweet, for sure."

I let out a gusty breath. "That's exactly what I was hoping you'd say."

"They've actually got a deep, rich peachy flavor and well-balanced but definitely more on the sweet side." He braced his forearms on the top post of the fence. "Normally, they'd all be gone by the last week of October, but we seemed to have a warmer month than normal. Funny since the weather seems to be turning cold quickly now." He pointed out toward the orchard. "That's the last of them there."

I could see some workers gathering the harvest on the trees farthest away up on a small hill.

"That's perfect."

"Can I ask why you don't want any moonshiners getting a hold of them?"

"Those peaches out there are going to be my secret ingredient for the winning flavor of the Green Valley Shine Amateur Moonshine Contest." And winning that first prize was going to be my ticket to opening my own distillery—Marly's Moonshine.

"Here's a deal. I keep you deep in peaches, and you keep me deep in moonshine. Even trade?"

"Even Steven."

"Well then. Guess you better drive your truck around to the barn so I can load up your winning ingredient."

I squealed then jumped up into his arms and hugged him tight. He laughed and patted me with a friendly hug.

"Oh, hell." I dropped my arms and stepped back, tucking the strands of my blond hair behind my ears nervously. "Sorry. I got carried away. I just get so excited."

"I see that." He laughed again. "Come on, Mad Marly."

I smiled and followed him back to my truck, not at all bothered by the familiar moniker. Chase used it playfully, and I knew I was an unconventional kind of gal. Of course, it did remind me yet again of Dad's last phone call and his command to stop chasing my crazy dreams. I winced then pushed that thought back out of my mind, focusing on the thrill of moving forward with my little dream.

CHAPTER 3
-WADE-

I was still mulling over my new possible poacher situation when I pulled up into Jed's driveway. Correction. Jed and Lola's driveway now. She'd moved in not too long ago and now they were engaged and planning a wedding. Though I'd always hoped Jed would get his dream girl that got away, it still surprised me sometimes when I realized my longtime bachelor buddy was no longer a bachelor.

Of course, I'd only been a bachelor for a few months before they started dating. But it had felt like I'd been alone for years. Kristie and I married because she got pregnant with Jake. We'd been friends through college, and I wasn't about to shirk my duties as a father. When I suggested we marry, she agreed happily. And we were both happy for a while…until we weren't. We realized that while we loved and cared for each other, we weren't in love. I wasn't even quite sure what that felt like.

To see Jed in so deep with Lola made me happy for him. It also made me uncomfortable. I was pretty positive Kristie and I had never acted the way they do or look at each other like it didn't matter if the world burned around them as long as they were together.

What made me more uncomfortable was knowing how long Kristie and I had stayed married when it was apparent neither of us were all that into each other. When her work as a pharmaceutical rep sent her on the road for weeks and even months at a time, that's when it became quite clear that we'd simply become roommates. It wasn't a difficult divorce, and I'm not sure if that's a good thing or a bad thing. Good, for Jake's sake, of course. That's all that really mattered.

Thankfully, Lola was the good sort and didn't mind me encroaching on them from time to time for help with Jake. Kristie now lived in Nashville. My parents had moved to North Carolina several years ago, building their retirement dream home on Fontana Lake. They don't live too far for visiting, but definitely too far to pick Jake up from school when I had to work late. My grandmother picked him up three days a week and kept him until I was done. But Nana and Pop kept early bedtime hours, so I didn't like to bother them when I worked past six.

Today was one of those days. The new guy Ben, who was barely twenty and eager as ever, spotted four-wheeler tracks on a game trail inside the national park border. We'd traced the ATV tracks back to a clearing not far off of the main road. There were deeper truck and trailer tracks that had been parked near a heavily wooded area on the northwest side of the park. It could've been kids joyriding. Or it could've been poachers trespassing and illegally hunting in the park.

We'd have to monitor the area closely this hunting season. If it was poachers and they'd gotten away with it, they'd be back.

Hopping out of my own truck, I grabbed the new puzzle book I'd picked up in Merryville this morning. Jake's school had recently identified him as a gifted student. I didn't know what that meant besides he was really smart. Got that from Kristie, most likely.

Being a good parent to Jake was my number one goal in life. So when I met with his teacher Ms. Hillary who explained he'd be pulled out for special gifted classes a few days a week, I asked what I could do to help him at home.

Being a single parent put extra pressure on me, but I was prepared to do whatever I needed to help Jake in every way I could. One thing she'd suggested was to find puzzles and brainteasers to help with critical thinking. So I'd been picking up different books I found when I made it to the Wildlife Resource Agency office near Merryville.

I ambled up to the front door and rapped a few times.

"Come in!" yelled Lola.

I stepped inside to a delicious smell and followed it into the kitchen where Lola was stirring something in a bowl, the counter littered with condiments.

"Hey, Wade. We made plenty of burgers so you and Jake can stay for dinner."

"You didn't have to do that. I don't want y'all to feel like you've gotta cook for us all the time."

It was true that whenever they'd take care of Jake for me, they always had dinner waiting when I picked him up.

"Nonsense." She shot a smile over her shoulder. "You can grab a beer in the fridge. Jed's outside at the grill."

"Thank you."

I certainly wasn't going to complain too hard because damn, it was nice having a hot meal waiting when I got off work. Of course, Jed did most of the cooking from what I understood. But Lola sure could make a mean batch of snickerdoodle cookies.

Popping the top off the Michelob, I carried the book for Jake outside. I smiled at the sight of him rolling around on the grass with Jed's yellow lab, Joe.

"Hey, man." Jed waved as he lowered the top of the grill and ambled over, beer in hand. "Y'all find anything?" he asked as he sat down on the porch across from me.

I set Jake's book on the table and shook my head. "Only tracks."

"You think it's poachers?"

I'd told Jed why I was going to be late. He had that concerned look he always got when we talked about possible troublemakers in and near the park. For him, that typically meant irresponsible campers who might leave a fire unattended, which could lead to a major catastrophe for him and the other firefighters of Green Valley. For me, that could mean criminals who knew how to use a gun and who didn't mind using one to get away from authorities. Both of which could be lethally dangerous.

"Could be. But could also be kids taking a ride on the game trails. We'll be on the lookout."

"Dad!" Jake shot across the yard, dropping a long stick he'd been holding. Joe loped along behind him.

I stood and wrapped him in a hug. "Hey, kiddo. Good day at school?"

"Yeah. I finished my math test early, and Ms. Hillary let me work on my Legos project."

"Which project is that?"

"I'm rebuilding a Roman city. But my aqueducts won't actually work. The water will just run off the sides, but Ms. Hillary said that was okay. It's just a model anyway."

I honestly didn't know quite what to say to that. He knew what the word aqueducts was and their purpose, and he wasn't even eight. "Sounds like a fun project, son."

His eyes lit up. "It is! But now I'm not sure if I want to be an architect or still be a paleontologist when I grow up."

"You've got time to figure it out," I told him, picking up the book I'd bought him. "I got this at the Merryville bookstore for you today."

"Oh, sweet!" he said, pulling it out of the bag. His eyes didn't have that shine they did a second ago.

"Did I already buy this one for you?" It was possible since I didn't keep track very well.

"No, I don't have this one. It's cool, Dad." He smiled back up at me in a way that I knew he was placating his old man. He plopped the book back on the table, walking swiftly backwards. "Me and Joe are fighting Visigoths."

"Visigoths?"

"Yeah. They're barbarians invading Rome! Come on, Joe!"

He grabbed his stick which was apparently a sword and he and Joe started chasing the invisible barbarians around the yard again.

"That kid," huffed Jed. "An architect or a paleontologist? I didn't even know what the hell those things were at his age."

"And Visigoths? I know what they are but how the hell does my seven-year-old know?" The little doubts that I wouldn't be able to steer Jake well enough on my own wiggled their way back into my psyche.

It wasn't that I doubted my parenting skills in general. As a father, I thought I was doing pretty damn good on my own. But Jake wasn't like me as a kid. When I was his age, I was catching tadpoles in a ditch or fishing in a stream. He had no interest in that at all. Instead, he'd rather be fighting medieval invaders and building aqueducts and Roman cities. Sometimes, I simply felt disconnected from him.

Like just now when he smiled at the book I'd bought him but obviously wasn't all that interested. His interests were vast and quickly changing and quite different from most kids his age. He would get interested in one topic then become obsessed over it, and then decide that would be his career focus until the next topic of fascinated interest came along.

I suppose I'd better order some textbook on Roman history or something. I don't know. This little disconnect between us often overwhelmed me with worries. Like one day the gap between us might be so big, I wouldn't be enough at all for him.

Lola pushed the patio door open and walked out with a glass of wine in her hand. "Potato salad is done. I can't promise it's as good as my Aunt Polly's, but I tried."

"I'm sure it'll be delicious," said Jed, his gaze raking down Lola, certainly not thinking about potato salad. I glanced away and drank my beer, smirking that these two couldn't seem to get enough of each other.

"You're just saying that to get on my good side." She plopped down in the chair next to me and stretched her feet onto Jed's lap.

"Since when am I not on your good side?" He wrapped his hand around one of her ankles, massaging lightly.

"When you make fun of my cooking."

"Lola, you know you're the best cookie baker in town. I've told you so a hundred times."

"Baking and cooking are two different things." She suddenly gasped and jumped up. "Dammit, I forgot about the cookies!" She tore off back into the kitchen.

Jed chuckled, his lingering gaze on the door where his fiancée had disappeared.

"I see things are still going well," I said truthfully, taking another swig of beer.

"Yeah, it's," he shook his head, dropping his gaze. "It's something else."

That had me grinning wider. "Glad to hear she was worth the wait."

He took a swig of his own beer, eyeing me thoughtfully. Too thoughtfully. "What about you?"

"What about me?"

"You still dating that girl from Knoxville?"

"Who?"

"The veterinary assistant or whatever. Stacy?"

"Stephanie. And no. That wasn't. She wasn't—" I heaved a sigh. "Think I'm done with dating, man."

"Done?" He laughed. "You're not even thirty."

"I feel like I'm eighty most the time." Jake's laughter pulled my attention to him and Joe in the yard. "I've got all the family I need anyway."

I felt Jed's penetrating gaze, and I didn't want to hear whatever encouraging words he had about finding the right girl. We didn't all need the perfect partner. Jake and I were just fine on our own.

"Speaking of eighty," I turned back to him, "Pop has a birthday coming up.

Eighty-one this year. Mom and Dad are coming in. Nana's baking your favorite red velvet cake. We'll have a small party at their house if you and Lola want to come."

"Come where?" asked Lola as she popped back outside.

"Pop's eighty-first birthday party. Just family and a few friends."

"Of course, we'll be there," said Jed, pulling Lola down onto his lap before she could take a seat. "What you gonna get the old man?"

"Hell, I don't know. The only thing he ever wants is moonshine, and I just got him a new jar the other day."

Jed grinned. "Bet he's mad as hell since he can't make his own anymore."

"You got that right. More ornery than ever."

"Your grandfather makes his own moonshine?" asked Lola with interest.

"He used to," I told her. "He's had some serious back issues and can't get around much anymore. He definitely can't haul his old butt up the mountain to his moonshine shack."

"Why's he gotta go up there to do it?" she asked.

"That's where the water is," I said. When she responded with a more confused expression, I added, "You need fresh spring water for good moonshine."

"Well, you can haul in fresh spring water," she replied with a touch of sarcasm. "There is this new thing called bottled water, and I'm pretty sure you can order by the gallon."

Jed squeezed her waist till she squealed. "Feeling sassy tonight?"

She laughed and twisted, grabbing his hand so he couldn't tickle her. "You like my sassy mouth."

"I sure do," he murmured low against her throat.

"Should I leave?" I asked.

"No!" they shouted together.

Chuckling, I swigged the rest of my beer. "Anyway, what you don't know, Lola, is my grandfather is a stubborn son of a bitch."

"So pretty much like all grandpas."

"Basically, yes. But he believes there's only one way to make good and true moonshine. And that's out in the woods using the natural mountain spring. And he can't do that anymore, so he has to send his grandson all over the territory, picking up new jars for him to sample and critique."

Jed chuckled. "I imagine he has lots to say on the deficiencies of local distilleries."

"Tons." I stood up, empty bottle in hand. "Think I'll get another."

"Grab me one," said Jed.

After grabbing two more beers, I returned to find Jed back at the grill, flipping the burgers onto a platter. Lola was sitting in his chair, her legs curled up beneath her, expression pensive.

She tilted her head at me. "It's funny we were talking about moonshine making."

"Why's that?"

"My friend Marly is going to enter the Green Valley Shine Amateur Moonshine Contest next month."

"I didn't know they had one."

"Yep, it's always mid-December as part of their holiday marketing. Then they launch the new year with the winner's flavor."

"Hmph," was all I could manage to say.

Lola stared at me, making me a little uncomfortable. Before I knew it, I blurted, "I saw Marly the other day."

"At the store?" asked Lola. "Yeah, she told me." There was a mysterious quirk to her lips that had me frowning.

"What?"

"Nothing." She replaced the smirky expression with one of innocence that made me more jittery.

"Nah. You know something. What is it?"

"She just had a few choice words to say about you."

"Me? What did she say?"

"She told me about Jake spilling the moonshine."

Jed walked up. "Burgers are ready. Wait. What did I miss?"

Because I was scowling at Lola who was still grinning like a cat that got the cream.

"What *else* did she say?" I asked gruffly.

She stood next to Jed, who was watching us. "She said you were super grumpy and she figured it was because you needed to get, uh, relieve some tension. With a female."

Then she giggled and walked into the house.

I looked at Jed. "What the hell are you grinning about?"

"Just the fact that she's probably right." Then he walked on into the house.

I followed. "I'll have you both know I've been grouchy my whole life, with or without a woman in it."

"That's what I told her," Lola said.

We settled in to eat after that. Jake had come in, grabbed his plate, and headed back outside to share his meal with Joe, mumbling about keeping his army fed.

Conversation switched to something else, but I couldn't seem to keep my focus. What the hell was Marly Rivers doing talking about me and my lack of a sex life?

Her feline image popped into my mind as I devoured my burger. There was something about her that was extremely cat-like. The tilt of her clear blue eyes always seeming to reflect the mischief going on behind them. The swish and sway of her softly rounded body as she moved from one place to another. She hadn't seemed to change since high school. Just curvier.

"She's still kinda crazy," I muttered.

"What was that?" asked Jed, smiling as he forked a spoonful of potato salad into his mouth.

"*Marly*," I snapped, revealing more emotion than I'd wanted. "She's still as crazy as she was in high school. A little ditzy too," I added spitefully.

"Don't go there, Wade." Lola sat straighter and pointed a spoonful of potato salad at him. "Just because she's blond and beautiful and a bit wild and carefree doesn't mean she's dumb. To be honest, she's the smartest person I know."

I'd clenched my jaw to keep from refuting and possibly because I'd added that last insult in a cheap shot at revenge for Marly's dig at my own personality.

"Why you say that?" Jed asked the question I'd wanted to know.

"For one, she told me I was dumb as dirt for breaking up with you." She pointed her spoon at Jed before eating it. "Besides, y'all just don't get her the way I do. I know she moves a mile a minute and says things perhaps she ought not to, but she's got more brains than most people give her credit for. All they see is Mad Marly doing something nuts again, but they don't know her like I know her. She's got the biggest heart in the whole wide world."

I kept my mouth shut after that, because I didn't know her. Not really. All I knew was that she was the girl always getting into trouble or doing some crazy stunt in high school. Her loud and proud personality always made me a bit uncomfortable.

One time she made me *really* uncomfortable. She'd lost a bet to someone our senior year and had streaked naked through the football locker room before our Homecoming game.

I remember it clear as day since I was one of the few players still suiting up in the locker room. I'd just put my pads on and was pulling my jersey from the locker when I heard that old eighties song *Girls Just Wanna Have Fun*. It was kind of low and drawing closer. When I turned to see where the music was coming from, my jaw dropped. Marly came parading through, holding her cellphone over her head, which was playing the music. She was naked down to a g-string, laughing and running—and *bouncing* beautifully—down the aisle toward the back exit.

And heaven above, what she had in high school had only filled out further to the kind of figure a man wanted to grab and hold on to.

Fucking hell.

I was not going to sit here at dinner and get hard thinking about Marly Rivers streaking through the locker room in high school. It was because Lola told me what she'd said. That's why my mind kept straying to her.

It was true. I hadn't been with a woman in a while. Not since Stephanie from Knoxville. And it hadn't been a problem until Lola had brought it up. When I knew Marly was talking about me. I could see her cat-eyes now, narrowing with mischief. And why that had my body tightening with arousal, I had no damn idea.

I drank the rest of my second beer down in three gulps.

"Well, we better go." I checked my watch. "Thank y'all again for helping out."

"So soon?" asked Lola. "I've got cookies."

"We'd better take them with us. Not sure if Jake has homework yet to finish."

I managed to appear grateful and not the surly grump I felt like as I gathered Jake and the cookies and ushered him out to the truck. What I needed was a long, hot shower and my bed. Or perhaps, a cold one. Either way, I wasn't going to think about Marly Rivers or her cat eyes or her hot body one more time.

CHAPTER 4
~WADE~

Mac pointed at the map I had spread out on the hood of my truck.

"Yeah. They were right about there. There's a sharp switchback right after the curve, and I know there's no one livin' up there. Just an old abandoned house."

"And easy access to cross into the park," I added.

Mac straightened, meeting me eye to eye, his brow wrinkled.

"That's what I was thinking."

Lola had texted me this afternoon that her sometimes co-worker Mac, a fry cook at Bucky's Bar and Grill where she still picked up shifts from time to time, saw some suspicious activity heading into work this morning. I immediately messaged him to stop by our office on the way home.

"And you said they had North Carolina plates?" asked Ben, who'd been typing everything Mac had said into notes on his phone.

"That's what tipped me off. The two men in the truck weren't from around here. And they were hauling a trailer with a big four-wheeler in the back. Heavy duty tires on that thing."

"Wish you'd called us sooner," said Ben.

"Sorry, man. I had to get to work. I texted Lola on my break since she didn't work today. Figured Jed would know who to contact."

I waved Ben off. "It's all right. We're glad to get the information. Now that we know that's one of their entry points into the park, we can keep an eye out on that area."

I held a hand out to Mac. "Appreciate your help."

He shook mine, then Ben's. "Happy to be useful."

"You've got my number now. If you spot them again, message me any time. Night or day."

"Will do."

I made a mental note to call Deputy Jackson James, so I could send the description of these possible poachers. He and the deputies could help us out and be on the lookout for these guys.

While Mac climbed into his truck and drove off, another truck—a Ford F-150—was driving in.

"Who's that?" asked Ben.

My gut tightened when I recognized the blonde driving the white F-150.

"Marly," I muttered.

"Who?"

But I didn't answer as I watched her swing into the small parking lot. When she hopped out of her truck, every muscle in my body locked up.

"What in the hell is she wearing?" I growled.

"Not much."

I shot Ben a glare, but his eyes were on Marly. Then mine were too. She wore an apron that hit her high on the thighs and a tank top with such skinny spaghetti straps she looked like she was naked behind the little apron. It was fifty degrees out here!

The visual effect as she swayed in our direction was demoralizing since I'd promised myself I'd never think about her naked ever again. That was after I'd spent a long, long time in the shower the other night, using that old memory of her and my own imagination to visualize what she looked like now under her clothes. As I'd crashed in my bed, I swore to myself I'd never think about her that way again.

But here she was, strutting toward me with those sultry eyes and pretty hair piled in a crazy knot on her head. Soft strands wisp around her face, taunting me with her natural sensuality.

Crossing my arms as if I could barricade my wayward thoughts, I stood rigid and tall, waiting for her to reach us.

She waved with a friendly smile. "Hi, there."

As she drew closer, I noticed a few smudges of dirt or something on one thigh, an arm, and her hands.

"Hey. I'm Ben Sharp and this is my boss, Wade. What can we help you with?"

She stopped in front of us, her smile widening. "We know each other," she told Ben as she kept her eyes on me.

A satisfying warmth almost made me smile. Almost. "What in the hell are you wearing?"

"It's called an apron."

"It's—."

"Adorable?" She propped her hands on her curvy hips. "Yes. I know."

"Indecent," I snapped.

"I think you look very nice," said Ben suggestively.

"Thank you." She tapped his arm playfully which had red flushing up in the kid's cheeks.

I heaved out a breath, arms still crossed. "Ben," I snapped, "you can go inside."

He opened his mouth to protest, but then he caught the look on my face and nodded. "Yes, sir."

Her innocent/mischievous expression never wavered as she watched Ben leave then turned her attention back to me. "Is something wrong? Or is this just the normal way you greet damsels in distress."

"You're not a damsel in distress."

"How do you know? Maybe I had an altercation with a wild raccoon or hit a deer on the highway and needed the help of my local Wildlife Resources Agent."

My heart skipped a beat, my gaze shooting to her truck, searching for dents or cracks in the windshield. Hitting a deer on the highway could be deadly to both the deer and the driver. Of course, she was still standing here, smiling pretty as you please, so she obviously hadn't had that sort of encounter.

"If you're in distress at all, it's because you're going to freeze to death in that next-to-nothin' outfit."

"Awww," she teased, batting her eyelashes. "I appreciate your concern, but I'm just fine."

Heaving a sigh, I asked, "What's going on, Marly?"

"I was going to ask you the same thing. What's Mac doing here?" she hooked a thumb over her shoulder, but Mac was already gone. For a second, I wondered how they knew each other, but she'd have met him at Bucky's at some point with Lola.

"We've got a poacher situation."

"Yikes! Is that serious?"

"It can be. But nothing for you to worry about. What's going on?" I prodded yet again.

"I was working and—"

"They let you work at Green Valley Shine in *that*?" I pointed at the next-to-nothing apron she wore over her equally minimal shorts and tank top.

She rolled her eyes. "I wasn't working at work. I was working at home. That's what I came to talk to you about."

She paused, biting her lip, which drew my focus to the plump lower curve.

Growing even more irritable, I snapped out. "Tell me what it is you need. I've got lots left to do."

She blinked those sea-blue eyes wide, her dark lashes making my gut tighten even more. "I want to meet your grandfather."

Of all the things I thought she was going to say, that wasn't even on the list. "Come again?"

"Lola mentioned to me that your grandfather used to make his own shine. Was really famous around here for the quality of his product. I wanted to ask him some questions."

"This about that moonshine contest?"

She nodded on a sigh. "Yeah. I've run a batch of my own, and it's good. Damn good. But I don't think my still is good enough. I've ordered a new copper still which should come in by Friday. Though hell if I know how to put one of these together. It requires welding, and I don't have that skill. It's an older style but all copper. Pot, condenser, thumper, cap, everything."

"How'd you put the one together you've got at your house now?"

"Jed helped me. Guess I can get him to help me with this one, too."

Something in that idea rubbed me wrong. I wasn't sure I wanted to identify the emotion because it was too close to jealousy, which was absolutely nuts.

"I know how to put them together," I offered quickly. "My Pop taught me."

"He did?" she asked excitedly. "Sounds like he knows all about the artform, doesn't he?"

And just like that, the tight knot in my chest loosened and fell away. Only the true moonshiners recognized it as an artform. The way my Pop always did.

There was chemistry to it, yes, but there was also an instinct and craft that elevated moonshine making. Pop would like her.

"Yeah, I can introduce you to him."

"Terrific!" She clapped her hands and looked at her watch. "How about in an hour? I'll run home and get cleaned up."

"*Tonight?*"

"Well, of course. I mean, I won't terrify him in my indecent apron the way I did you. I'll go get a shower and put on some jeans."

She rubbed her arms where goosebumps raised along her skin.

"You aren't freezing to death, dressed like that?"

Hell, the temps were in the fifties and dropping as the sun went down.

"I wasn't earlier because I was moving my mash around in my shed. Had to dump it in the still and everything. Anyway, I don't like to restrict my movement when I'm working and it was hot enough in the shed with the still and my chiminea going. How late are you working?"

Taking a second to absorb her string of words, I answered, "My grandparents actually keep my son Jake on Mondays, Wednesdays, and Fridays, so I've gotta go pick him up anyway."

"Perfect! Should I just meet you there?"

"Now?"

"Of course now. I can't waste any time. That contest deadline will be here before you know it, and I've gotta make at least five batches to find the best one."

After another minute of her blinking up at me looking sweet as pie, I grumbled. "I prefer to have time to plan things. I'm not a spontaneous sorta guy."

"I'm well aware of that." Her face barely shifted, but there was a definite crinkle at the edge of her eyes telling me she was making fun of me.

"Fine," I finally grumbled, determined to not be the stiff guy she saw me as. I held out my hand. "Let me see your cell phone. I'll put the address in your Maps."

She pulled out her phone from some invisible pocket behind the tiny apron and handed it over. Focusing on pulling up her Google maps, I stiffened as she'd moved close beside me, leaning over to see what I was typing in. A wisp of her hair brushed my wrist, sending a sudden jolt of heat low and deep.

Trying not to react, or rather overreact, I subtly shifted away. Still, I could smell the sweet lavender of her shampoo and the campfire smoke clinging to her hair as well as lingering cinnamon and the warm, unidentifiable scent of her skin that must be her own. That knot began to tighten again in the center of my chest.

This was all extremely uncomfortable. I didn't like it. Not one bit.

I had no idea how I'd wound up freely giving Marly Rivers directions to my grandparents' house after I swore to avoid her at all costs and not ever think of her again in any intimate way. But heaven help me, the sweet scent of her combined with those almond-shaped blue eyes and her nearly naked self was going to kill me.

"There." I handed over her phone and took a step back. "See you there in an hour," I said gruffly over my shoulder as I stormed back toward our office.

"Thank you, Wade!" she said, and I heard laughter in her voice as she walked away.

I didn't care what she was laughing at. Whether it was my abrupt and rude behavior that she found amusing or something else going on up there in her head. What I did care about was the fact that I was now thinking about Marly Rivers far too often.

Rather inconvenient when I'd decided to swear off dating. I mean I wasn't totally against finding someone to settle down with. The whole dating thing was simply awkward and messy and I hated all of it. Besides, Marly was not the woman a man settled down with. She was the one who took him on a wild ride and left him bewildered when she was done.

None of my ponderings mattered anyway. I couldn't mess around with Lola's best friend, knowing we'd be at every family/friend event together from now till the end of time. Nope. I'd help Marly with her moonshine then be done with her. And that was all there was to it.

CHAPTER 5
~MARLY~

"Thank you, Ms. Kelley." I took the cup of coffee from Wade's grandmother.

"Call me Nana, dear. If you're a friend of Wade or Jed's, then you're practically family."

I didn't correct her that while I was a friend of Jed's, I was pretty damn sure Wade would never put me in that amicable category.

"Did you get to his twelfth birthday pictures?" she asked, pointing to the photo album stretched out over my lap. "He and Jed went deer hunting with Darren, Wade's father, but a rainstorm blew in and you can see the result when they got home."

I eagerly flipped to the next page, unable to hold in the burst of laughter. "This is…amazing."

"Aren't they the cutest?"

"The absolute cutest," I couldn't help but agree.

"There was no way I was letting them track all that mud into the house, and then I couldn't help myself but snap a picture."

Younger versions of Jed and Wade stood outside next to a mud-covered four-wheeler in their tightie whities. Both of them looked toward the camera, surprise and fear in their expressions at being caught with their pants down. Literally.

Their faces, necks, and arms were mud-caked as well, but their adolescent white bodies stood out in stark contrast. Wade held a hose in one hand and Jed was leaning over, reaching for it. Granny had caught them mid-wash.

Even at twelve, they were big kids who would grow much bigger together over the years. Here, they were still gangly and wiry. Warmth swept through me at the sweetness of the picture.

"Dad looks white as a ghost," said Jake over my shoulder.

"He does, doesn't he?" I grinned up at Wade's son who'd welcomed me with a hug when I showed up twenty minutes early.

The loud stomp of footsteps coming up the porch announced Wade's arrival a few seconds before he strode through the door. His stern gaze swept the room and landed on me, his jaw clenching when he saw what was in my lap.

Instead of growling at his Nana, he hugged Jake who leaped into his arms. While I watched him greet his son, that warmth in my chest blooming hotter, I whispered to Nana, "Can I take this picture to make a copy for Lola? She would love to have this."

"Sure, sure. But you best not let him know you have it." She nodded toward her grandson then stood and walked into Wade's arms for a quick hug and a kiss.

That was all the time I needed to slide the photo out and into my purse next to me on the sofa.

"You're late. Your friend's been waiting for you."

"She's early," he grumbled, glancing past his grandfather to me. "Have you gotten all your questions answered?"

"Hell, no," barked Pop. "Margaret wouldn't let us talk business till she had coffee and all."

"Watch your language, Bernie," said Nana. "It's polite to get acquainted with new guests before you start boring her with all the moonshine talk."

"She wouldn't be bored, Margaret," he argued, leaning forward in his recliner with a hand on his walking stick. "That's why she came here, dammit."

"Language," she warned him.

He looked mildly abashed and softened his expression.

"Oh, don't worry about me," I chimed in, sipping my coffee. "I haven't been bored one minute."

Wade's scowl returned to my lap, but I'd already closed up the photo album so he couldn't see how far down the embarrassing childhood picture trail I'd gotten.

"Well, then. Jake, why don't you come help Nana put frosting on that choco-late cake."

He took off after her back into the kitchen. Wade sat next to me, leaving a large gap between us.

"Now then," said Pop, leaning back in his chair. "Tell me what you're after, and I'll set you on the straight and narrow."

I turned my body toward his chair which also angled my body toward Wade who was a giant presence I couldn't seem to ignore even if I wanted to. Focusing on the information I needed, I relayed to Pop the recipe I was using, the time I'd let my corn mash ferment, and the distilling cycle I used.

"Wait a minute," he stopped me before I even started. "Where do you keep your mash?"

"I have it in my shed. I know it's been kind of cool, so I've been running a heater."

"Unless your shed is insulated, you're likely not getting an even temperature. And it drops cold at night. That can make the yeast go dormant."

"Yeah, it quit bubbling, so I figured it was done." I thought my space heater was doing the job, but it's been dipping into the thirties some nights. And my shed didn't have the insulation to keep an even temperature.

"How long are you fermenting your mash?" he asked.

"I've only distilled one of the three batches so far. It was seven days today, so I went ahead and tried a batch."

He scratched his gray grizzled beard, looking at Wade.

It was Wade who spoke up first. "Not long enough. Not in this cooler weather. You'll need to go at least ten to fourteen days. I'd lean toward twelve or thirteen."

Surprised Wade seemed to know something about moonshine making, I turned my attention to him. "Well, I've got the other two still going."

"In the shed?" Mr. Kelley. When I nodded, he added, "I'd get them indoors. Not close to a fireplace or anything but somewhere in the house where you can keep them at room temperature round the clock."

I nodded, wondering if I could balance my pots on the dolly and get them into the house. When the mash was finished, I let the liquid run out of a spout into a smaller barrel I could actually lift and pour into the still. But the two ginormous pots I had the mash in were entirely too heavy to carry on my own.

"I'll come help you move them." Wade observed me with those hazel eyes. "After work tomorrow, I'll swing by and take care of it."

For once, I didn't have a smart comeback. All I could say was, "Thank you."

"The other thing you've gotta be damn sure you do," Mr. Kelley said abruptly, "is jar the hearts, not the heads or tails."

"Yes, sir. I know that trick, for sure. I've watched them make it at Green Valley Shine plenty of times. But it's different when you're using a small still and not making it using a commercial tank."

"It's a hell of a lot better when you hit right too," the older man added with a wink and a smile.

"That's for damn sure," I agreed.

He smiled wider.

"What's the flavor?" he asked.

"I'm going with a peach flavor. Using some late harvest peaches from Chase's peach farm. Of course, I'm trying different spices. I like the cinnamon and cloves with peaches."

"Good combination," said Mr. Kelley, but it was Wade's slight nod that dragged my attention back to the giant man shadowing me on the sofa. "I'll look through my old recipes and see if I can find one to give you some ideas."

"I'd love that." My usual charm had vanished under so much generosity and kinship in something no one except fellow employees and the owners of Green Valley Shine could understand. "Well, I better get going."

"Us too." Wade stood with me. "Jake! Come on, son."

The quick pitter-pat of little shoes and Jake came running, chocolate smeared around his mouth. I laughed and pulled him close by the shoulder.

"Hold up, Jake." I used the hem of my sweatshirt to wipe his mouth clean.

He laughed. "Thanks." Then hugged his great-grandfather and took off out the front door.

When I glanced up at Wade, he had a funny expression on his face. Frowny as usual, but less angry frown and more into the pensive territory.

I leaned down to Mr. Kelley's chair and reached out, taking his big, bony paw in both of my hands. "I can't thank you enough. I can't wait to use your advice."

"Not at all," he beamed. "Now I expect a sample of this next batch."

"Yes, sir. Absolutely."

"But you know what?"

I stood straight. "What's that?"

"If you truly want the best batch, then you need to take your mash out to the mountains and do it there. Up at my moonshine shack." He nodded to Wade looming behind me. I could feel his heat at my back. "Wade could take you out there and get you set up."

"I couldn't impose like that." I didn't even want to look over my shoulder at the grumpiest man alive, most likely scowling even harder at his Pop's suggestion.

"Nonsense! You take her on up there to the cabin when she's got that mash ready."

I fully expected a growling rebuttal and protest, but all I heard was a low, "I can do that, Pop."

"Course you can."

Before I could spin around in shock, Nana dashed out of the kitchen, wiping her hands on a dish towel and wrapped me in a hug. I had the warm fuzzies when Wade followed me out into the dark and down the walkway to the drive.

"You don't have to do all that." I finally chanced a look at him over my shoulder. "What your grandfather said." Though secretly, the idea of making moonshine out in the woods the way the old-timers used to shot a thrill through me.

His gaze was on my hair. "You shouldn't leave the house with wet hair this time of year. You'll catch a cold."

I laughed. "Wow. Wade Kelley, you are such a mom."

His scowling expression deepened, which I could just make out by the porch light.

"I'm not quite sure what that means."

I turned and leaned back against my car door. "You say lots of mom things."

He stared at me, his eyes skimming over my face. "I've had to be both Mom and Dad for a while, so I guess that makes sense."

Something in that response stung me. "Sorry. I didn't mean to offend you."

"You didn't."

A heavy silence crept between us where we were both standing there in the dark, staring at each other. The porchlight cast shadows over his face. I'd never noticed the attractive slope of his throat from his Adam's apple down to the sexy dip between his collarbones. He swallowed, the Adam's apple I was staring at bobbing. Then he cleared his throat.

"I'll swing by tomorrow after work and move your mash into your house for you."

"That's really sweet, but you don't have to."

His frown returned, seeming to examine me closer. "You're going to move them by yourself tonight, aren't you?"

"I can't waste any more time."

He cursed under his breath. "I can come by at lunch if you're going to be that hard-headed."

I bit my bottom lip, and he frowned even harder if that was possible.

"Goddammit, Marly. You can't wait a few hours?"

"A few hours? You're talking about fourteen or fifteen hours. That's a long-ass time in the life of my contest-winning mash."

"Fine, fine. Hell," he growled and turned abruptly. "I'll follow you to your house now."

"No, Wade. You don't have to. I've got a dolly and I can—"

He spun and shot me a glare over the hood of his truck. "Get in your truck, Marly. I'm not going to hear through Jed and Lola that you broke your back or your neck or cracked your pretty skull open trying to haul heavy barrels of mash into your house late at night by yourself."

He hopped in his truck and revved the engine, while I grinned in shock that he thought my skull was pretty.

He let me back out first. I drove slower than usual, because Lord knows he drives like a PawPaw. I'd lose him around a curve if I went my regular pace with him poking along like a turtle.

"Shit," I muttered, trying to remember how dirty I'd left the house.

When I'd run home to shower earlier, I'd flown through there like a tornado, slowing down only long enough to take Scooter and Pooter out of their kennels to go potty. I'd left them in the yard, knowing I wouldn't be too long.

When I pulled into the driveway, I sprinted inside, leaving the front door cracked so they could walk in. Hurrying to snatch up clothes and shoes I'd left in the living room, I ran it all to the laundry and dumped it on the floor, quickly closing the door.

Then I went to the back door and let my dachshunds inside. "Hey, kiddos! You missed Mama?"

They danced around me and yipped then took off, nails click-clacking on the wood floors as they hauled ass to see who was walking in the front door. I followed them through the kitchen, my gaze snagging on Wade without his jacket or his uniform shirt. He wore only a thin white t-shirt, one of those undershirts that allowed me to ogle the outline of his sculpted and quite broad chest.

"I didn't want to get anything on my uniform," he explained when I stared a little too long.

"Of course."

I tore my gaze away and looked down at Jake sitting on the floor with both my dogs jumping and licking all over him.

"They're so cute," he laughed. "What're their names?"

I squatted down beside him. "This one here with more brown on his nose is Scooter and the other one is Pooter."

Jake laughed and petted them.

Wade raised his brow. "You named one of your dogs Pooter?"

I stood up again. "You would too if you'd seen how gassy he was as a little baby. Come on." I turned toward the kitchen. "I won't keep you long. The mash is in the outside shed. We can put it on the dining table."

He followed me through the kitchen, seeming to take in my renovations. "How long have you owned this place?"

"Since my Granny Mae died three years ago. It was hers and the house my dad grew up in."

"You've done a good job with the remodel."

"Thank you. I can't say I did it all myself. Leffersbee & Green Construction did the renovations. Miles and Walker were super nice and got the job done fast."

He followed me out the back patio door and along the stepping stones to the shed.

"I just haven't done anything out here. Granny Mae used to keep goats," I told him.

"Goats?"

I laughed. "Yeah. It took me quite a while to get the shed, which was originally a goat barn, cleaned out properly."

"I imagine so."

It took me a minute to unlock the door, and while I was fumbling with the old latch—something I hadn't updated yet but had opened a million times with no trouble before—all I could think about was the giant wall of a man standing at my back, his body heat seeping into my shoulders, his warm breath close enough it sent tingles up my neck.

"Here we go," I said weirdly, because I never said things like that as I swung open the door. "The pots are there on that table. Should I get the dolly for you?"

He arched a brow at me like my question was ridiculous, and I swear that look had a direct line to my panties. All I could do was stand there and watch as he hefted one giant pot with a grunt.

"Lead the way," he growled.

I opened the door for him and rushed ahead to get the patio door that led into the kitchen. "Right there on the table." I pointed.

He set it down and made sure it was steady before following me back toward the door. When he didn't come out right after me, I backtracked to the doorway to find him looking at the calendar on my fridge.

"Oh. That's the Green Valley Firefighter calendar."

"Yeah," he grumbled, turning toward me. "I know what it is."

I couldn't make out what that expression was on his face, so I walked on ahead of him, rambling. "It's a fundraiser for a good cause."

"Mmhmm."

I tried not to laugh, because he seemed disgruntled that I had a bunch of hot, shirtless men tacked to my fridge.

"Jed's the month of February."

"Yeah. I know he's in it."

Still that unreadable response. He likely thought I was a little pervy, which I was. He was so straight-laced that it made me giggle. I wondered what it would be like to ruffle his rigid and stuffy exterior.

"What's so funny?"

"Nothing."

"Might as well tell me," he said, following me back into the shed. "You want to anyway."

"It's just that you're so prim and proper."

"And that's funny?"

"To me. Yeah. I mean, I can't even imagine you posing for one of those calendars."

Rather than make a comment, he leaned down and hefted the second pot, his biceps straining against the short sleeves of his threadbare t-shirt and gave me one of those serious Wade looks. I swear, every drop of saliva in my mouth evaporated as he stalked by me and kicked the door open with his boot then kept walking.

Suddenly, I absolutely *could* imagine him posing for one of those calendars. That wide, muscular chest, those big biceps, that tight slab of an abdomen. Since when did my thoughts of grouchy, uptight Wade Kelley turn into growly, sexy thoughts?

He set the second one down and maneuvered it so it wasn't on the edge. "So, did you want to use Pop's cabin?"

I couldn't hide my surprise. "Are you serious?"

That all-consuming Wade stare didn't waver. "Why wouldn't I be?"

"I don't know." I huffed a little laugh. "It seems a rather romantic notion to drag all my stuff out there to make my moonshine in nature rather than just bring in spring water here."

Yet again, his expression didn't shift the teeniest bit. He blinked heavily then said, "It's idealistic, I suppose. But Pop's not the romantic or idealistic sort. He's pragmatic to the bone. Like me. And he's right that the best moonshine is made directly from a fresh mountain spring. So if you want the best, I'd take his advice."

"You don't have to twist my arm. Just tell me where it is, and I'll get my stuff up there a little at a time."

He gave me that heavy blink again. "I'll need to take you up there. It's off the beaten path, and I haven't been in a while. When's that new still coming in?"

I pulled my phone from my back pocket, quickly pulled up the email, and clicked on the tracking number. The link popped up with the delivery estimation.

"Still scheduled for Friday. I'll call Jed tonight and see if he can come and put it together Saturday morning."

"Don't bother." He walked past me toward the living room where we could still hear Jake giggling and the prancing of my dachshunds on the wood. "I'll come by Friday afternoon."

"You don't have to, Wade, I—"

"Weren't you the one telling me you couldn't waste time?"

"Yeah, but—"

"Then I'll be here Friday night." I followed him while he was still talking. "Best to get it done, because cleaning the cabin may be an all-day job."

"I can't Friday night, though."

"Why's that?" He turned to face me.

"I've got a podcast date. Can't break it, because we need to record next week for this one."

That familiar frown dented his forehead. "That's fine. I can work on it while you're on the date." He glanced down at his son, rolling on the carpet. "Jake can occupy your dogs while you're out."

"Really?" My face split open into a wide smile. "That would be amazing."

He stared a few seconds then dipped his chin. "Not a problem. Come on, Jake. We need to get home."

"Aww, man," he whined, dragging himself up onto his feet. "Dad, can we get one of these wiener dogs?"

"No, son." He opened the door.

"But you can come play with mine on Friday, Jake," I told him excitedly.

"I *can*? Awesome!" He patted Scooter and Pooter's tiny heads one more time then ran out the open door.

I followed them to the porch. "I don't know what I did to get so much help from you, but I certainly appreciate it. I can pay you for your time. I know you're busy."

"Nah." He paused on my walkway, his body angled sideways in the shadows, his head tilted down so I couldn't see his face. "You're Lola's friend, and I know this would make my Pop happy, so don't worry about it."

Then he marched quickly to his truck and pulled out without looking back at me again. I guess he wasn't really doing me favors so much as keeping his best friend's fiancée and his grandfather happy. The why didn't matter really, but it was strange to have so much help on my pet project I wanted to turn into a career. A career my own father would laugh at if he knew. *When* he knew.

Pushing those thoughts away, I headed into the kitchen to fix something for dinner. I did have that macaroni and cheese I could make. The sight of my two giant pots of mash now on the dining table sent a little zing of excitement through my belly. Friday couldn't come soon enough.

CHAPTER 6

~WADE~

I tried not to think about why I felt it necessary to take a shower and change clothes after work on Friday before Jake and I headed to Marly's. I also tried not to think about Jed's smirks and prodding questions when I borrowed his welding kit yesterday.

When I told him it just didn't make sense for him to waste a Friday night welding when he could be at home with his girl and I had nothing better to do, he said, "Yeah. Sure. Thanks for doing me a favor." But his asinine grin told me he thought I was moving in on Marly.

I'd already well and truly decided that dating Marly was off-limits. One, she was Lola's best friend and the fallout when we ended it would be awkward and uncomfortable. My least favorite state of being.

Two, we weren't compatible so the only thing that might happen between us would be scratching a particularly persistent itch that started every time I saw her.

Three, I doubt she'd even be interested. I wasn't her type. And she wasn't mine. I couldn't understand her wild, impulsive ways. Hell, she was going on a date tonight, so why was this even on my damn mind?

"What's wrong, Dad?" Jake asked as we stepped onto her porch.

"Nothing's wrong. Why?"

"You keep making that grumbly sound in your chest. That means you're aggravated."

"I'm fine," I assured him, squeezing his shoulder with my free hand, the welding tool kit in my other hand, helmet under my arm.

Footsteps and the yipping of dogs announced her approach to the door. When she jerked it open, I ground my back teeth together so my mouth wouldn't fall open in surprise.

She wore a t-shirt that hit her upper thighs and had no pants on. Her hair was loose and wavy down to her breasts that didn't seem to be covered by a bra if that thin t-shirt revealed the truth of it.

"Hey!" she squealed excitedly, waving us in with a mascara wand in her hand. She smiled wide down at Jake. "I've got something for you, little man."

"Me?"

"Come see." She left the door open and spun to walk toward the sofa, her t-shirt dangerously close to revealing the panties she wore underneath.

Averting my eyes, I stepped inside and closed the door, looking around the living room to avoid her near naked appearance.

"No way!" laughed Jake.

That drew my focus back to them.

"You haven't read this one yet, have you?"

"No, I haven't." Jake was already flipping excitedly to the front of the book.

That got my curiosity going. I ambled over. "What book is it?" I read over his shoulder. "*Captain Underpants and the Perilous Plot of Professor Poopypants*?"

Jake and Marly fell into giggles.

"Something funny?" I asked.

"Dad, you said poopypants."

Then they started laughing harder, which had me frowning down at them. Marly's eyes actually started watering.

"I don't understand what's so funny."

"That's what's so funny." Marly finally wiped her eyes and sucked in a deep breath then cleared her throat. "Go sit and read to Scooter and Pooter," she urged Jake with a nudge.

While he did just that, I stepped closer to her. "Yeah, you should probably go finish getting dressed," I nodded down.

She looked down, then back up at me, her smile turning wicked. "They're just legs, Wade."

"You're half naked, Marly," I hissed in a whisper, glancing at Jake who was smiling while reading his book on the sofa. "I can practically see your under-wear," I added gruffly.

"Who said I'm wearing any?" she tossed back, which hit me like a sledge-hammer to the chest as she walked away.

I stood there, grinding my teeth and failing to *not* look at the brush of her t-shirt hem on the back of her rounded thighs, hoping like hell to find out if she was indeed wearing panties or not.

Fucking hell.

This woman was trouble with a capital *T*. Finally, I jerked myself into motion, lumbering to the kitchen where I saw a large box beside the dining table. Setting the welding toolbox and helmet on the table, I opened the top flap to see the shiny copper parts wrapped in bubble-filled plastic wrap.

Not wanting to weld in her kitchen, I hefted the box and carried it outside into the shed, relieved at the gust of cold air hitting my heated face.

She said that just to embarrass me. She seemed to enjoy irritating me. But irritation wasn't what had my blood simmering and pooling below my belt. I put my mind to the task at hand and pulled out each part from the box, unwrapping them and laying them on the table that had held the mash buckets earlier this week. After pulling the largest piece out last, the copper kettle which made up the bottom, I inventoried again. Everything looked in order, so I headed back inside to get the welding tool kit.

When someone knocked on the door, I found myself bypassing the toolkit and heading straight for the front door. I opened it to find a tall, bearded guy in jeans and leather jacket. I sized him up, wondering if that blank expression he was wearing hid some kind of creepy perv.

Marly was the best friend of my best friend, and I couldn't allow her to go out with some douchebag who had nefarious intentions. Unfortunately, I couldn't tell if he was the villain my imagination was conjuring or just a grouchy son of a bitch like me.

"You don't look like her type," I finally said to the man I was blocking from entering Marly's house.

He grunted, frowning. "Who are you?" he asked. "Her brother?"

Marly whipped open the door beside me. "Hi, Arthur," she said pleasantly. "I don't have a brother. This is Wade. He's just a friend."

Arthur stretched out his big paw to shake my hand, but my gaze had snagged on Marly's tight, skinny jeans and fitted red sweater. Hesitating a few seconds more, I took his hand and shook it hard.

"Where are you taking her?" I demanded.

"Wade," Marly said with warning, the first time I'd ever seen her frown, but my eyes fixed on her lips painted deep red, outlining the perfect bow-shape.

"What?" I snapped defensively, gaze tracking to her eyes then back to her pretty mouth. "I'm just asking where he's taking you."

"You don't have to sound like you're accusing him of murder."

Arthur cleared his throat and answered with a deadpan expression. "We're going to the movies."

"You don't have to tell him," she said, taking Arthur's arm and guiding him away from the door and down the porch. "You can lock up if you finish before I get home, Wade."

"We'll wait," I informed her and *him*, crossing my arms. "Don't be too late."

"Yes, Daddy." She tossed a sinful smirk over her shoulder, swaying her curvy ass all the way to Arthur's truck.

I couldn't help but picture spanking that ass for her sassing me. My mind quickly conjured another image of what she could do with that mouth. I curled my hands into fists, the itch to touch her skin a little too bright in my imagination. Before they backed down the drive in Arthur's truck, I slammed the door and headed to the shed to do what I came to do and get the hell home where I belonged.

"I'll be working in the shed out back if you need me, Jake." I took my watch off and set it on the coffee table, not wanting to damage it while welding.

"Okay, Dad." My son was still cuddled up on the sofa with Marly's dogs and his new book.

I don't know why I'd told Marly we'd wait for her, because why the hell should I? It wasn't my responsibility to make sure she got home safe and sound from her date. Arthur seemed okay, unless he was hiding some deviant serial killer beneath his polite exterior. Would he try to kiss her? Maybe we should wait.

Stomping through the kitchen, I glared at that fireman calendar with one of Jed's coworkers posing shirtless, aggravated that this irritated me too. I was going to walk on by when something else caught my eye on the fridge. It was the picture of me and Jed when we were kids, standing in the yard in our underwear while we washed off the mud from a deer hunt.

Nana must've given it to Marly the other night. I stepped closer, smiling at the two of us, looking so young and caught like deer in headlights by my grandmother in our underwear. I chuckled at the memory of us being terrified that she'd somehow use the picture against us. She only brought it out on occasion to embarrass us in front of the family. And now, with Marly.

Funny, I wasn't really embarrassed at all. I'm not quite sure what I was feeling that Marly had decided to put it at the top of her fridge, front and center. But it had the tension loosening from my muscles, the tightness easing from my chest.

Tapping the picture, I then marched outside, pulled open the shed door, and sat on the stool next to the table. I'd get this still built for her, then Jake and I would head home.

Maybe.

CHAPTER 7
~MARLY~

Giddiness fluttered in my belly when Arthur pulled up into my driveway behind Wade's truck. He'd waited. The fact that I was elated to return from a date to find another man's truck in my driveway should've given me pause. But I couldn't help it.

Arthur was a nice guy, but I didn't want to tell him that I knew our date would be getting low rankings on the date-o-meter for the podcast. He barely said ten words the whole time we'd been together/ After a quick bite at Bucky's where I'd rambled on to fill the silence, he took me to see a romantic comedy. I suppose he thought that was a good date movie. But no movie was a good date movie on the first date.

That was something Lola and I had discussed early on. Movie dates needed to be saved for the third date or later. First dates required places where you could actually talk and get to know the person. All I knew about Arthur was he wore a beard well, didn't like to talk, and rigidly followed his routine.

When I mentioned we could get some coffee afterwards, he'd looked at his watch and said he couldn't because it was nearly his bedtime.

I'd bitten my lip to keep from laughing, because he was the only adult I knew under seventy who had a bedtime. It was barely nine o'clock. He further explained that he had to work early, and he had to keep to his schedule.

Though Arthur was a polite, handsome, likeable guy, he had zero game and his rigidity was a bit much for me. We also lacked any sort of chemistry. His frowns and basic broody demeanor didn't have the same effect Wade's had on me. Funny, that.

Speaking of which, Wade was waiting inside my house, and I couldn't wait to get in there.

"Thank you for a nice night, Arthur. I'll see you this week for the podcast recording?"

"Sure. Let me come open your door."

"No, that's okay. I've got it. Goodnight!" I hurried to hop out then practically sprinted up my walkway and into the house.

My heart nearly melted right into my stomach at seeing the sight on my sofa. Jake was curled up, both of my dogs cocooning him, Pooter by his belly, Scooter laying at his feet with his chin propped on Jake's ankle. Scooter peeked open his eyes then closed them again, neither moving a muscle to greet me. Seems they found a new favorite person. I couldn't even be mad about it, because Jake was the sweetest boy on earth.

Then I smelled coffee and heard the tinkle of a spoon on glass. Pulling off my jacket, I tossed it on the club chair and ambled into my kitchen to find Wade pouring a shot of moonshine into a coffee cup.

"How was your date?" he asked, pouring a second shot into another cup.

He added some vanilla creamer I had in the fridge then passed one over to me.

"Moonshine in coffee?" I asked, wondering why I'd never thought of doing that.

"This was Pop's idea of a nightcap when I was sixteen. I think he thought since it was a coffee drink, he wasn't contributing to the delinquency of a minor."

A bubbly warmth filled me at the thought of his Pop corrupting his grandson with moonshine coffee drinks. I sipped from the mug, my eyes widening with the burst of sweet fire on my tongue.

"Mmm. What's in this?" I glanced at my counter, seeing cinnamon next to a jar of Salted Caramel moonshine I'd brought home from work last week.

"Just what you see there. I usually use unflavored moonshine with Pop, but," he hesitated, glancing away from me, "I thought you might like the cinnamon."

"I love cinnamon."

He nodded and sipped his coffee, a heavy silence filling the space between us. His intense hazel eyes took a trip down my body, and I felt it everywhere. I hoped my girls weren't giving him a nipply salute, because they were definitely trying to show off for his inspection.

"How was your date?" he asked again.

I shrugged. "Fine."

"Going out with him again?"

His voice was casual but there was a steeliness to his stance. Did he care if I went out with Arthur again?

"No. It was just a podcast date."

"You don't go out with podcast dates more than once?"

"Sometimes." I watched his shoulders stiffen. "But not this time."

He watched me a few seconds more, and I was perfectly fine with the awkward quiet spreading between us. Funny how I didn't like it at all with most people. This was a new experience. Perhaps that's because his tense body language and heated gaze were saying plenty all by themselves.

He knocked back the rest of his coffee and set the cup in my sink. "Come see your still." Then he turned and marched out the back door.

I was getting used to his abrupt nature, and I don't know why but his sharp commands and curt manners were revving my engine. Quite unusual seeing as I tended to like the playful, wild guys. He was anything but. Still, there was no mistaking the fluttering going on in my belly and heat happening between my legs told me that I was more than attracted to the big, growly bear.

I drank the rest of my coffee, humming at the pleasant burn down my throat then followed him. That had me pondering some flavor combinations for another moonshine for my own distillery. I was contemplating that while also ogling Wade's nice ass when he opened the shed door. He'd started a fire in my chiminea while he was working apparently, but it had died down to glowing embers. Even so, the golden light reflected off my still standing on the table in one piece, looking like a shiny copper trophy.

"Oh, my God!"

I was rarely astonished, but for some reason I hadn't expected to feel a kind of euphoric pleasure at the sight of my new still all put together. I ran over and wrapped my arms around it then pressed a kiss to the top of the kettle.

When I stepped back, laughing and jumping a little in place, I knew Wade would be wearing his confused expression. He totally was.

"Are you always this weird?" he asked.

Rather than answer his question, I walked over and wrapped my arms around his waist and squeezed, my cheek landing right at the base of his throat.

"Thank you so much."

Hesitantly, I felt his arms come around me, enveloping me in his warmth. I inhaled his lovely, masculine scent. It was woodsy. Cedar maybe. Or pine. There was also a citrus scent like oranges, probably from his soap or shampoo. But then there was whatever the hell scent Wade created from his own body. That had my heart kicking faster. This was so not good. But also, it was very, very good.

"You're welcome," he said in that deeper register that made me tingly. He patted my back, seeming to become uncomfortable. "It's not that big a deal," he rumbled, and I felt his words vibrate against my cheek.

I huffed out a laugh and released him, backing up and tucking my hair behind my ears. Staring at the still, all shiny and perfect like my dream, I didn't bother to tell him that my own father would never in a million years help me as much as Wade had already.

"Marly? Are you okay?"

He looked at me with concern. I didn't want to tell him about my father and why this *was* a big deal to me.

"I'm just excited," I told him, which was true.

He nodded. "All right then. I better get Jake home."

"He's going to have to visit Scooter and Pooter," I said as I followed him back into the house. "I'm afraid my little boys have fallen in love with him."

Wade's expression was softer than I'd ever seen it as he held the door open for me, thinking about his son. I wanted to memorize that look, maybe take a picture and keep it forever.

"I suppose I'll have to break down and get a dog soon now." But he didn't seem that mad about the idea.

"Sorry about that."

He smiled. "Not your fault. He's been begging for a dog since forever. He loves animals. I'll get him a pet eventually."

I nodded, feeling a little intrusive on him and Jake for some reason. They were a sweet duo, and I couldn't help but want to be a part of their tiny circle.

Glancing around, I asked, "Where's your welding kit and stuff?"

"Already put it in the truck." He stood there, hands low on his hips, staring at me, his eyes flitting between my own and my mouth.

No. *Way.* Was he thinking about kissing me?

"I better get Jake home."

"You said that already."

I didn't break the tension, because I was enjoying simmering in its scintillating goodness. What was obviously uncomfortable for Wade revved me up with heart palpitations and heated arousal.

He cleared his throat and dropped his gaze first, walking directly into the living room. My phone buzzed from my jacket pocket while Wade leaned over the sofa, dislodged my puppies gently, and scooped Jake into his arms.

Pulling my phone from my jacket, I then checked the text and cursed under my breath.

"What is it?" asked Wade, coming closer with his son tucked against his chest, Jake's head on his shoulder.

My breath caught a second at the tender sight of him holding his son so protectively close.

"Nothing. I forgot to send Lola her nightly meme. She was wondering if something was wrong and if I'd made it home okay."

"Your what?"

I clicked on my Gallery app and found the folder for the funny and somewhat naughty memes I collected so that I could send one to my best friend every night. It was a tradition I'd started years ago, and I rarely missed a night.

"It's a private joke. See." I turned my phone screen to face him. "Here's the one I just sent." I turned my phone screen to face him.

He read what I'd just texted to Lola. It showed two old men running away from a drug store, arms full of Viagra. The caption read: *Police are looking for two hardened criminals.*

Wade's frown deepened. He didn't laugh, just gave me that same look he did that day at Green Valley Shine when he'd found me and Jake hiding behind the bar.

"Yeah, I know. It's not one of my best. I've got some better ones."

"You send her one of those every night?"

"We're very good friends. I'm dedicated."

"I see that."

"You want me to send you one? I can see you're a little jealous."

He blinked at me. "I'm not jealous."

"Whatever you say."

His scowl deepened which only made me smile wider.

"Would you get the door for me?"

I was starting to worry about myself, because every time he grumbled at me in that deep, gruff voice, heat simmered and pulsed between my thighs. I'm pretty sure I had a growling fetish now, and I didn't even know that was a thing.

I grabbed the pink throw on the back of my sofa and wrapped it over Jake. "It's getting chilly outside."

Wade stiffened as I tucked the throw between Jake and Wade's chest. His wide, hard chest. Too bad Wade wasn't a fireman, because I'd love to see him on that calendar.

"Dammit," he muttered, "I forgot my watch. Can you grab it from the coffee table?"

I turned and picked up the hefty silver monstrosity. "Dang, this is a serious watch. What's this little thing in the corner?"

"It's a compass."

"A compass? You an explorer?" I teased.

"Never know when you're going to lose your way in the woods with a job like mine."

"I bet you know where every direction leads you in a fifty-mile radius."

His heavy gaze was fixed and focused. "I do." His serious nature made me laugh and turned me on all at the same time.

"Thank you again, Wade." I tucked the watch into the front pocket of his jeans, having to work to wedge the big thing in there, which had me wanting to glance down at his other big thing. I resisted the temptation since it seemed a little too pervy while he was holding his sweet son. Rather than fondle the poor man any more than necessary to give him his watch, I stepped back. "I really do appreciate your help."

"Not a problem." He swallowed hard. "I'll be heading to Pop's cabin tomorrow to clear things out for you to use. I haven't been up there in a while, and there might be limbs blocking the road."

"I'll come with you," I offered quickly. "I should help."

I fully expected him to protest, but instead, his darkened gaze swept over my face for a few seconds then he said, "I'll drop Jake off with my grandparents and pick you up around nine. Is that too early?"

"Not at all. I'm an early bird."

He grunted.

"What does that mean?" I asked, resting my hand on Jake's back, enjoying the feel of him breathing beneath my palm.

"I just took you for a night owl."

"Well, I do stay up late too. I'm just one of those people who doesn't sleep much. I feel like I'm missing out on something if I sleep too long. You know what I mean?"

"Not one bit," he grumbled, his voice low so as not to wake his son. But the effect was that his voice rolled like low thunder with a vibrating timbre that sent arm tingles along my skin. "I like sleeping in when I can."

He wasn't saying anything sexy. Like, at all. But still, I imagined him lounging like a big bear in his bed, spread out naked under his covers.

"Pick you up at nine then." He moved to the door.

I opened it for him, then I hurried ahead of him to open the passenger door of his truck so he could lay Jake on the front seat. He managed to loop the seatbelt around him in his prone position and tucked my pink blanket around him, which made that sweet warm feeling return tenfold. The way he loved his son was too adorable.

He rounded the front of his truck and got in, rolling the passenger window down.

"Get back inside, Marly."

I stepped back to the walkway, crossing my arms in the chilly air. "Good-night, Wade."

"And lock your door."

He was still using *that* voice. I shivered, and not from the cold, then hurried back inside. I locked the bolt and peeked through the window blinds next to the door. Wade was sitting in his truck, frowning at my front door, like he could detect if I'd obeyed his orders or not. I'm not sure why that was so hot, but I was well and truly turned on.

Then he looked down at his sleeping son and reached an arm to drape over him as he backed out of my drive. The tenderness of it sent another kind of warmth through me. Flustered and confused and still aroused, I headed to bed, excited to head out into the wilderness with him tomorrow.

CHAPTER 8

~WADE~

As I drove down Marly's street, I tried not to analyze why there was an unnatural burst of excitement humming through me this morning. Why the last person I thought of before I fell asleep was Marly. When I went to Jake's bedroom this morning, she was there again as I remembered Jake sleeping on her sofa, snuggled by her dogs.

Scooter and Pooter? Those were the craziest damn names I'd ever heard of. Maybe that's why my blood pumped with a thrill to spend the day with her. Because she said and did things that were so unexpected.

It was more than that, and I knew it. Something about her had stirred the lustful—and for the longest time, dormant—animal inside of me. It was in the tilt of her feline eyes, the arch of her slender brow and the mysterious smirk she wore that had me thinking of dark rooms and what we could do to each other in them.

Which was absolute insanity!

I had to stop thinking about her like this. Keep it friendly. Not just for my sake, but for Jake's too. He loved his Mom and she loved him, but just like in the last several years of our marriage, she wasn't around much. Even less so now than when we were. When she picked him up for their weekends together, Jake lit up like a firefly, basking in her motherly affection.

I'd even noticed how Jake often gravitated to Lola when we were with her and Jed. He'd even sit on her lap and let her rub his back. So no, it wasn't lost on me that Jake was in need of a more frequent, or rather, permanent feminine fixture in his life.

That's why I had to tread carefully here. I couldn't get his hopes up about Marly then let the poor kid get heartbroken when she suddenly disappeared from his life. Because I was pretty damn sure that Marly wouldn't consider anything permanent with me.

Thankfully, Kristie was coming in two weeks and keeping him for several days before she headed overseas for a conference. I'd okayed his absence with the school since his mother wouldn't see him for a while. They said it would be no problem and he could easily catch up what he missed over the Thanksgiving break. Maybe by then, my part in helping Marly get her still going at Pop's cabin would be finished, and he'd forget about her.

Something pinched in my chest at the thought as I hopped out of my truck and headed up her walkway. She popped open the door and pulled it shut behind her then hurried down the porch steps before I'd made it halfway.

"Look at you, Wade Kelley. Being the gentleman and coming to my door to get me."

"How the hell else would you know I was here?"

I inspected her to be sure she was bundled up properly for today's travel into the mountains. A cold front blew in last night. The sky was slate-gray and didn't show a chance of sunshine all day. And it was colder than a witch's tit up there.

"Oh, I don't know. You could honk this little thing called your horn on your truck. Or better yet, send me a text."

She was standing in front of me now, all bright smiles and hypnotic eyes.

"My mother taught me better than to honk a horn for a lady to come running," was all I could manage to say as I soaked in this radiance she beamed.

"A lady?" Her ocean-blue eyes widened. "Wade, you don't have to flirt with me to get my attention. I'm already riveted."

Flinching at her forwardness and surprised at her sort of admission of attraction, I argued, "I'm not flirting."

I couldn't even respond to the last thing she said. I was pretty damn sure that if Marly offered me anything, I was going to take it. Morals and best friend boundaries be damned.

She laughed, that rich throaty sound making a straight line to the growing bulge in my jeans which made me glad to have on my longer wool coat. I glanced down at her hands.

"Where are your gloves? You need them today."

"Oh! They're in my pocket."

She dug around in her puffy purple jacket's pockets, then pulled out two leather gloves and waved them at me.

"All ready, Papa Bear."

"Don't call me that," I growled and marched back to the truck.

"Okay. How about *Daddy* Bear?"

I jerked opened the passenger door and glared down at her when she stopped right in front of me, bold and brazen as you please.

"Don't call me that either."

She shivered, her eyes slipped half-closed as she whispered almost innocently, "How about just Daddy?" But there was no way she intended that to be innocent.

"Marly," I warned. "Get in the fucking truck."

She grinned as she brushed by me, her breasts grazing my chest as she slid sideways.

Fucking hell, I was in serious trouble.

I slammed her door shut and hurried round the front to get in. Once I watched her buckle herself in, I did the same and pulled out of her small neighborhood, taking the highway up the mountain. We were both quiet, but I didn't want her steering the conversation, because she always took it somewhere that left me perplexed and dumbfounded.

"So did you always want to live in your grandmother's house one day?"

"I'd never given it one thought until she died, really."

I drummed the steering wheel with my fingers, realizing I'd touched on a sensitive subject by the hint of pain in her voice. She'd seemed okay the other night telling me about her Granny Mae, but apparently it still hurt more than I realized.

"Sorry. I didn't mean to bring her up if it's a tough subject."

"It's not my Granny Mae," she said more softly. "I love talking about her. She was the greatest person I ever knew."

I glanced sideways to find her staring straight ahead, her expression grimmer than I'd ever seen it.

"It's the fact that my father didn't think twice about selling her house the second she was in the ground." She huffed out a breath. "I mean, I know he wasn't glad his mother died, but you'd have caught whiplash if you'd seen how fast he'd put her house on the market, glad to finally be rid of his last tie to Green Valley."

"He doesn't like Green Valley?" Because that seemed unheard of.

"It's not that exactly, it's that he doesn't see this as a place of opportunity."

"Opportunity how?"

"As in professionally and for a rising attorney."

I was more confused than ever. "You want to be a lawyer?"

"No. I don't," she stated with disdainful emphasis. "Not that there's anything wrong with that. It's just not for me. But my father is a pushy S.O.B., and he doesn't like it here or more to the point, he doesn't like me being here, or any ties to his small-town past. He was one of those who grew up, dying to bust out of here and make a life in the bigger city."

That was quite a bit to take in. "But you are here. He's got ties here whether he likes it or not."

"I wasn't here for a while actually. After college. I lived and worked in Knoxville." Her words were tempered with something like sadness, but a little harder. "I used to stay the weekend with Granny at least once a month. And when she died—"

She broke off, looking out the passenger window now. The leafless limbs of the trees whipped by as we headed deeper into the woods.

"You didn't want to let her go," I offered gently.

She turned her head to look at me. No tears glistened on her cheeks or in her eyes, but the sadness dripped from her in addition to a small smile of gratefulness.

"I didn't. So I told Dad I wanted to buy her house, and wow"—she let out a laugh with no hint of humor in it— "that nearly started World War III in my family."

"But why?" I asked, honestly confused.

"Because at the time, I was working for my father. He never particularly liked growing up here. Shot out at eighteen to attend UT and then law school and only came home on holidays. So when I told him I wanted to move to Green Valley and buy Granny Mae's house, he was angry. And when I told him I was quitting as one of his paralegals, he kind of lost it."

"Oh." I couldn't imagine having a parent like that. My parents have always been loving and supportive, no matter what I chose.

When Kristie got pregnant during college, and we were getting married, they completely supported me, even though they had their doubts about the marriage. When I decided I wanted to quit college football and not take the opportunity to go pro because I wanted to raise my son close to home, they were perfectly supportive. When I told them I was getting divorced, they never were anything but loving parents to lean on.

"Yeah." Marly shook her head on another loaded laugh. "Oh."

I didn't quite know what to say since this was obviously a difficult subject, and it wasn't my place to pry. Even though I wanted to know more about what happened to put that cynical note in her voice regarding her own father when I'd never heard her sound that way about anyone ever. Not even in high school.

So I drove us higher up the mountain in silence till I saw the turn-off onto the narrower road that wound toward Pop's cabin. Her gaze was fixed out the side window. It was a good forty-minute drive from Green Valley's town center, but it was a peaceful one too.

"Good heavens, it's beautiful up here."

She must've been thinking the same thing. Her voice had lightened too. A knot dislodged in my chest and loosened my limbs. "It is."

"This is all your Pop's property?"

"Not all." I pointed to our left. "Most of that side belongs to the Pruitt family. They all live in Nashville now, but they keep the property for hunting and logging. Both ours and Pop's property line butts up against the park. It's really quiet up here."

Though the light gray clouds seemed to be pressing lower, the bare woods with some evergreens dappling the monochromatic landscape was lovely in a stark kind of beauty. These mountains had always been a place of peace for me. I couldn't imagine being like Marly's father who wanted only to leave them.

"You used to come here with your Pop?" she asked.

"And my dad when I was younger. All the time."

"You even made moonshine with Pop?"

I felt her intense gaze on me while I focused on the road.

"Yeah. Now look up ahead," I told her.

In my peripheral, I saw her head snap front where I pointed.

"You see that tree that looks like a giant Y? The trunk forks in two?"

"Yeah, I see it."

"That's the turn-off toward Pop's property. It's hard to see, and you'll miss it if you're not looking for it."

"What's the name of the road?"

"There's no sign marking it, so just remember the tree."

"So there's no name to the road?" she asked in disbelief.

"There's no sign, but it does have a name." I turned onto the road leading onto Pop's land.

"Is it a state secret or something? Why won't you tell me?"

Heaving a sigh, because I knew what her reaction would be, I said, "It's called Y-tree Road."

She burst into laughter which made me feel suddenly warm in her presence. "No way."

"You think I'd make that up?"

"Who named it?"

"It doesn't matter," I snapped.

"You did! Stop it right now. You did, didn't you?"

She looked so pleased I thought she would burst with excitement.

"I did," I finally clarified, because I loved this side of her, the bright and happy one, not the sad one from before. "When I was nine."

Still laughing, she angled to look at me. "Of course you did. Even back then, little Wade was logical in his road-naming skills. I bet when you played G.I. Joe, you actually called him Joe."

"What else would I call him?"

"Stop!" She tilted her head back, a full-on throaty laugh filling my cab. "You didn't."

"No, I didn't. Because I didn't play with G.I. Joe. That would require imagination."

"What did you play with?" she asked, teasingly but also seeming interested.

"I liked sports. And board games."

"Why's that?"

"Because there are rules you had to follow."

She was quiet a second. When I glanced over, she was staring intently at me. "What?"

"Nothing. That just makes a lot of sense. Rule-following seems to be your thing."

I wasn't sure what that meant, positive or negative in her book—probably negative—but I wanted her mind on the road. "Pay attention. I don't want you to get lost when you come up here on your own."

"You're going to let me come on my own?"

"Well, I imagine you'll be brewing up several batches in the coming weeks. I can't guide you up here every time. That reminds me." I picked up the shiny silver key from the cup-holder on the middle console and handed it to her. "That's a key to Pop's cabin."

"You made a key for me?"

"Yeah." I'd gotten up and hit the Eager Beaver's Hardware and Lumber store before eight to make sure I'd have time to make her one. But I didn't tell her all that.

"You're giving me my own key?"

"How else are you supposed to get in?"

She was quiet, which was not a normal state of being for Marly. I glanced over to find her staring at me with the sappiest expression I've ever seen.

"What?" I asked, genuinely confused.

"I can't believe you're being so sweet to me, Wade. I was so wrong about you."

"The devil knows what you thought of me before, but I'm just being practical." Though it did make me wonder what she *had* thought of me before. "Pop wants you to use it. He'll get bragging rights that the winning moonshine was made on his property. That is, if you win."

"I'm gonna win."

"And I can't coddle you and carry you up here every time you want to come work. But hear me now, Marly Rivers." I slowed the truck and put it in park, turning on her with the full force of what Jake called my scary-dad-face. "Do not come up here after dark and do not stay up here after sundown. That means, you leave here by four o'clock every day to be sure there's enough daylight to find your way down the mountain. The woods get dark fast even before the sun is fully gone down. I don't care if you're brewing the best batch of moonshine in moonshine history, you leave it and get moving."

Her blue eyes were round and her expression blank for once. I couldn't read what she was thinking.

"Do you understand me?" I asked low and deep, just to be clear.

"Yes." She nodded, her voice husky. "I understand."

Letting my gaze linger on those impossibly blue eyes and full, pouty lips, I leaned back and shoved the truck into drive again.

"People easily get lost up here, and there's hardly any cell phone service. Oh, that's another thing. I've got a satellite walkie-talkie radio for you. One that connects to me and Ben and any other Wildlife Resources Agent in range. So if you need something, you can use that to reach one of us."

She became extraordinarily quiet. But when I glanced at her, she was simply looking ahead thoughtfully.

"There are two different forks off this main trail. We take a left here," I told her as we veered left at the fork onto a gravel road, leading us deeper into the woods. "Then a little ways up, we go right."

"What's down the other forks?"

"Nothing really. We used to go deer hunting that way, but I prefer to hunt closer down in the valley now whenever I want to go."

"Why's that?"

"Have you ever hauled a two-hundred-pound deer up a hill?"

"No. But isn't that why hunters use ATVs?"

"Yes, darlin'. But ATVs don't go everywhere. My grandfather's land is extremely hilly with lots of dips and valleys in the woods. His moonshine shack is on the most level piece of the property out here."

I felt her stare again. When I chanced a look, she was grinning like a maniac.

"What now?"

"I like the way you say *darlin'*." She drawled it with a sexy lilt.

"Don't start, Marly," I warned though some part of me heated with pleasure when she flirted with me.

But that was just it. Marly had been a flirt all her life. It didn't mean anything, and I know she got some sort of twisted kick out of making me uncomfortable. Right now, I was growing more and more uncomfortable with the way my hard dick was pressing into my jeans.

"Now look up ahead," I ordered, "this is where we go right at the fork. So from the highway, it's a right off the road at the Y-shaped tree."

"At Y-tree Road," she butted in with a sassy look.

Scowling, I said, "*Yes*. Then first fork left, second fork right. Got it?"

"Right then left then right. Easy peasy."

"Why don't you type it in your notes on your phone?"

She scoffed and stuck her hand in her pocket. "Do you really think I'm that dumb?"

"No. But it's an easy thing to get mixed up. And dangerous if you get lost out here by yourself."

"Oops." She laughed. "I can't anyway. I left my phone by the front door."

I cursed under my breath. "This is why you'll keep your walkie-talkie in your car. Shit." I stopped the truck suddenly. "I was afraid of this."

A small tree had fallen across the road. I hopped out and crunched across the dried leaves. Marly slammed her door shut and followed me over.

"Do you need help?"

I lifted one end. "Nah. It's rotted through and light enough."

She watched me as I hauled the upper half of the dead tree and heaved it into the underbrush along the side of the road. Something I couldn't read glimmered in those crystal eyes.

"What if it was bigger?" she asked.

"I've got a chainsaw in my truck for just the occasion."

"Always prepared, aren't you, Daddy Bear?"

I didn't answer or take her bait in riling me, but I did stand there and watch her hips and her tight ass as she sashayed back to the truck. She'd worn her blond hair in a ponytail. It swished against her purple coat, and I was having visions of wrapping my fist around it, bending her head back so I could kiss the fuck out of her. Before those thoughts carry me away even further, I got back in the truck and drove the last mile to Pop's cabin.

We came out of the trees to a wide flat piece of land. Pop's cabin didn't look too bad, except there was a heavy limb on the roof. I could see I'd need to replace some shingles from here.

"Wow." Marly clapped her hands over her mouth.

"It looks a little rough," I admitted, "but I'll get it fixed up pretty quick."

"Are you kidding me? You and Pop called it a shack. This isn't a shack. This is the cutest cabin I've ever seen in my whole life!"

As soon as I shifted into *Park*, she hopped out and ran around the front of the truck, standing there staring at it. I met her and tried to see it from her eyes.

It was about a thousand square feet total. A porch wrapped all the way around. The entire cabin was built of pine, coated in a natural stain to protect it from weathering. It had a gable roof and two dormer windows at the top.

I pointed to them. "I used to sleep in the loft when Pop and Dad and I stayed out here when I was younger. There's a great view of the stars from up there."

Those years came tumbling back to me, and I realized something.

"You don't bring Jake up here?" Marly asked, standing close to me now, like she was reading my mind.

"I haven't." I shook my head, wondering why. "Kristie hated it up here. She's a city girl, and so I kind of got out of the habit of coming." I stared at my childhood home away from home. "But you're right. I should bring him."

"You should." She fiddled with something in her hands, then I realized she was fitting the key I'd given her onto her keyring. Then she dangled the keys in front of me, grinning like a fiend. "Now I've gotta see the inside."

She ran across the round stones that led to the front porch. I helped Dad lay those when I was thirteen. Once she fitted the key into the rusty lock on the door, she shoved it open. I was right behind her. A wave of nostalgia hit me like a brick. It was dusty but still exactly the same, except for the tarps laid over the sparse furniture we'd hauled up here so many years ago.

Marly walked inside and did a full circuit of the open kitchen, living room, and bedroom. There were no walls to speak of. A double bed was shoved against the far wall, overlooking the back porch and woods that curved steeply downhill.

The kitchen was just a countertop, a sink with plumbing hooked to the pumping well. In the corner squatted a fat black wood-burning stove with a cylindrical black venting pipe that went straight up and out through the roof. A small fireplace in the living room was surrounded by a sofa and two chairs made of wood and not very comfortable cushions, if I recall correctly. Then there was a wooden ladder that led to the loft which held nothing more than a mattress.

"Wade. This is *not* a shack." Marly huffed out a laugh.

"Depends who you ask, I suppose. Nothing like those cabins up by Gatlinburg and Pigeon Forge." I lifted the coverings over the furniture. "It ain't luxury living, but it's a good, well-built cabin. We don't have a running toilet. Just an outhouse in the back. But we do have fresh spring water. Which of course you'll need for your still."

"Where's that?" she asked excitedly, her eyes glowing like a kid on Christmas morning.

"This way." I went to the door next to the kitchen and opened it up, leading her into the workshop-like room which was specifically built as an afterthought for making Pop's moonshine. Light shone in from the large windows. There was a new hole in the ceiling, unfortunately. "It looks bad, but I can fix that later."

It was dirtier than the rest of the cabin. Leaves had fallen through the hole, leaving the room with a mustier smell than the dry cabin.

"You brought roofing supplies?" she quirked a brow at me.

"No. But we have some extra tin around back I can use to at least cover it for now."

She laughed. "I was going to say if you happened to have roof tiles in your truck then you truly are the most well-prepared person I know."

I didn't bother telling her that I typically kept a little of everything in my toolbox, including material that might patch a roof. She already found my over-preparedness amusing enough.

She raised her arms and spun in a circle, letting out an excited squeal. "This place is fantastic!" She whirled on me, bright eyes beaming. "Wouldn't it be awesome to live out here?" she asked with a kind of breathless awe.

I blinked at her a second. "Hell, no. It would be a nightmare. There's no plumbing or hot water." I shivered, remembering the creek baths Pop would make me take when we stayed out here for more than two days at a time.

Her burst of laughter was so infectious, I didn't mind it was at my expense. "You are such a grumpy bear, Wade."

"I'm practical. You take a bath in that creek down below and tell me how long you want to live out here."

She rolled her eyes. "I do believe I spotted a stove inside. You can heat up water."

"To fill a whole tub?" I shook my head. Pop, Dad, and I never once bothered to consider doing something so frivolous as heat water for a bath. "Besides, we don't even have a tub."

"There are portable ones. You do know that, right?"

"You and your smart mouth," I rumbled, staring at that part of her anatomy with too much interest.

Her bright smile dimmed a little, her gaze drifting down my chest then lower. Marly flirted with everyone, that was true. But that look right there, the one that told me she appreciated what she was looking at, that was going to start something I wasn't sure I was ready for.

I suddenly broke from her gaze and stepped up the two stairs into the main cabin, stopping to look back. "Why don't you get started cleaning up in here, and I'll work on the roof. There's a broom in the supply closet. I'll get a fire going first though."

It was still below freezing. I didn't have to look at the gauge we kept on the porch to know it. Even with coat and gloves on, she might get cold. A discomforting feeling lodged in my chest at the thought, so I walked straight through the cabin and out toward the woods to gather kindling, wanting to make sure Marly kept warm.

CHAPTER 9

~MARLY~

I stood in front of the fireplace, brimming with a warm, fuzzy feeling. This wasn't the kind I was used to wallowing in. Excitement, giddiness, frustration, humor. Those were my typical modes of operation. But this fluffy, cottony emotion that had me smiling at absolutely nothing as I looked around the well-cleaned cabin while warming my hands behind my back? I wasn't quite sure what brought it on.

Wade had removed the branch and covered the hole in the roof while I cleaned out the room where I'd be making my moonshine. He hauled out a small ice chest from his truck, handing me a turkey and Swiss sandwich, a bag of chips, and a water. "Didn't know what you liked. You can have the ham and cheese if you want," he offered gruffly.

After recovering from the fact that Mr. Always Prepared had thought enough to pack us a lunch, we settled next to the fire and ate quietly before returning to work. I suppose I hadn't realized how long this would take. But Wade had and he'd packed us a lunch. It made me smile like a fool and had stirred to life this soft, lovely sensation I was currently enjoying.

After lunch, I'd cleaned the rest of the cabin, wishing I'd found some clean sheets to make the bed. I'd bring some up here along with Scooter and Pooter when I came to make my first batch. I wasn't planning on taking a nap or sleeping here, but something made me want to fix everything up perfect and pretty up here.

My dogs were wily, curious little pups. They'd love exploring out here. Earlier, Wade nearly had an apoplectic fit when I mentioned how great it would be to live out here.

Granny Mae always said I was a romantic stuck inside a warrior princess's body. I never quite understood her metaphor, but now I got it. She was right. I was a fighter who liked feminine things. And underneath my Mad Marly exterior, I had a deeply romantic heart. This place reeked of nights under the stars, cooking hotdogs over the campfire, drinking hot coffee while watching the sun come up over the valley behind the cabin.

Wade stomped in from the moonshine shed as I'd started to call it. The room was closed in and more comfortable than a shed, but it was bare except for some sturdy worktables. There was a door that led outside to the back pump for getting mountain spring water straight out of the ground. It was absolutely perfect.

A new wave of elation bubbled inside me that this would be the perfect spot to test out all the flavors I wanted for my own distillery. Of course, I knew I'd eventually have to purchase commercial-sized equipment, but I needed to start small.

I didn't plan on being Green Valley Shine's competition. Hell, I honestly didn't want to be. I learned so much from working there and appreciated all they'd taught me. I wanted to be a boutique-sized moonshine distillery, changing my flavors like a seasonal chef changes his menu. I'd already spotted a place in town near the Donner Bakery that would be perfect.

"I don't even want to know what's going on in that head of yours right now," Wade grumbled as he pulled off his gloves, cupped his hands over his mouth and blew into them.

"Come over here and get warm." I'd taken off my jacket and set my gloves aside while I stood here, spinning dreams in my head.

He tromped closer, his heavy boots loud on the wooden floor, his gaze wary for some reason. "I primed the pump and it's good to go. I was worried it might be frozen at the top, but it's clear."

"Thank you. That's great."

He stretched his giant hands out to the fire. I noticed he had some freckles scattered across the backs and knuckles. He didn't have any on his face or neck. Then I found myself wondering where else he might have them.

"I stacked up some kindling and firewood for you on the porch too, in case you want to start a fire."

Yeah, I knew he had. I'd watched him from the front window. I'd been sweeping the kitchen area when I saw his jacket draped over the hood of his truck and heard the sound of the chainsaw. That's when I got the glorious sight of Wade using said chainsaw to cut a giant fallen tree into small pieces.

Look, I subscribed to one of those hot lumberjack YouTube channels who showed off his muscles while hacking up stumps with his ax. But there was something near primal about watching Wade go to work on a tree as big around as a cow and nearly as long as a football field, manhandling almost the whole damn thing into neat stacks of firewood with far too much ease. That's when I took my own jacket off and tried to get comfortable, because watching the man was making me sweat.

"The wood stove will heat up the room as well if you want to just start the fire in there and cook something while you're out here. I know it usually takes four to five hours to distill one batch so you may need to bring something to eat."

"I might do that."

I never seemed to remember how big he was until he was standing right next to me. He didn't take his eyes off his outstretched hands he held to the fire, but I couldn't take my eyes off of him. The firelight made his hazel eyes a warm gold, his auburn hair more red. Even his beard which was a shade darker was cast in a lovely golden-red hue by the firelight. It hit me rather hard all of a sudden.

He was beautiful. I mean, *really* beautiful. You might not notice beneath his constant scowls and glares but right now, he was relaxed, his features soft and tranquil.

"I like you like this," I told him, fully expecting him to ruin the moment and frown at me.

But when he turned to meet my gaze, there wasn't a hint of his usual ornery self in his expression.

"Like what?"

I shrugged a shoulder. "Less bear-like."

Again, he surprised me by huffing out a laugh rather than growling something at me.

Then something caught my eye from the window. "No. Way!"

I squealed and ran across the living room then barreled outside and down the porch onto the crunchy leaves. Opening my arms, I stared up and caught the tingly snowflakes on my palms.

"What in the hell are you doing? You need your jacket!"

"Look how beautiful." I ignored him, spinning in a circle.

"You'll catch your death. Come get your jacket if you're going to stand out there like a lunatic."

"Uh oh." Laughing, I kept spinning slowly, loving this vertical view of the snow coming down in puffy flakes. "The bear is back."

"Marly, I'm serious."

Looking down at my palm, I caught a few flakes and peered closely at their unique crystalline patterns as they melted against my skin. Then I walked over to the elm tree beside the porch where the snow was already accumulating on the long, slender branches.

"So pretty," I whispered.

Our snows are few and far between. Usually, it doesn't stick for long. I'd always found it so lovely, how it put a powdery white coat on everything around. I had a friend from Michigan who said she was pretty sure that hell was cold and white and covered in snow, because where she's from it was a painful nuisance. But here in the Smoky Mountains where snow sprinkled glittery flakes in soft waves on occasion felt like magic trickling from heaven.

I figured Wade must've gone inside, but when I turned, he was simply standing on the porch staring at me with that deep, thoughtful look. His expression was soft, but his eyes were intense and focused on me.

"Come on, Wade! Come play in the snow!"

"There's nothing to play in. It'll likely stop before there's an inch accumulated on the ground anyway. You're going to get sick if you don't get out of it."

"You are the biggest glass half empty person I've ever known."

"Just stating facts, sweetheart."

I know he didn't mean anything by it, but my tummy flipped all the same when he called me by the endearment. I tromped back over to the porch and up the steps, grabbing both his hands.

"Come on."

"Why? So I can get cold again for no damn good reason."

"There is a damn good reason." I smiled, because he was letting me pull him down the porch. Lord knows if he'd dug his heels in there was no way I was moving this behemoth.

"Enlighten me."

I tugged him to the center of the yard in front of the porch, still holding onto his hands, neither of us wearing gloves. His rough callouses and big, strong hands felt divine in mine.

"For a new perspective. Now." I stopped him and put my hands on his biceps. Then swallowed at the feel of the massive firm muscles he was hiding under his coat. "Look up."

For a moment, he simply stared down at me and I gazed right back, both of us caught up in a hypnotic daze. He lifted a hand and swept a flake from my eyebrow, his fingers coasting down my cheek and along my jaw before the warm tips fell away. I held my breath then he blinked heavily and tilted his head up. I did the same, still holding onto his biceps, like he might try to bolt for the warm indoors if I let go.

"I love the first snow. It's like hope and happiness floating down from heaven in pretty, fluffy flakes." I laughed at myself, knowing how sappy that sounded. But I felt it all the same. "Isn't it beautiful?"

He said nothing but kept looking for what felt like ten minutes but was probably closer to two. He tilted his head back down. "It is."

My heart thumped heavily in my chest, then I realized I was still holding onto him. This close, it felt nearly like a hug. I had a feeling if Wade ever wrapped those strong arms around me, I might never want to leave.

"Do you always do nonsense things like this?" he asked in a serious voice.

"Yeah." I laughed. "It makes life fun."

"I think I'm too logical for fun."

I couldn't even giggle at that. He was so somber, almost sad about a fact he just confessed to me.

"You should adjust your perspective sometimes," I told him softly as the pillowy snow whirled down around us. "Put away your grumpy face and do nonsense stuff that makes you happy."

"That's hard to do."

"Why's that so hard to do?"

He huffed, his breath puffing out in a swirly gust. "Because I've got responsibilities. A son to raise on my own. Hell, I've got parenting books to read that make no sense at all, but I keep reading them so I don't screw Jake up." He stepped back, my arms dropped, but he didn't go far. Then he added, "He's a special kid. And I know parents always say that about their own, but Jake's smarter than me and I'm terrified I'm just not—" He didn't finish the sentence, his gaze back on the ground where snow slowly piled between us.

"He is special," I admitted gently. "And he's got a special dad who cares so much for him. Don't you?"

He scowled at me, his frown deeper than ever. "Of course I do. I love him more than anything in the world."

My heart squeezed at the sincerity and passion in his voice. "He's a lucky kid. And I bet he'd love to join you in some nonsense things that are fun. Not everything has to be logical and reasonable."

"I wouldn't know where to start, Marly. I don't think like you do."

I did laugh then, which drew his dark gaze to my face. "Take him to a movie on a school night. Or take him to that goat roller coaster over in Pigeon Forge."

"They have goats on a roller coaster? That can't be legal."

"No, Mr. Wildlife Agent. The goats are in a petting zoo at the bottom of the coaster." I snapped my fingers which barely made a sound, my fingers starting to numb from the cold. "I know! Camp out in your own backyard."

"What's the fun in that?" He looked honestly confused how that could possibly be fun. "We've got camping sites all over the place."

"Good Lord, Wade." I wrapped my arms around myself. "You are such a Negative Nancy. It's fun because it creates an adventure in a place of comfort. It puts joy in the mundane."

He stared like he was trying to figure out a puzzle.

When he said nothing, I added, "Sometimes you've gotta fill up on the small joys in life."

He grunted. "Are you telling me to stop and smell the roses?"

"No. Yes. Well, maybe. I'm telling you to loosen up, step out of your comfort zone, find those little joys with Jake."

He nodded with a quiet, "I'll try."

My heart pinched at the thought of having such a devoted father like Wade. It was obvious he lived and breathed for his son. Not that my father, my parents, didn't provide me with everything I needed. It's just that my dad was always trying to fix me, make me something I'm not. Make me more like my sister who had gone to law school and was now partner at a firm in Knoxville. Wade simply wanted to be the best dad possible. I glanced away, blinking away the tenderness, rubbing my hands together.

His gaze dropped from my face to my shirt and shaking arms, that familiar scowl even fiercer. "Let's get inside. You need to get warm."

This time, I listened to him, because I was actually starting to shiver. When I stood before the fire, holding the hem out so the cold wetness of melted snow wasn't against my skin, he looked down at my shirt.

"Hang on. I'll be right back." Then he stormed back out to his truck.

I spent the minute and a half that he was gone gathering my wits.

Then he marched inside and said, "Take off your shirt."

My wits up and scattered again. I spun, grinning. He held a long-sleeved black t-shirt in his hand.

"Not even a kiss first?"

He flinched, a crimson flush crawling up his cheeks. "That's not what I meant."

I grabbed the hem of my shirt and flung it over my head anyway, glad I'd put on one of my demi-cup, pretty bras in black lace.

"Jesus, Marly." He turned away, flustered. "Here! Put this on." He held the shirt out, averting his gaze though I caught him sneaking one more peek before he added, "I'll—I'll wait outside."

He cursed something fierce all the way out the door. I smiled like the fiend I was as I slipped on his shirt. Of course he'd carry a spare in his truck. Through the window, I could see him facing away, hands on his hips, his mouth moving, still cursing I'm sure. I pressed the sleeve of the shirt to my face and inhaled the lovely, piney scent of Wade. After rolling up the sleeves to my wrists, I pulled on my jacket, lifted the hood and slipped on my gloves.

I opened the door. "You can look now."

"Are you sure?" he huffed with exasperation and probably a little sexual frustration.

"Yes. I am sure that I am fully dressed."

He turned slowly like he didn't believe me, his gaze dropping to where the hem of his shirt hit my thighs.

"See?" I said sweetly. "I can be a good girl." I gestured toward my hood. "All buttoned up like you want me."

He clenched his jaw as the molten gold of his eyes darkened and devoured me from head to foot. "Get in the truck," he said gruffly.

"Yes, sir," I replied just as pleasantly as before, knowing I was poking the bear and loving every second of it.

I hurried out to the truck while he banked the fire and covered the grate with a screen. I could see him through the big picture window of the cabin. He stalked out to the truck and started it up. There was still a warm glow in the windows of the cabin as the sky darkened, puffy flakes still fluttering down. The cabin looked even more picturesque.

Wade tossed his phone in the center console as he reversed and wound back up the gravel road.

"You broke one of your rules," I told him.

"What's that?" He turned up the heat and pointed two vents toward me. My hair was a little damp from the melted snow.

"It's five o'clock, Mr. Kelley. We're an hour behind curfew."

"No, ma'am." His mouth quirked into a sexy smirk that made my stomach flutter. "You mistake the rules. *You* are not to be here past four o'clock."

"How come you can and I can't?" I asked, a little miffed. "Is this a macho man thing?"

"No. This is an I-know-these-woods-and-roads-and-you-don't thing. If you get stuck out here after dark, you can easily miss the turns and lose your way."

On the one hand, I felt offended on behalf of women everywhere that he didn't think I could follow directions well enough to find my way in and out of these woods. On the other hand, maybe it wasn't about that. Maybe he was just worried…about me.

That had me shutting my smart mouth, that warm, fuzzy feeling from earlier returning ten-fold. We rode in contented silence back down the main highway, taking the sharp turns at a leisurely pace.

When his phone buzzed, I nearly jumped out of my skin. Jed's name popped up on his phone. He clicked hands-free on his wheel so the call came through on the truck's speakers.

"Yeah," said Wade.

Why did guys answer phones like that? The proper greeting was *hello*.

"Hey, Wade. Do you know where Marly is today?"

His penetrating gaze slid to me across the cab. "Yeah. She's been with me."

"With you?" Jed's voice rose in surprise.

"Hi, Jed!" I announced myself. "What's up?"

"Hey, Marly." He exhaled a relieved sigh. "Lola's been near hysterical because she's been trying to text and call you all day and you haven't answered. She thought something had happened."

"No. I just left my phone at home by accident."

We heard Jed muffle the phone and relay those exact words to Lola in the background. Then I heard Lola's higher pitched voice say something that sounded like *ducking bell* but I was pretty sure wasn't.

"She wants to know what y'all are doing," said Jed, sounding amused.

Then more muffled sounds and Lola's voice filled the cab. "Hey! What the hell have y'all been doing all day?"

She sounded very pleased and accusatory.

"Well," I started, "First, we went skinny dipping over at Bandit Lake. Then we had a picnic lunch, naked, where Wade fed me strawberries and whipped cream. Then we massaged each other with coconut oil and—"

"I took her to my Pop's cabin to clean all day," interrupted Wade with a bellowing voice to drown out whatever else I was planning to say. "So she can use it to make her moonshine."

I bit my lip and watched that blush crest his cheekbones again.

Lola laughed. "We're headed over to Genie's for a bite to eat if you two want to meet us there."

Before Wade could answer, I piped up, "Yes! That sounds great. Our picnic lunch was good and all, but I'm starving now."

"Sounds good. See y'all in a few."

He clicked the button on the wheel again and glared over at me. "Must you always be so crazy?"

He was irritated with me because I embarrassed him. I knew that. But the sting of his words—or one particular word actually—along with the annoyance in his voice made my heart fall like a stone into the pit of my stomach. I turned away before he could see the hurt on my face and said as lightly as possible, "You know me. Mad Marly."

CHAPTER 10
~WADE~

Marly was upset. She hadn't said a word since Jed's phone call, and it wasn't the contented quiet we'd shared on the way here this morning. Whatever had stolen the joy out of her—and I was afraid it was me—was winding me into a tight knot.

I'd called Nana on the way down the mountain to be sure it was okay to leave Jake a little longer while we stopped to eat. She'd said he'd stuffed himself on his favorite, her spaghetti and meatballs, and was currently beating Pop at Battleship He was perfectly fine.

Marly didn't comment when I'd hung up or when we'd pulled in and parked at Genie's Country Western Bar. As we walked toward the entrance, I couldn't stand it any longer.

"Are you all right?" I opened the door for her, honky tonk music blaring from inside.

"Yeah. I'm great," she piped back, flashing me a smile that had no spark at all in it.

Placing a hand gently on her back, I guided her around the few couples dancing to the back booth where I knew Jed and Lola would be. Sure enough, Jed had found our favorite booth empty. It wasn't all that crowded but busy enough.

"Hey there, moonshiners," Lola greeted us with a grin.

They were already sitting on one side of the booth together, looking mischievous. When I sat beside Marly, taking the outside seat of the booth, my knee brushed against hers. She didn't flinch away and neither did I. I widened my thighs, actually hoping to get her to snap at me with that smart mouth. But she didn't say a word or even look at me.

Fuck. What did I do wrong?

"No moonshining today," she said, reaching over and grabbing Lola's beer to take a swig. "Just cleaning up. But I'll move the still up tomorrow and brew my first batch."

"You don't have to work tomorrow?" asked Lola.

"No, I cut back on my hours this month. I need more time to work on my moonshine."

That struck me as odd. "You cut back on work hours for a contest?"

The contest winnings came with a cash prize, but I wasn't sure it was worth cutting regular work hours over.

"Yeah." Those blue eyes snapped to mine, her chin tilting up in challenge. "If I'm going to win it, I need to dedicate more time to get my recipe just right."

I stared, completely confused. That seemed fairly irresponsible to me. I figured this was just her weekend hobby. But I wasn't stupid. I kept my big mouth shut. When she went back to ignoring me to chat with Lola across the table, my gaze slid to Jed. He seemed to be wearing the same baffled expression I was, except his was tempered with amusement.

"Did y'all order dinner?" I asked him.

"Yep. Ordered both your favorites you usually get here too."

That small reminder that we were sitting across from both our best friends made me feel even more awkward. I had no idea what the hell was going on between me and Marly. I'd determined that there was no way we should date, but I'd also spent nearly the entire day checking out her hot body, basking in her pretty smiles, and worrying about her safety while at the cabin. In short, I was acting very much like a man interested in dating this particular woman. I was already feeling strangely possessive and protective, and I had no idea if she even thought of me like that or if her flirting was nothing more than part of her personality.

Right now, all I wanted was for her to smile or tease me the way she had been all day. But she was flat-out ignoring me.

She suddenly turned and asked me, "Something wrong?"

"No. Why?"

"You're making that growly noise in your chest."

Jake said I did the same thing when I was aggravated, but I wouldn't give her the satisfaction of knowing she was responsible for my current piss-poor mood.

"I'm hungry," I answered gruffly.

She gave me a once over then returned her attention to Lola, telling her about the cabin. I should be happy that she was so pleased with Pop's cabin. It was a source of family pride and sentimental nostalgia to me. But I wasn't happy at all. I wanted her attention back on me, and I specifically wanted her buoyant, bright personality filling up our space with her liveliness.

Genie's daughter, Patty, stepped up to the table with a tray, setting it down on a stand so she could pass out the burgers and fries and a basket of fried chicken to Marly. Jed had gotten me the double cheeseburger with extra bacon which was my favorite here.

"Y'all need anything else right now?" she asked.

"I'll have a Michelob." Then I turned to her. "Marly?"

"Bourbon and Coke, please."

"So, your Pop's old cabin is still in one piece?" asked Jed before he bit into his burger.

"In one piece?" Marly scoffed "It's perfection. I told Wade I didn't know why he didn't live out there year-round, and he nearly had a heart attack at the idea." She shoved a fry in her mouth.

She was exaggerating, but she was also slightly turned toward me and paying me the smallest bit of attention so I didn't bother correcting her.

"It's got no plumbing," Jed pointed out, reaffirming one of my least favorite things about the cabin.

She shook her head. "You men are so prissy. Y'all complain about such trivial matters when you've got a penis and can pee standing up. If I had a penis—"

I choked on my bite of burger, coughing hard while Marly pounded my back. Jed slid his beer back to me so I gulped it down.

"You okay?" she asked sincerely.

"Fine," I rasped. "But please don't talk about having a penis."

"Why not?" she mused. "If I had a penis, I bet it would be big." She winked at Lola who snickered down at her plate.

"You'd have big balls, that's for damn sure," I added before picking up my burger.

"Thank you, Wade," she said with gooey sweetness, pulling the crispy skin off her fried chicken. "I think that's the nicest thing any guy has ever said to me."

Warmth flushed through me at being her focus again but also, *that* was the best compliment she'd ever gotten from a guy? What the fuck? What idiots had she been dating?

Patty set our drinks down and swished on to the next table.

"Speaking of guys," added Lola, "don't forget we have podcasting Tuesday with Arthur."

"I haven't forgotten."

"How'd the date go?" asked Jed. "Any sparks flying there?"

He wore that conniving grin of his, like he knew this line of questioning would bother me. But how would he know? I didn't even know it would bother me till they were talking about it, and it was *so* fucking bothering me.

"It was good." Marly gave a one-shoulder shrug and took a sip of her Bourbon and Coke.

"You told me it was fine," I had to add.

"Good. Fine. Same difference."

"Not really. Fine leans toward not great. Good obviously leans the other way."

"Does it matter?" She arched that brow at me, a hint of ice still in her voice.

"Guess not," I mumbled, pushing my plate away, feeling more agitated and frustrated than before.

With cool dismissal, she turned back to Lola, "Hey, can y'all give me a ride home? I'm sure Wade is tired of playing chauffeur and he's gotta pick up Jake."

I ground my teeth and locked my jaw before I spat out a protest. She was cutting me out. I wanted the playful, teasing Marly back and she was giving me the cold shoulder. We were about to pay checks and then she'd go off with Jed and Lola. I'd drive home alone and stew over this all damn night and not get a wink of sleep.

No ma'am. We weren't playing that game.

"Hell," I muttered, pulling myself out of the booth. I held out a hand to Marly. "Come dance with me."

I ignored the stunned, wide-eyed looks coming from Lola and Jed, keeping my focus on the blonde now blinking up at me.

"You don't like country music," she stated plainly.

"I fucking hate it," I admitted, but she already knew that after the argument we'd gotten into the night we helped Lola get Jed back. I curled my fingers in a come-here gesture. "Marly. Take my hand."

I realized I was being rough and demanding and sounded like a complete asshole, but I wasn't letting this night end till we hashed it out. I'd done something to piss her off after one of the best days I could remember, after she'd been nothing but sweet and kind and wonderful all day. I wasn't letting this go.

Without another protest, she took my hand and let me haul her up. Wrapping my bigger hand around her delicate one, I pulled her behind me to the dance-floor. Thankfully, it was a slow song, so I pulled her in close, one hand cradling hers, the other at the small of her back.

"This is mighty forward of you, Mr. Kelley."

"What's wrong?" I snapped.

"What do you mean?"

"Don't play coy, Marly. We had a perfect day together then all of a sudden you shut me out on the way here. What's wrong?"

Her gaze softened. "You think we had a perfect day together?"

Faltering that maybe I was saying too much, letting her see too much, I didn't answer her, but kept on my original track. "Why are you mad at me?"

The hand she had on my shoulder slid around to cup my nape. I shivered at the skin-on-skin contact. She slid the pad of one finger along the collar of my shirt, caressing my skin intimately. "I'm not mad."

"You're lying. And you're trying to distract me."

She pressed her perfect tits against my chest, her body flush to mine. "I think it's working."

"Stop that."

"Why? You're enjoying it." Her flirty smile was back, widening with mischief. "I think Daddy Bear likes me."

"I told you not to call me that."

I squeezed her closer on instinct, my body responding without my brain. Which was new for me. After an unexpected pregnancy that led to a marriage that fell apart, I was very careful with women, never encouraging unless I was one hundred percent sure and interested.

But Marly? She wiped away all my pre-set intentions. I couldn't let her go or push her out of my arms if I tried. Then she made it even worse.

She curled her fingers at my nape, scraping her blunt nails along my skin. She whispered low and sultry, "Don't growl at me, Daddy Bear."

"Marly."

Tilting her face up, she caressed me with her body on each sway to the music. "Though I kind of like the way you make me feel when you growl."

"Goddamn, woman."

Enough.

Spinning her body in front of mine, her back to my front, I gripped her by the hips and pushed her toward the door. Her throaty laughter drifted back to me as she complied, letting me guide her outside.

"Around the corner," I told her as we burst out into the cold night, still behind her and pressing her forward.

It was full dark now except for the two lights in the parking lot casting a soft glow. Once we'd turned the corner of the building, I spun her around and pressed her back against the wall.

"Tell me how this feels," I purred as I cupped her face firmly, tilted her chin up with my thumb, and brushed my lips across the pillowy curve of hers. And she was so ready for me, leaning in, wanting me right back.

Fuck if she didn't taste like sweet paradise. Warm and wet and luscious.

She moaned as she wrapped both arms around my neck, trying to take over the kiss. But I wasn't having it. This woman had tied me into knots and had been driving me crazy all day. Longer than that, actually. I needed control of this.

I nipped her lip in warning then coasted my mouth along her jaw. "Slow down, Mad Marly."

A little whimper escaped her throat, and I vowed to myself that I'd hear all her sensual sounds before this thing was through. She rocked her body forward when I scraped my teeth down her throat then placed a suckling kiss at the base of her neck.

"Your skin's like hot silk," I whispered against her fluttering pulse.

"You should feel between my thighs."

"You and that dirty mouth." I nipped the soft skin of her neck with my teeth.

"Love that beard," she whispered right as my chin brushed over her collarbone.

I licked a line up her neck then purposely brushed my beard in its wake. She hissed in a breath and combed her fingers into my hair, squeezing fists of it till it stung. I chuckled against her throat.

"I want to feel what beard burn feels like." She bit my earlobe. "On my inner thighs."

Groaning, I fisted one hand in her hair and held her still while I kissed her hard, licking my tongue inside with feverish need. Suddenly, she gripped my shoulders tight while she hoisted herself up to wrap her legs around my waist.

I rumbled appreciatively against her mouth, swimming in hot desire as she ground her hot pussy right over my cock. Cupping her ass with one hand, I held her steady, grinding hard as I kissed her fiercely the way she wanted, the way I wanted.

She mewled into my mouth, making my dick even harder. When she rubbed just right and leaned down to bite my neck, I fisted her hair tighter on a hiss.

"Bet you're always trying to top from the bottom, aren't you, sweetheart?"

"Trying? I usually am the top, Daddy Bear."

Then we were kissing like mad again, dry-fucking each other in the freezing cold in the shadows of Genie's bar. It was like something wild took over us both. All the arguing and snapping and growling had culminated into this unhinged mess of tongues and teeth and moans.

My logical brain was telling me to stop what I was doing, get a hold of myself before someone caught us acting like randy teenagers in the parking lot. But another side, the one that wanted to let go and have fun, the one that Marly awakened was along for the ride.

I reached my hand between the flaps of her open coat, which she hadn't taken off inside, and jerked up the hem of my shirt she was wearing to slide my fingers up her ribs. Without warning, I pulled the cup of her bra down and mounded her full breast, her tight nipple beading in my palm.

"Yes. Fuck. Pinch it," she moaned, still riding my jean-clad dick like a cowgirl. "Pinch me hard, Wade."

I did just that, watching as she dropped her head back to the building. Thrusting harder against her, I kissed and sucked below her ear, rolling her nipple with my fingers between giving quick, sharp pinches and tugs.

"You're going to come right now, aren't you, beautiful?" I whispered, leaning back to watch her face. "You're going to cream in your jeans, wishing I was inside you."

"Yes, yes, I'm coming!"

I heard someone exiting the bar right as Marly started trembling, her moan rising to a scream.

"Shit," I hissed, jerking my hand from under her shirt and clamping it over her mouth. Then I whispered in her ear while she continued to tremble and grind against me.

"That's it, sweetheart. Come hard for me. Soak these jeans through."

Fuck if she wasn't gorgeous, completely wild and free, her eyes broadcasting her intense pleasure. She was smiling behind my hand, her moans vibrating against my palm. I'm not sure I'd known anyone like Marly, who always said what she wanted, felt what she wanted, and let everyone know it.

She grabbed my wrist, jerked my hand away, and latched her mouth to mine, thrusting her little tongue inside. I rumbled with pleasure, gripping her ass with both hands, rocking against her again. She bit my lip, her voice sultry and soft when she started her attack with dirty words.

"My panties are ruined," she whispered against my lips. "I kept thinking how good it would feel to have your giant cock inside me, fucking me senseless."

I growled, pressing my forehead to hers, and closed my eyes.

"How good it would feel if I was riding your dick, my tits bouncing. You sucking them till they were red and swollen, puckered from your mouth and teeth."

"Marly," I warned, hearing people chatter and shuffle to their cars in the parking lot. "I'm putting you down."

She squeezed her legs around my waist, latching on like a python, one of her hands disappearing under my shirt.

"Tit for tat, Wade Kelley." She pinched one of my nipples, and I swear, a laser of hot pleasure shot directly to my cock.

I couldn't believe this. She wanted me to come in my jeans, and I was about to.

"Next time," she whispered, "we're going to try this without clothes. I want to feel this," she ground hard against my length, "thrusting inside me. I bet you'll stretch my tight pussy to bursting. Ride her till she's worn out. You can spank me too for being such a bad girl. I like being spanked."

"Fuck." The image of her ass in the air while I spanked and fucked her sent me right over the edge.

I groaned on a long, deep rumble, opening my mouth over her throat and biting while I spilled my load in my jeans.

What the ever-loving fuck just happened?

CHAPTER 11
~MARLY~

It had been a fantastic day after a fantastic night. I couldn't wipe the smile off of my face. I'd run my first batch at Pop's cabin and was now racing back down the mountain toward Wade's office with a sample jar. My smile slipped when I realized my first thought wasn't to run to Lola to show her. No. It was Wade.

Did making out with loads of dirty talk last night in Genie's parking lot mean we were dating?

We didn't say a word on the way home. Jed was leaning against Wade's truck with his cell phone in hand, grinning with an accusatory look, when we'd finally ventured out of the shadows, a little breathless and a lot befuddled.

Jed had told us they'd taken care of the bill and then handed Wade his cell phone he'd left on the table. He then whispered something to Wade who shoved him and growled something back then Jed joined Lola who was heating up the car for them. Those two scamps knew exactly what had happened.

Well, not exactly. They might be appalled if they knew *everything*.

Wade didn't seem to want to discuss it as we drove away. I didn't mind. I was enjoying post-orgasm bliss and the discovery that Wade was sexy as hell when he growled naughty words with his mouth and hands on me. And *damn*, could he kiss. I wanted to know what else he could do with that mouth of his.

He'd dropped me home first. He handed me the walkie-talkie he wanted me to use up at the cabin then walked me to the house. Unlike me, I was feeling a little awkward about how to end the night. But I didn't have to worry for long. When I turned at my front door, he scooped a hand around my neck, bent and placed a soft kiss to my lips, lingering a little before he said, "Goodnight, Marly."

And that was that.

I wasn't positive what was going on besides the fact I was pretty damn sure this wasn't a one-off. I hoped it wasn't. Wade was so much more than I realized.

My pulse raced ahead as I veered into the parking lot of his office, which was really a cabin-style building on the outskirts of Green Valley. Interestingly, Wade and Ben were outside just like last time, but they were loading some big cage or something into the back of Wade's truck.

They both looked up and watched as I pulled into a spot. I couldn't read Wade's expression from here. It might be too presumptuous to show up at his work the night after we made each other come in our jeans like teenagers behind the bleachers.

Oh, hell. I didn't think this through. Like always. Should I have texted first? Should I have waited a day? He might think I'm being clingy by showing up here at his work. Too late now.

With a sigh, I grabbed the jar of moonshine I'd cradled in a basket for the ride down. I'd left the other jars stacked in a crate marked Batch #1 back at the cabin. Thankfully, there was plenty of room there to organize each batch.

I slammed the door behind me and walked toward the guys with a lightness to my step. "Got my first batch of peach moonshine."

I hoped he'd be okay with me coming to his office again. He frowned as I approached, but that was his normal look. Today, his gaze was heated and telling. My tummy flipped at his swift perusal of my body as I walked his way.

"Taste my peach, Wade." I teased when I stopped, holding out the jar, breathless. "You've never tasted anything so good."

He clamped his jaw tighter, not responding, but Ben quickly stepped in. "I'll taste your peach, Marly."

Wade turned to him with a death glare, "Go away, Ben."

"Yes, sir," he grinned and hustled back into the office like last time.

"It's so good. Come on, I know you're on the job, but just one taste."

Wade took the jar from me, twisted off the top, which had my gaze wandering to his big, veiny hands. I shivered at remembering how good they felt on me last night.

He smelled it first, which made me smile. A true moonshine connoisseur move. Then he took a good sip. When his brows shot up in surprise then he smiled, I jumped in place and clapped my hands.

"Good, huh?"

"Damn, Marly." He closed the lid on the jar, with a shake of his head. "That's really good. That's your *first* batch?"

"Yep. I have several jars of it. I thought your Pop might like that one."

"Thank you. I'll give it to him."

"You're welcome."

I was rocking on my heels, hands in my puffy purple jacket. His gaze lingered on my shirt. Well, his shirt. Damn, I forgot I pulled his shirt on this morning. Oh, hell.

"Oh, don't worry, these are different jeans," I assured him. "And panties."

A blush of pink crested his cheeks as he cleared his throat.

"I showered too when I got home last night," I added. "I just…liked your shirt."

I liked that it smelled like him. Even big and baggy, it felt delicious on me.

Then he did something I wasn't expecting. He laughed. The sound gave me a heavy dose of euphoria with that great big smile of his aimed directly at me.

"You wanna go for a ride with me?" he asked, surprising me.

I glanced at the cage in his truck. "Where you goin'?"

"We had a call about an orphan fawn. I need to set this up so we can catch her."

"Then what?" My heart rate spiked with fear. "You're not going to kill Bambi, are you?"

He actually rolled his eyes at me. "No, Marly." Then he was in my space, nudging me toward his truck. "We don't kill baby deer. We've got a rehabilitator in Green Valley who takes in orphan animals for us."

"Really?" I asked, suddenly interested in this aspect of his job I wasn't aware of.

He followed me around to the passenger side and opened the door for me. "Yep."

Once he was settled into the driver's seat, he placed the jar on his console. It didn't fit in the cup holder, but he managed to wedge it so it was pretty secure.

"So Wildlife Agents don't just police for poachers and check for fishing and gaming licenses?"

"Nope."

He didn't elaborate, but I could tell he was amused by my questioning. I liked that he wasn't wearing that grim expression he wore when talking to Ben about those poachers they were still looking for. He seemed almost playful at the moment.

"You save little Bambis too?" I continued.

"We've caught quite a few orphans before."

"Like what other kinds?"

"Last year, I caught two baby raccoons. The year before, someone had found a baby owl on their porch. It had hit something and blinded itself in one eye. It would've definitely died without a keeper. The rehabilitator we work with kept her since we couldn't safely release her into the wild without knowing she'd make it. She named her Hedwig."

"Awww! That is the cutest."

"Naw, the cutest was a baby black bear I caught my first year on the job. He was rummaging through this old guy's garbage every night, caught him on his garage camera."

"A black bear? Your rehabilitator knew how to care for a black bear?"

"No. We took him to the zoo in Knoxville. They had the resources for him there."

"I wonder what happened to his mother."

"Could've been anything." He shrugged. "Disease, an accident on the mountain, another predator got her defending the baby."

My heart sank. "That's so sad."

I felt his gaze on me. "You've got a tender heart, don't you."

He was smiling at me again, making that tender heart race faster. "I'm not sure I could handle that. Knowing every orphan lost its mother tragically."

"I don't think about that. I think about saving the baby animal. Getting it to someone for proper care so it can be released back into the wild where it belongs."

My feelings for this man were growing exponentially. And that was terrifying. I still had no idea if we were dating. And he hadn't given me any indication one way or another, besides asking me to ride along so he could play superman to a baby deer. My heart was a puddle of mush right now.

"You didn't take the walkie-talkie with you today, did you?" he asked accusingly.

Damn. "Um, I forgot actually."

"I figured. I tried to call you several times."

I couldn't read anything in his voice but was thrilled he'd tried to call me. At least, I think I was. Was he just checking on me, or was he trying to reach me to tell me something in particular? Like, maybe what happened last night at Genie's was a mistake.

"You need to remember to bring it with you," was all he said.

"I will," I promised, remembering that I had tried to use my cell phone to call Lola around lunch time, but I didn't have any service.

I glanced down at his walkie-talkie radio, noticing the letter/number combination written in silver sharpie on the side—WR-GV-2.

"Hey, I noticed mine has letters and numbers too. What's that stand for?"

He saw me looking down at the console. "It's so we can track the radios. That one is Wildlife Resources, Green Valley, two. We keep radio number one in the office at all times. I keep the second one on me, and Ben has number three."

"Mine has WR-M1. What's that for?"

He was blushing again. He cleared his throat. "It stands for Marly, number one."

I gasped with joy, exhaling a laugh. "I have my own walkie-talkie?"

"It was an extra. We weren't using it." He specifically avoided looking at me as his ears turned pink.

"Why Marly number one? Is there a Marly number two out there somewhere?"

"No. I, uh, I don't know." He laughed. "I'm just so used to numbering everything."

"Mr. Orderly." I reached over and poked him in the ribs. He caught my hand before I could pull it away. "There better not be a Marly number two waiting in the wings somewhere to take my walkie-talkie, Wade."

He held my hand, rubbing his thumb along the center of my palm then he finally glanced over at me, capturing me with a piercing look. "There's not," he said like a dire promise.

Then he dropped my hand and made the next turn. We rode on in silence, but that squishy feeling was back, and I was perfectly okay with it.

A few minutes later, he checked Google maps on his phone and turned onto a gravel road. A half a mile into the woods, a white house appeared. A small, quaint but pretty one with rose bushes in the garden. Though not blooming now, I recognized them. I still had a few left over from my Granny, which I tried to keep up as best I could. An older woman stepped out onto the porch and waved. Wade parked and we stepped out.

"Mrs. Jennings?" he asked.

"Yes. You're Mr. Kelley?"

"Yes, ma'am. Let me grab the cage." He did that while I walked closer on her walkway.

"Hi. I'm Marly. I bet your rose garden is pretty in the spring. Are these Double Knock Out roses?"

Mrs. Jennings smiled brightly, stepping down onto the pathway with me. "Why yes, they are. You know roses?"

"Only a little. My grandmother grew them and I still try to keep them up. I don't recognize these though."

"Those are Floribunda. I've got the sunset and the yellow."

"Wow, I bet they're gorgeous in the spring."

"And smell so good," she added sweetly. "Are you," she hesitated, "a wildlife agent?"

"Oh, no. I'm just along for the ride. Wade and I are—" he stepped up beside us with the cage— "we're friends."

That flicker of a smile touched his lips again, once more hazing my brain and turning my belly to butter.

"Mrs. Jennings, why don't you show me where you've seen the fawn?"

"Oh, of course. Follow me right around the back."

"Do you need help?" I asked, because that cage looked big and heavy.

He only frowned at me and nodded for me to follow Mrs. Jennings.

She guided us past her carport and toward the woods that lined the back of her house. "She comes every morning and every evening. Eats the corn feed I put out for her. But every time I try to get close, she takes off."

"Can you get some of that corn feed for me?"

"Absolutely. I spread the feed right there under that big pine tree."

Wade nodded, carrying the giant cage like it was nothing. He opened the hatch and set the mechanism that would drop the door shut once the deer was inside.

"I can't believe the deer would fall for this. It looks like a trap. Don't they have better instincts than that?"

"Normally, yes." He stood and scanned the woods. "But she's alone and desperate. And she's been safely getting food right here for about two weeks Mrs. Jennings tells me. She isn't afraid of the smell of Mrs. Jennings or her place. Odds are she'll ignore the prickle of danger and take a chance on filling her belly."

"Here you go," said Mrs. Jennings, carrying a small bag of corn feed and handing it to Wade.

He sprinkled some at the far end of the cage so the deer would have to go completely inside to feed. "I'd say don't let her see you on the back porch when she comes. She might be hesitant at first, but if she sees no danger, she'll go right in and we'll have her."

"And your rehabilitator said she'd be able to care for her?" Mrs. Jennings was worried, which made me worried.

"Good question. Can your person care for a baby deer?"

Wade glanced from Mrs. Jennings to me, seemingly amused at our grave concern. "Yes. I've talked to her and she's got a pen set up in her yard already. She's cared for deer before and knows what to do."

Mrs. Jennings and I shared a look of relief.

"Thank you so much, Mr. Kelley. I'll call you as soon as we have her."

"Ben and I will be waiting for the call."

"It was nice meeting you," I told her.

"You too, sweetheart," she said, walking beside me while Wade went ahead. "You too sure are a cute couple."

The blood drained from my face, because she definitely said it loud enough for Wade to hear. I saw him turn his head to the side like he was listening, but he didn't look back.

"Oh, um, well, thank you." I thought it would be awkward to explain that we weren't really a couple. I shook her hand at her front walkway. "Bye, Mrs. Jennings."

We hopped into the truck and turned back down the gravel road. An awkward silence filled the cab. Or at least, it felt strained to me, but I wasn't sure if it was one-sided on my part.

"I didn't know what to say about her couple comment," I finally said. "Thought it easier not to correct her."

His gaze just flicked my way with one of those enigmatic smiles. This was new. He had rarely ever smiled at me before. I took that as encouragement, but also I needed clarification.

"I mean, not that we're a couple, mind you."

Rather than put me out of my misery on that topic, he asked, "Why were you mad at me at Genie's last night?"

"I wasn't mad. I thought it was pretty clear when I climbed you like a monkey. That's me, not mad."

A laugh gusted out of him. "Before that. You were upset. Don't lie."

The sting returned. I heaved a sigh. "You're going to think I'm dumb."

"No, I'm not, Marly. Just tell me. How do I know not to do it again if you don't speak to me?"

Jeesh. A man who wanted open communication and to know my feelings? This was new and revolutionary.

"After the call from Jed and Lola," I started, wondering if I should confess this or not as I did so, "you called me crazy. And it just hit me wrong. The way you said it."

"I've called you Mad Marly before and you didn't get mad."

Yeah, when he said it while we were making out, he kind of growled it all sexy like. It didn't have the same ring to it as the *crazy* comment in the truck.

"You just sounded…like my father for a minute." I looked out the window, watching the bare trees as we passed by.

He didn't say anything for a bit then, "You don't get along with your father at all?"

I snorted. "It's not that exactly. It's that he thinks I'm *crazy*." I emphasized the word with disdain. "When I bought Granny's house and quit being his paralegal and decided not to go to law school, I was *crazy*. When I got a retail job at Green Valley Shine, I was *crazy*. When I took the position as manager, I was wasting my life *and* being crazy. And when he hears what I've got planned next, I just know it's going to send him over the edge. They might have to hospitalize him."

Another beat of silence, then Wade asked with genuine interest in his voice. "What do you have planned next?"

Finally, I turned to look at him. He watched me between watching the road, sincerity in every groove of his expression.

"I want to win this contest not just for the prize money. I've learned from working at Green Valley Shine that the winners become famous among local moonshiners. It would give me the boost I need to open my own moonshine distillery."

His brow shot up. "You're going to open your own distillery?" Rather than call me crazy like I thought he might, like many others already had, he asked, "Do you have a small business loan yet?"

"I don't need it. Granny Mae left me some inheritance money. It's not a lot, but enough to open my own shop. I've done all the calculations. My research. I just want to be sure it's a success. I don't want to waste what Granny left me. If it fails…" I shook my head.

"How long have you been planning this?"

"Seriously planning it? Since last year," I admitted, knowing I hadn't even admitted to Lola I'd been thinking of it that long ago. "But I've been dreaming about it since the day I took the job at Green Valley Shine. And when I saw last year's winner get so many accolades from locals. And tons of people would come in asking for the winner's moonshine, it just gave me the idea."

"Why moonshine?" he asked.

I frowned. "What do you mean?"

"I mean, if you could open any kind of store, why moonshine?"

"I love making moonshine. I remember the first time they gave me a tour of the distillery. I was amazed at the process. I've always loved chemistry. But it's more than that. It's how you can subtly change the flavors after the distilling to come out with unique flavors. It's like baking, but with alcohol." I shrugged my shoulders with a smile. "I just find it fun and exciting. Satisfying. And I've always wanted to be my own boss."

"That doesn't surprise me."

He was grinning at me as he pulled back into the Wildlife Agency parking lot.

"What is that smile for?" I asked.

"I can just tell it makes you happy. That's a good sign you're on the right track."

"Yeah?" I knew that I was. I believed strongly in my dream but hearing his affirmation of it seemed to light me up inside. "Thank you, Wade."

He shoved his truck into park and turned to me. "Come sit with me a minute. I want to talk to you."

Then my heart plummeted. Was this the breaking up part before we were even together?

"Okay."

I followed him up the walkway, enjoying the view of him in uniform and how fine he looked from behind, internally sighing that we were having *the talk* before we'd even gotten started. Most guys waited at least until we'd slept together.

I knew I was a lot and it would take a special guy to appreciate me, but I also knew I was worth it. That's why when a man gave me the gentle shrug-off, like I thought Wade might be giving me right now, it was fine by me. It just meant they weren't the one, and weren't worth the time if they didn't appreciate who I was. I only wanted the man who was meant for me.

If that had always been true, then why was my heart beating so erratically with the fear of what was about to come out of Wade's mouth?

Around the back side of his office building, there was a small courtyard, like an outdoor eating area. There was also a bench facing the field under some trees that probably provided pretty shade in the spring and summer. Right now, it looked rather bleak and an appropriate place to get *the talk* I was used to getting.

"So what's on your mind?" I asked as I sat, because I wasn't going to make it easier on him.

I'd heard quite a few of these speeches, but I decided long ago that I'd let the man struggle with getting the right words. Sometimes I found their struggles entertaining, sometimes educational. Like the one who told me, *you're really beautiful, but you're too wild*. Wild, I'd thought? So I wasn't boring and that's why he was breaking up with me? Good riddance.

I clasped my hands between my thighs, angling toward Wade as he took a seat next to me. Then he pulled one of my hands between both of his big calloused paws. I tried to ignore the sweet tingly feeling it gave me as he looked down at my hand, palm upward, his thumb tracing the fine lines. He was trying to find the right words to say to me, I knew that, but the way he was holding my hand with such care was…well, rather gutting. It was sweet and tender and sexy as hell.

But I simply held still and waited for him to get his speech together.

"Marly," he finally said, his voice gravelly and deep, "I want you."

I blinked, shocked and slightly elated. "Wait, what?"

Those piercing hazel eyes lifted to mine. "I just want to take it slow… because of Jake."

"I never quite understood what taking it slow meant," I admitted. "Does that mean we have to obey the three-to-five date rule before sex? Or that we can't go out on weeknights? Or that we can't hold hands in public?"

My eyes fell to where he clasped my hand resting on his knee, engrossed in the way his thumb swept up to the tender part of my wrist and back down, somehow feeling intensely sexual.

"We're not in public right now," I offered, not wanting him to stop.

That smile that I rarely saw on his face slid wider as he let out a little laugh. "I hadn't thought of any rules."

"Good. Because I really don't want to wait three-to-five dates before we have sex."

He shook his head. "You just say whatever you're thinking whenever you're thinking it, don't you?"

"Life's too short to waver in doubt and confusion, Wade." When he just stared, I added, "I'm a *carpe diem* sort of girl."

"I noticed."

"That doesn't bother you? That I'm, you know, kind of…wild?" I didn't like the c-word. And I don't mean cunt. I rather liked that word, especially when whispered amongst other dirty words during sex.

He bit his bottom lip, which was entirely too distracting that I had to shake myself to tune in when he started talking again.

"Do you remember when you lost that bet in high school?"

"I lost a lot of bets in high school. You'll have to be more specific."

His grin widened. "It was the time you had to run naked through the football locker room. Senior year."

"Oh!" I laughed. "Yeah. I'd bet Lola she couldn't fit ten hot dog wieners in her mouth at one time. Who knew she had such a big mouth? I lost, obviously." That day came back in a rush. "I remember you were in that locker room."

I didn't date football players in high school, so I'd never really looked their way. It was Lola who'd had her terminal lovesickness for Jedediah Lawson on the football team. That was the only reason I really even knew who they were and could tell them apart. They were all big, muscly jocks, which had never been my type. I preferred the quirky, sarcastic, cerebral type. Or the grungy, poetic, garage band type. Which was why my current situation—me lusting and slobbering over the literal biggest jock from high school was kind of hilarious.

"I remember you too."

Oh, boy. The way he said that, and the way he looked at me just now was electrifying. I felt the sizzle between my thighs.

"I'm embarrassed to admit it, but for some reason I'm going to," he paused, leaning back against the bench and lacing his fingers with mine, keeping them on his knee. "I thought about you quite a few nights after that. When I was alone. In my bed."

A thrill of adrenaline shot through me as I turned more to him. "Oh, yeah? Why are you embarrassed to tell me? All teenage boys masturbate. Well, girls too. And not just teenagers." I arched a brow at him meaningfully.

"No. Not just teenagers." Again with that sensual smile, his hazel eyes sweeping down to my mouth, broadcasting his thoughts.

Good Lord, where had he been hiding this sexy side of himself?

"So," I finally said, "explain this taking it slow thing to me, because I don't know how that works."

"I don't know either." He shook his head. "To be honest, I've barely dated since Kristie and I split up."

I crawled on top of him, straddling him on the bench. Rather than stop me, he blew out a heavy breath, his big hands gripping my hips as I settled right where I wanted to.

"Is this too fast?" I teased. "I don't want to shock you or rush you."

Then his fist was in my hair and his mouth was on mine. For a big, rough man, his mouth was so soft, his lips warm and delicious. I pressed my body against his, sinking into the kiss. He squeezed my hip and tightened his grip in my hair, but didn't let his hands wander while we tasted and explored each other with our mouths.

When we broke the kiss, panting, I asked, "When do we get to have sex?"

He burst out laughing, his hand loosening in my hair now, combing through it softly. I'd worn it down today after watching the way he looked at my hair so much. I'm pretty sure he loved my hair. And the way he was feeling and touching it, tucking it behind my ear while staring, I knew I was right. Admittedly, it was one of my best features. Next to my sparkling personality of course.

"Marly," he said fiercely with that deep-barrel voice of his rumbling against my chest, "once I'm inside you, I'm going to want more." He leaned in and bit my bottom lip. "A lot more."

"I see no problem with this situation. You're saying it like it's a problem."

"Not a problem. Just that...sex complicates things."

I rolled my eyes. "No, it doesn't. Sex is very uncomplicated. It's pure chemistry. Animal magnetism. Whatever you want to call it. It's the least complicated part of a relationship. I mean, it's pretty obvious that's the one thing we definitely both want." I ground down a little to emphasize that I knew this by the giant pipe poking me through his uniform pants.

He shook his head, examining me intently, that fiery gaze of his sweeping across my brow, down to my mouth then to my breasts then back up to me.

"Why don't we start with dinner first?" he asked, still combing his thick fingers through my hair. I felt like a cat in his lap, wanting him to keep petting me like that.

"You are welcome to feed me before you fuck me."

He laughed again. "Stop that."

"What?" I knew what, but he needed to understand something. "This is who I am, Wade Kelley. Take it or leave it."

Then my heart skipped a beat. I said it flippantly and without forethought, like I said and did everything, but suddenly I didn't want him to leave it. I really, really wanted him to take it. And then slap it and spank it. And kiss it.

Without any effort at all, he stood from the bench and set me on my feet. Scooping his fingers into my hair, he cupped my cheeks and pressed a short, sweet kiss to my lips.

"How about dinner with me and Jake at my house tomorrow night?"

"I thought taking it slow because of Jake meant you didn't want him to see us together too much."

"I'm going to admit that I don't know how to do this, but Jake and I, we're a package deal. Take it or leave it," he tossed back at me.

Grinning, I went up onto my toes just trying to get closer to his handsome face, "I'll take it. What time?"

"How's six o'clock?"

"Sounds perfect."

We stood there, staring at each other for another lingering minute before he glanced at the tree line where the sun had already disappeared. Then he leaned over and took my hand. "Let me walk you back to your car."

We walked, hand in hand, my insides slowly liquefying with his sweetness. When we made it to my truck and he opened the door for me, he said, "I really do love your peach moonshine."

"I bet you say that to all the girls."

He chuckled. "Just you, Mad Marly."

For some reason, the way he said that old nickname felt like the sweetest endearment.

"Just wait till you really taste my peach, Daddy Bear." I kissed him while he growled then hopped in my truck. "See you tomorrow night."

He simply closed my door and crossed his arms, watching me drive away.

CHAPTER 12

-WADE-

"She's here! She's here!" yelled Jake from his spot in front of the living room window.

I'm not sure what I was thinking asking Marly over to dinner with me and Jake as our first date. I'm pretty sure that when it came to Marly, I wasn't thinking much at all except that I wanted her near me.

I'd told myself that we should try dating privately before letting Jake know too much. I knew how easily Jake fell in love with people. So the smart thing to do would've been to wait and see if this was going anywhere before I had her come hang out at the house.

But like I said, when it came to Marly, I wasn't thinking straight. So here we were having our first date at my house. I smiled, wondering if she'd like what I had planned. It wasn't much, but I had a feeling she'd embrace it.

Marly knocked on the front door.

"I've got it," I told Jake who was already unlatching the door.

He swung it open before I could get there. "Hey, Marly!" He bounced excitedly.

"Hey there, handsome." She pulled him into a hug and ruffled his hair, which had him beaming.

The sight made something pinch behind my sternum.

When she went to pull off her apparently favorite purple jacket, I stopped her and readjusted it. "You may want to keep that on." I kept my hands on her collar, checking out the low, scoop-neck, white sweater underneath.

"You like my sweater, Wade?" she asked, blinking innocently at me.

"Yeah, Marly." I blew out a gusty breath then dragged my gaze back to hers. "I like it a lot." I'd like it even more on the floor of my bedroom, but that certainly wasn't happening tonight.

"Come on. You've gotta see what Dad and I did." He grabbed her hand and dragged her toward the back patio door.

"Do you mind?" she asked over her shoulder as she was being bodily hauled away by my son.

"Not at all," I answered honestly, following behind them.

I wanted to see her face when she realized what our date entailed. Jake pulled her through the screen door and opened his arms wide.

"See! Isn't it awesome? Dad put up the tent. He said we can both sleep out here tonight. Come look what I've got."

Marly followed, taking in our camp site in the back yard, not saying a word, which was rare. She bent down at the flap of the tent where Jake was now sitting, showing her the battery-powered lanterns I'd bought.

"I finished the book you bought me," Jake was saying, showing her the copy of *Captain Underpants*, "but I thought I could reread it and some others. And Dad put some movies on the iPad so I can watch those out here too. Look, we even built a little table for it."

He pointed to the makeshift table I'd built out of scrap wood that would allow his iPad to sit up on its own and had space for one of the lanterns and his juice box. He also had a particular pink blanket stretched out in the tent. It had become his favorite when he woke up the morning after I'd put that still together for Marly. When I'd told him it was Marly's, he seemed to love it all the more.

"Your dad made that?" she asked, now sitting cross-legged on the cold grass.

"Oh, yeah. He's really good at making things."

"Aren't you lucky to have a dad like that."

"Uh-huh. And I know all kinds of things how to survive in the wilderness."

"Really? Like what?"

"Like don't ever, and I mean ever, go to the bathroom near your campsite."

"Why's that?" she asked attentively.

"Because it attracts bears and mountain lions and such."

"Then I'm definitely not doing that."

"Also, if you need bait for fishing, you can trap minnows using your t-shirt as a net. Just spit in the water and they'll come right up and you can trap them with your shirt."

"Interesting." She tilted her head. "Is there something in spit that attracts them?"

"No. They just think its food of some sort. Dad told me that trick. And another is you can use mud to keep mosquitos from biting you and toothpaste to help with stings if they do bite you."

I smiled at her gentle laugh.

"This is all very valuable information, Jake. I'm storing it away for when I need it."

"Oh, come see what we're having for dinner," he added excitedly, now back outside the tent and trying to drag her by the arm.

"Jake, go easy, son," I told him, walking closer to the firepit I'd bought today on my lunch break.

Marly laughed as he dragged her to the circle of chairs and table with tonight's dinner laid out.

"We're having hot dogs and s'mores. And any kind of chips you want." Jake rattled on. "Dad got the variety pack because he said he didn't know what kind of chips you like and you can pick any kind. You can have more than one kind even if you want. My favorite is Funyuns. What's your favorite?"

His rambling bubbled with excitement.

Marly laughed. "I love all chips, but Doritos are my favorite."

"Those are good too," he agreed. "Oh! I forgot the iPad in my room." Then he took off into the house.

I sidled up closer, hands in pockets, admiring the way the firelight kissed her skin with a reddish glow.

"This will likely be your least fancy first date ever."

Her smile was sweet, her eyes bright with joy. "I don't need fancy. Don't much care for it actually."

"So hot dogs and marshmallows are okay?"

"I always love a good, hot wiener, Wade," she teased. "Did you get the foot-longs? Those are my favorite."

"Stop that," I told her as I pulled her close and kissed her mouth to keep her quiet. And just because I wanted to kiss her.

I couldn't remember the last time I'd had this sort of urge with a woman, the impetuous feeling to grab and hold and touch. This need to simply have my hands on her and keep her close was a maddening compulsion.

When I gripped her by the upper arms and pulled her away enough to see her pretty eyes, I was rewarded with the sort of expression that would stay imprinted in my memory. It was a heady combination of excitement, happiness, adoration, and sensuality. How Marly could wear all of her feelings for the world to see like that boggled my mind. And jostled my heart.

But she wasn't wearing them for everyone, was she? She was wearing that look just for me.

"Thank you for coming," I whispered low, our faces close, both of us staring and admiring each other.

"Thank you for asking me." She looped her fingers through my beltloops. She tugged slightly like she wanted me closer.

"I liked your idea about camping in the backyard," I told her, stupidly stating the obvious.

"I see that." Her smile beamed wider. "You like my pink blanket."

"Jake loves your blanket." Her expression softened even more.

Then Jake came tearing out of the house, and we subtly parted and moved toward the fire. I passed out the metal skewers and we settled in, cooking our hot dogs and enjoying the warmth of the fire on a cool night. The snow that had fallen a few days ago had already melted, the temperatures in the forties now.

Our date consisted mostly of me watching my son entertain Marly as well as hoard all of her attention. To my surprise, she didn't seem to mind at all. Even more surprising, I didn't mind either. I enjoyed simply watching her, listening to her. She seemed genuinely interested in everything Jake had to say, particularly when he told her about the table-top catapult he made in his new gifted class.

Making s'mores reminded him of the project they'd completed two weeks ago. They'd apparently used marshmallows as their cannonballs which they'd shot from the catapults engineered out of rubber-bands, small wooden dowels, and plastic spoons. Marly listened and laughed. I watched and listened.

When Marly glanced at the time on her phone, my stomach sank a little.

"You work tomorrow?" I asked, knowing she did.

"Yeah, I open. And there's inventory I need to check since I took Monday off."

"Jake, say goodnight to Marly."

"Aw, man. You've gotta go already?"

"Afraid so." She stood, and I stood with her.

"Well, can we come to your house next time and play with Scooter and Pooter?"

"Jake," I snapped, "you don't invite yourself to other people's houses."

"She's not other people. She's Marly."

Of course, Marly simply laughed and tousled his messy hair on his head. "Of course. Next time, dinner is at my house." She gave me a wink.

"Goodnight then," he said, giving her a hug then running to his tent.

"I'll walk her to her car, son. Be back in just a minute."

"Okay!" he yelled from inside the tent, the flaps closed.

With a light hand on her back, I nudged Marly toward the door. "Sorry about that."

"About what? That your son is ridiculously adorable and is a social butterfly?"

"No." I laughed. "And yeah. I was thinking more of the fact that this wasn't much of a first date in getting to know each other."

"Oh, I got to know you plenty," she said as I guided her through the back door that led through the open garage.

"Did you now?" I'd left the carport light off, lacing my fingers with hers.

"You've got a motorcycle?" She was looking at the covered old Harley parked against the far wall of the garage.

"Yeah. Haven't ridden in a while though."

"Why not?"

"For one, I don't have much time to joy ride anymore. And two, it's dangerous. I don't like to take chances with my life, knowing someone else depends on it so much."

She nodded, her expression pensive. "Makes sense." She smiled up at me. "But then I bet you'd be the safest rider on the road."

I tugged her toward her truck. "Tell me."

"Tell you what?" She leaned back against the truck then flinched away. "Cold." She laughed.

I took her truck keys and got in, then turned it on and cranked the heat all the way up. Shutting the door I clasped our fingers in mine again and pulled her back into the garage where there was no chilly breeze. Opening my jacket, I pulled her against my chest and wrapped the flaps around her body. "Now. Tell me what you were going to say."

She slid her hands up my back between my jacket and shirt, her touch a tease of what I really wanted. "I don't remember what we were talking about." She snuggled her breasts against my chest. "I can't think straight when your big body is all up over me."

"I ain't over you yet," I let slip before I bit my lip.

"Mmmm," she hummed, staring up at me. "I like that word *yet*."

"You said you got to know me plenty," I reminded her.

"I did. I learned that not only do you love your son but you strive to make him happy. Even if that means listening to the ideas of a crazy girl."

I hugged her tighter, her warmth seeping through my clothes to my skin. I wanted to feel her skin on skin. Craved it.

"You're not crazy," I told her. "Mad as a March hare, maybe."

"You're sweet to say so, Wade. I'm getting used to the moniker. Maybe I need to fully embrace it."

She smiled, her fingers finding their way underneath my shirt, blunt nails now gliding on the skin of my back.

I grunted, my hands squeezing her tighter. "I could think of a few other words to define you."

"Yeah?" Her brow rose. "Do tell."

Leaning my head down, I brushed a kiss across her forehead. "Beautiful." I swept my lips lower, kissing the bridge of her nose, her eyes closed now. "Sweet." Then my mouth found hers as I whispered, "sexy as fuck."

Her smile widened before I slanted my mouth over hers and delved inside, sweeping my tongue in on a groan. Her nails dug into my back deeper. I cupped her ass and hauled her against me. She kissed me back with the same fierce need, both of us seeming to try to crawl inside one another. But when she rocked her hips against my painful erection, I broke the kiss and pulled her away from my body.

"No, ma'am. We are not repeating Genie's." I tossed a look toward the door leading into the kitchen, half expecting Jake to be gawking at us with a grossed-out expression. "Come on."

I took her hand and hauled her back to her truck, hustling her inside. She was beaming from ear to ear as I buckled her seatbelt, the cab nice and warm now.

When I caught her grinning at me like a moon-eyed puppy, I asked, "What?"

"You called me sweet." She cupped my face, one of her thumbs brushing my beard then my lips, where her eyes were focused. "Just for that, Wade Kelley," she whispered in a not-sweet-very-sultry voice, "I'm going to give you the best blow job of your life on our second date."

"Goddammit, Marly." I closed my eyes to pull myself together, her filthy mouth driving me absolutely crazy. Fisting her hair, I held her still and kissed the hell out of her. Only when she finally let out a whimpering moan did I ease up, letting her full bottom lip slide between my teeth. "Text me when you get home so I know you made it safely."

"Yes, sir."

I slammed her door, knowing I was scowling. But only because it made me want to haul her inside and fuck her on the kitchen table. And I should not be having thoughts like that with my son inside.

She put her truck in reverse then stopped and rolled down her window. "Thank you for dinner. And the company of two very handsome dates. Tell Jake it's at my house next time."

I nodded. "Roll up the window before you let all the cold air back in."

She rolled her eyes and did as she'd been told as she backed the rest of the way out of the drive. Once I saw her turn the corner down the street, I marched back inside, through the house, and out the back door. Jake was watching a Pixar movie on his iPad, his eyelids drooping. I went back to the campfire and started picking up the food when my back pocket buzzed.

I pulled it out, seeing a notification from Marly. She couldn't be home already. I quickly opened, terrified she'd wrecked on the road or something. Up popped a meme.

It was a cartoon of two Tyrannosaur Rexes having sex. The speech bubble for the female read: *Pull my hair!* The male mounting her was saying while waving tiny arms: *I'm fucking trying!*

I burst out laughing. The ellipses rippled a few seconds before a text popped up from her: **I like my hair pulled too. But I doubt you'll have trouble reaching. Goodnight.** She added a winky face at the end.

No. I wasn't going to have trouble reaching.

CHAPTER 13
~MARLY~

"It just surprises me, that's all," Lola was telling me over the phone as I took the first turn toward the cabin. I was using hands-free mode in my truck.

After our podcasting session this week with Arthur, I'd left abruptly. Lola was calling me on it, accusing me of avoiding this conversation. She was right. I was.

"Surprises you how? Like, I'm not Wade's type?"

"I didn't say that," she answered. "Actually, I think y'all match perfectly."

"Shut up." I turned right by the giant Y-shaped tree off the main highway onto Y-tree Road, smiling at the silly name, and the cutest, probably most serious boy there ever was who named it. "We are so different."

"Exactly. You could use some grounding in your life, and Wade could use some spontaneity in his. I'm actually surprised y'all didn't get together after the prom re-do night."

"All we did was fight that night."

Lola laughed. "Looked like foreplay to me."

"I wish."

I'd been doing a lot of daydreaming about foreplay with Wade. And during-play and after-play. I'd teased him by sending that t-rex sex meme three nights ago, but the truth was I wasn't teasing. I wanted that man something fierce. All I had to do was think about him scowling or growling at me, and I was wet and ready.

I wasn't the kind of woman who experienced sexual frustration. I owned every gadget under the sun to satisfy my own pleasure. Typically, I could go to my drawer of merry sex toys, find the right one and take the edge off. But, right now, nothing was helping. Least of all me daydreaming of the ways I'd like to ride Daddy Bear Wade.

Because I'd opened and closed Green Valley Shine the past three days, and Wade was busy at work, we hadn't seen each other since the campfire night. Not that I needed to see him every day, but also, I *wanted* to see him every day.

What was this euphoric feeling that made me giddy at just the thought of him?

Obviously, I was infatuated. Maybe a little more than that. When I thought of how he was the other night with Jake, remembered how he patiently showed his son how to put a hot dog wiener on a skewer then roast it without burning it, my entire insides melted with overwhelming affection. He was such a good father. He was such a good man.

And he liked *me*…Ol' Mad Marly. Don't get me wrong. I was weighed down with far too much confidence. I had no doubts that I was a very likeable and appealing person. Any man would be lucky to catch me. It just seemed highly unlikely that a guy like Wade Kelley would be the one chasing me. That he would be as into me as I was him. But his frequent texts in the past couple of days assured me I wasn't alone in this. We were both smitten which put a dopey smile on my face all the damn time.

I also loved the way he made me promise that I'd never walk to my car alone, to text him when I was safely home and locked my doors. They were small ways of showing that he cared. I didn't even mind when he yelled at me for forgetting to text him last night after work. I loved all of his attention, even the grumpy, growly kind.

"Marly? Are you listening to me?"

Oops.

"No. I absolutely was not."

Lola snorted on the other end as I took the next turn toward the cabin.

"I was asking if you were going to his Pop's birthday party the weekend before Thanksgiving."

"Wade hasn't mentioned it yet. It may be too soon to do the family gathering thing."

"But you've met his Pop and Nana already. Jed said he knows Wade's Pop would want to hear all about your moonshining up there."

I tapped the steering wheel as I made the climb around the last bend and up the small hill, the picturesque cabin coming into view. My heart fluttered.

"We'll see. I'm not sure Wade is ready for that sort of commitment yet," I added cavalierly just as I wished with all my heart that Wade would invite me. "I've gotta go, girl. I'm at the cabin now."

"Yeah, I can tell. You cut out a second ago."

I patted the walkie-talkie Wade had given me which was sitting on the passenger seat, thankful I'd remembered. Actually, I just never took it out of the car once he'd given it to me.

"Real quick," she added, "I know Bekah is up for the next podcast date, but do you have someone lined up for yours after that? I saw this new hot guy going to work out at Cage Erickson's gym."

There were lots of hot guys who worked out at Cage' gym. He was a former MMA fighter and had a good reputation for training that seemed to keep his gym abundantly full of hotties. But it did nothing for me.

I sat there, frowning at the idea of going out with another guy while Wade and I were doing this thing. A sickly feeling washed over me.

"Marly?"

"I don't like muscly guys."

"Since when? Also, Wade is kind of muscly."

"And I don't need you finding me dates. I can do it myself."

"Ouch. What is that voice for?"

"What voice?"

"The mean Marly voice. I haven't heard that in a *long* time."

"Your hearing is off. Besides, I don't have a mean voice."

"Stop lying." She laughed. "If you don't want to go out with anyone for the podcast since you're wrapped up in someone else, just say so. We can do a series on best dates for the holidays since they're around the corner. Bekah can take over the podcast dates for now."

A giant weight I didn't realize I'd been holding fell off of me.

"Good grief," I muttered.

"What was that?" asked Lola, her voice cutting out a little.

"Nothing," I answered. "Just wondering what the hell I'm getting myself into with your fiancé's best friend.

She laughed again. "Bye, Marly. Happy moonshinin'!"

We hung up, and I hopped out, keys in hand, grabbing the backpack and big bag of stuff I had shoved behind my seat. I'd almost brought Scooter and Pooter today, but I was also afraid of them wandering too far and getting lost while I was working. They were just a year old and listened to me only half the time.

Once I opened the cabin door, I found it nice and tidy just as I'd left it. I hated to tell Wade this but I was starting to think of this place as my own private sanctuary. If things didn't work out, I wondered if he'd let me come visit from time to time after the contest?

After pulling the sheets and one of my Granny Mae's patchwork quilts out of the big bag I'd brought, I made the bed, nodding at how that completed the cozy vibes in the cabin. I started a fire in the wood stove rather than the fireplace to heat up the place and then set my mini-cooler on the kitchen counter. I brought some homemade beef stew and cornbread muffins for lunch.

I walked back to my truck and backed it up to the door that led directly into the moonshine shed. Then I hauled my covered bucket of mash inside. The bucket was half the size of the giant pots Wade had moved for me. There was no way I could haul those up here. I'd divided those two in half into these buckets with lids. I figured I had enough mash to run two more batches after this.

My first batch was so damn good, I was pretty sure I already had a winner. But unbeknownst to many people, except Lola who knew me better than anyone, I was a perfectionist. Besides, I wasn't going to waste my mash.

After pouring the mash into the kettle and lighting the burner under it, I settled into work. I hauled fresh spring water from the pump out back and poured it into the kettle. Then I checked the temperature to be sure it didn't boil and placed my jar under the coil for when the alcohol would eventually start trickling out of the spout. This process would take a while, so I left it to go work on my peach flavoring inside the cabin.

For the first batch, I'd used fresh peaches, cinnamon, cardamom, and vanilla extract. This time, I wanted to try using the preserves I'd made from Chase's Octoberfest peaches. The additional sugar in the preserved peaches might be just what my moonshine needed to take it to the next level. For this batch, I was going to try using ginger, clove, nutmeg, and vanilla extract for flavoring.

I'd decided on four different flavoring combinations to try, but it would also depend how each one came out. So far, the first one was banging.

The day whirred by as I strained the preserves and mixed my concoction of peach flavor #2, while going back and forth to check the still. I'd ended up starting a fire in the fireplace simply because it made the one-room cabin look so snug and comfy with the light of flames flickering in the room. I enjoyed my homemade beef stew with butter beans, carrots, potatoes, and black-eyed peas by the fire, dipping my cornbread muffins the way Granny Mae and I used to do.

"Wade is the crazy one," I mumbled to myself. I could live up here the rest of my life. This place was a quiet slice of heaven to me. So what if I literally froze my tail off going to the bathroom in the woods. There were worse things in the world than a cold ass.

By mid-afternoon, the distilling process was nearly complete. I'd dumped the first jars of the moonshine, what we called the heads. I'd collected the hearts, the middle of the batch into several jars. I let the tails drain off into a small bucket I'd have to dump as well. The heads had too much alcohol, the tails too little.

I took the jars of hearts inside and added my new flavoring mixture. I tasted, then added some more.

"That's pretty damn good," I told myself right when I heard a truck engine from outside.

Through the big window, I saw Wade's truck parking alongside mine, my heart pounding faster and my tummy somersaulting at the sight of his grouchy, handsome face through the windshield.

Setting the jar aside onto the small square card table I'd hauled up here for this, I wiped my fingers on the dish towel and nearly ran out to the porch to greet him. I propped my hands on my hips.

"What a nice surprise!" I yelled, grinning shamelessly.

He was out of the truck and eating up the distance between us with long strides. Per usual, he was scowling. There was a burning in those green-gold eyes that didn't quite equal anger but something akin to it.

When he was halfway to the porch, he bellowed, "You didn't bring your walkie-talkie like I told you, Marly."

"Yes, I did." My pulse quickened even more. "Oh, shit. I left it in the car."

"It doesn't help having it in the car when I'm trying to reach you."

"You needed something?" I asked as he bounded up the steps.

"Fuck yes, I did," he barked fiercely. Then he grabbed me around the waist, his giant paw cradling the back of my head. "I needed this."

He crushed his mouth to mine, invading me with a feral groan and a questing tongue. My lady parts combusted into flames as I clawed my way up his body, wrapping my legs around his waist. After stroking and sucking my tongue with his, he broke the kiss and bit his way down my jaw, scraping his teeth down my neck. I thought I was going to come in my jeans again.

"I fucking want you, Marly. I need you." He emphasized the need part by thrusting his hard dick against me.

"Yes," was all I could manage at the moment, my senses spiraling, my body so damn happy that her dreams were finally coming true. "Let's get naked."

He yanked the door open and kicked it closed with his boot, lifting his head long enough to glance around. He made a grunt-like sound at the sight of the made bed and headed that way.

"I hope you don't mind I took the liberty of dressing things up in here."

"It's about to come in handy," he said before tossing me onto my back.

Rather than attacking me, which I was one hundred percent expecting and hoping for, he kicked off his boots, while tossing off his jacket. Then he unbuttoned his uniform shirt and pulled off the white t-shirt underneath. The whole time, I lay there panting, unmoving, a little hormone-dazed and frozen at the unbelievable sight of his shirtless body and aggressive behavior.

"Good heavens," I murmured.

Then he was pulling off my Converse shoes and socks. He placed one knee on the bed and went straight for my jeans, unzipping, curling his big fingers into the seam of both my jeans and panties then pulled them off and tossed them aside. So there I was, laying there bottomless, completely shocked at this quick turn of events and entirely aroused.

He grabbed my ankles and dragged me till my ass was near the foot of the bed. He was staring at my top like he wanted to murder it. "Take it off."

"Yes, sir," I answered without any sass whatsoever as I complied.

Still, his hot gaze burned back up to mine, and I was almost scared of the intensity I saw there. Sex tended to be fun frolics for me, but this felt more potent than my normal encounters. As soon as I'd gotten my bra off, he knelt at the foot of the bed and bent between my legs. His body was so big that I had to lay my knees nearly flat on the bed to accommodate him.

"I can't stop thinking about you," he admitted, his gaze on his hand now mounding my breast, thumb circling the tight peak.

Oh, yeah. The girls had woken up and were perky and ready for him the second he drove up the hill.

I bit back a whimper. "Seems we have the same affliction." I watched his head dip to my chest, his hand holding my full breast while he flicked and swirled his tongue around my nipple.

"Oh, God."

My hips came up but his abdomen had me pressed down.

"Been thinking about you for three days," he gritted out as he opened his mouth over the pink tip and sucked hard, his gaze locked on mine.

"Shit, shit, shit." I rocked up again. "I'm going to come again." Too quick. Too fast. I'd never come from titty play, but it looked like that was going to happen.

"But it's this sweet pussy I've been wanting to taste since you left my house three days ago." Then he had my ass cupped in his big hands and his tongue on my clit.

I cried out at the sudden, blinding pleasure as he flicked my nub softly then trailed down to my entrance, fucking me with his tongue. My hands were in his hair, and I was grinding up against his beautiful mouth and heaven-help-me that delicious, raspy beard.

Yes, like that," I murmured on a gasp as he opened his mouth wider, lapping with his tongue and sucking me into nirvana.

"Mmm," he hummed in that rough way that vibrated against my clit. "You taste better than peaches, sweetheart." Then he swirled his tongue around my nub.

"I'm coming," I moaned.

He opened his mouth on my clit and sucked hard, sliding one thick finger inside me. My neck and spine bowed as a pulsing orgasm ripped through me. I screamed while he finger-fucked and sucked me through my climax. But before I'd even come down, he was on his feet.

He pulled a foil package from his back pocket and dropped it on the bed before he stripped off his uniform pants.

Picking up the condom, I read, "Magnum."

I arched an eyebrow at him with a sassy grin but it all fell away when I caught sight of what he'd been hiding in those pants.

"Oh, my."

He scooped me under my arms and hauled me up the bed, crawling between my legs before he sat back on his heels. Gripping his cock, he gave it a heavy stroke and my mouth watered. It took me a minute to absorb that Wade was completely in proportion everywhere. The ruddy organ in his hand jutted straight up, the tip wet.

"Come suit me up."

"If I recall correctly, I promised to give you a blow job on our second date."

"This isn't a date, and I'd come too fast. I want to feel you, Marly. And I want to watch your face when I make you come again."

I'm not a fool. I wasn't going to argue. Sitting up, I lifted the condom and tore the package open. "You sure are confident. What if I can't come twice?"

He took the condom from me since apparently I was taking too long and he stroked it onto his giant cock. Then he slid his hand around the back of my neck and squeezed, leaning close till our lips were nearly touching.

"We aren't leaving this cabin till I feel you come on my cock." He didn't kiss me, but he bit my bottom lip till it stung a little then he licked it, reminding me what his tongue could do.

My sex fluttered, and I must've made a funny noise because then he smiled that sexiest smile that made me all melty.

"Don't be afraid," he whispered against my lips as he came over me, pressing my torso back to the bed.

"I'm not scared," I told him.

He reached between us, holding his weight on one forearm beside my head. "You look a little scared."

I felt the head of his dick slide through my slick folds before he pressed to my entrance.

"It's only natural," I breathed gustily, his face only a few inches from mine. "I didn't know you were packing a monster in your pants."

That sexy smirk widened and it was so utterly hot, my belly fluttered again as he aimed that lethal look at me.

"Don't worry, beautiful." He nudged in a few inches and stopped when I gasped. He was fucking big. "I'll go slow till you take me."

"Then what?" I asked, because I could see the fire burning bright in his eyes.

"Then I'm going to fuck this pretty pussy till you forget every man but me, Marly Rivers." He pulled back and stroked in again, slowly wedging himself deeper inside me.

I whimpered, clawing onto his shoulders. It had been a while since I'd slept with someone, and I was tight.

"Shhh," he murmured against my lips. "Look how perfect we fit together," he assured me. "You feel so good. So fucking good, sweetheart."

Like I needed reassuring. The slight sting of him stretching me felt heavenly. I wasn't joking that I enjoyed spanking and hair-pulling. What I hadn't realized was that I'd enjoy an oversized dick barreling its way inside me so much. I shifted my hips to accommodate him more.

"There you go," he whispered in that deep, husky voice that made my nipples tighten even more. "Good girl."

"Fuck, Wade," I closed my eyes. "Don't say things like that. I'm going to come before you even start moving."

His chuckle vibrated against my chest. His beard brushed my neck as he nipped the sensitive spot below my ear and seated himself fully inside me. "You want to be my good girl, Marly?"

"Yes," I hissed, rocking up to try and get him to move, but he wouldn't. And this was one man I couldn't move if he didn't want to. "Please, yes."

An appreciative sound rumbled in his chest, his mouth coasting back up my jaw to my mouth. "You're soaking wet for me." He nipped my lip. "I love that."

"Of course, I am," I admitted, surprised to find my voice shaking. "I've wanted this for a while now."

He kept perfectly still, impaling me to the bed, his gaze on mine now, eyes dark and feral. "Since when?"

I could barely think, wanting him to move so badly I was squirming, one hand fisted in his hair, the other clawing at his broad back. "Since you yelled at Ben for ogling me in my apron."

If possible, his eyes darkened further, his jaw clenched before he rumbled, "I wanted to punch him out, bend you over the hood of your truck, and fuck you right there."

"You don't need a written invitation anymore," I huffed, tightening my fist in his hair which didn't seem to faze him at all. "You're buried balls-deep inside me right now, Wade Kelley. Let's get on with it."

He quirked a brow that would seem almost menacing if I didn't know him better.

"Don't worry, sweetheart. I'm going to fuck you properly."

"Thank you," I snapped with feigned impatience.

I wasn't impatient. I was enjoying every single second. One of his hands slid up my thigh to my knee where he bent it up and pressed me wider. Then he started fucking me. Properly.

All my smart comebacks vanished as I dug my nails into his shoulders and he thrusted inside me over and over, every long, thick stroke sweeter than the last.

"Let me see those eyes." He squeezed my thigh to get my attention.

"It's hard when they want to roll back into my head."

"I know, baby," he said almost compassionately. "But I need them on me when I make you come. Need to see you."

Who in the hell knew that Wade Kelley was a dirty-talking sex machine? While he angled and stroked inside me, hitting me just right, I marveled at how I never imagined it would be like this with him. Oh, I knew it would be good, because I'd felt his monster dick through his jeans at Genie's. But I didn't know the man himself would be a sex god with his raspy words and dark promises while he used his body to do irreparable damage to mine.

Damaged. Ruined. That's what I was, what I became as he fucked me into oblivion. What man could come close to this I thought as my second orgasm climbed higher and came faster.

"That's my girl," he murmured, letting my thigh go so he could slide his hand between us and circle his thumb along my slick clit. "Come for me, Marly. Let me see you. Let me feel you."

The intimacy was unbearable, and yet I couldn't look away as I panted and moaned, rocking my hips to meet him as best I could while he drove inside me faster and harder. When the second one hit, I couldn't help it. I squeezed my eyes shut and arched my neck with the agonizing pleasure pulsing through my pussy.

"Fuck, yes," he groaned, scooping an arm around my waist and hauling me upright with dizzying speed.

I couldn't even move while he maneuvered me like a limp puppet. Sitting back on his heels, he wrapped an arm entirely around my waist and hammered up inside me, while my climax continued to throb.

He cradled my lolling head by the back of my skull and forced my mouth to his, kissing me hard and deep, growling deep in his chest. All the while, he fucked up inside me with mindless speed and intensity, the sound of flesh slapping, the smell of sex slick between us.

When he finally rumbled a dark groan, biting my shoulder but not hurting me as he drove up hard and held me down while he throbbed inside me, I nearly cried at the heady emotion. I shivered out a sigh and combed my fingers along the back of his hair and nape, wondering what had just happened.

Sex had always been a release for me. A way to relieve the stress, to let go of bottled emotions and tension. A way to feel free. That's not what had just happened. That's not how I felt.

The emotions hadn't been set free. They were swirling with increasing speed and force inside my chest, winding tighter. I didn't feel free either. I felt tied, linked to this behemoth of a giant still pulsing inside me. Somehow, I didn't think I'd ever be free again, forever tethered in the most unexpected and blissful way.

CHAPTER 14

~WADE~

We hadn't said a word since I'd pulled out of her, disposed of the condom, and then hauled her under the quilt with me. I could've told myself that I was giving her post-sex cuddling, but as my fingers continued to trail a path across the small of her back and up to her hip I knew this was more for me.

I wanted to be with her, skin on skin. This need to map her body with my hands, to know every curve and line, gouged its way into my heart. I wasn't a cold-hearted bastard in bed. I'd always seen to a woman's pleasure, but I never felt this uncontrollable craving to keep touching, to keep her close after. Always.

I hadn't slept with a woman without a condom since Kristie got pregnant in college. Even after we married and she'd assured me she was on the pill, I was too paranoid, wanting to be sure I took care of business. I never saw Jake as a mistake, but I knew we weren't ready for another one. I think some part of me knew then that we weren't going to last.

But right now, all I could think about was sliding back inside Marly with nothing between us. Was this a primitive thing to want to plant my seed like a goddamn caveman? And why now? Why was Marly Rivers driving me insane with desires I'd never felt?

"Wade Kelley is a cuddler," she whispered against my chest where her cheek was pressed. She'd been trailing her own palm up and down my abdomen, petting me the way I was petting her.

"Don't tell anyone," I commanded, my voice rough.

I didn't admit that I'd never been a cuddler before. That she'd broken my brain and my body, stolen them both from me apparently.

"What if I'd have said no?" she asked playfully, "When you came charging up that porch."

"Then I'd have begged you," I found myself confessing.

Her palm stopped moving and she pressed up on me to stare with wide eyes. "*You* would've begged?"

I didn't answer, letting my small smile tell her the truth of it. She examined me for a few more seconds then pressed her cheek back to my chest. A tenderness swept through me when she pressed herself close to me again.

"I should've said no," she whispered. "I'd like to have seen that."

I didn't respond. There was nothing to say. I'm sure it would've been a sight, but I was telling the truth. I wanted her desperately. Still did. Once wasn't enough. I was starting to learn that Marly had well and truly dug under my skin, deeper even to that organ I kept locked away from women. Worse, I wanted to give it to her, but I wasn't sure if this was all fun and games for her.

"So you came up here just to get some?" she asked, her fingers grazing back and forth low on my abdomen at the top of the quilt.

If she kept that up, I'd have to get the other condom in my uniform pants. That was another thing. I was still on the clock, yet when she didn't respond to my third call on the walkie-talkie, I'd immediately told Ben I was taking off early then headed up the mountain. But not before I grabbed a pack of condoms at the Quick-n-Go.

She pinched the skin at my hip. "It was the t-rex meme, wasn't it?"

"No." I pinched her butt back.

"Ow!" She laughed.

"I missed you," I found myself admitting, holding her close when she tried to wiggle away. "I needed to see you."

She flattened her palm below my navel. "Wade Kelley," she declared in that know-it-all voice of hers, "you like me."

I chuckled. "If me mauling you and eating your pussy within two minutes wasn't proof enough then yeah, I'll admit it. I like you. Quite a lot."

She let out a little laugh then was quiet. "I like you too. If the screaming orgasms didn't give it away."

I settled my hand on the full curve of her hip, loving the feel of her. She felt so right in my arms. My pulse pumped faster as I squeezed her hip and said, "Jake likes you too."

She lifted her head and propped her chin on the back of her hand to stare at me. "I like Jake quite a lot. He's such a funny kid. A good boy, too."

Her voice had taken on a quiet sweetness, almost shy. That wasn't the normal tenor of her voice. I was used to the bold and brazen girl who told everyone what was what.

"You're good with him," I admitted.

"What's that look for?"

"What look?"

"You looked sad all of a sudden."

Heaving out a sigh, I combed my fingers through her hair, watching it fall across my chest. The sight of the blond strands spilled across my skin tightened the knot behind my sternum.

"I just wonder sometimes. Jake and I don't always connect. You two seem to get each other so easily."

"That's because I have the mind of a child. But you're absolutely crazy if you think you and Jake don't connect."

"I know he loves me. And he knows I love him. I'd die for him. I just mean, in some ways he's just like every other kid, but in other ways, he's not. I don't always get how he thinks. I wonder if I'm giving him everything he needs."

She sat up, looking down at me. Of course, I couldn't help but get distracted by her perfect, full tits.

"Don't even look at the girls, Wade. Look at me."

I snapped my gaze back to her face, a little shamed. But not a lot.

"You do realize you're a very smart man." She barreled ahead without a response from me. "Giftedness is hereditary which means he's smart because you are."

"Or he got it from his mother. And how do you know that?"

"I researched it when you told me Jake was gifted." That shocked me, but I kept silent. She asked, "What is it you're afraid of? That you're not enough for him or something?"

It was like she pulled my greatest fear right out of my head. And my heart.

"Well, that's dumb, Wade," she added, reading me too easily. "If you could see the way he lights up when you're around."

"I know he loves me. I'm his father. I can't quite explain it."

"So try."

I huffed out a laugh. She was so pushy and demanding. Normally, that would be a turn-off, but with Marly it felt…right.

"It has nothing to do with intelligence," I added. "It's just that since Kristie officially left, since the divorce, I've wondered if I can do this entirely on my own. What if I fuck him up and he ends up in therapy the rest of his life?"

"So what? Lots of people go to therapy. I went for over a year when I moved to Green Valley."

"Country life that bad?"

She gave me a sad smile. "No. It was that good actually, but I had all this guilt about quitting a job working for my dad and his expectations looming over me. They still are," she admitted softly.

I sat up, leaning back on one hand and cupping her face with the other. "You shouldn't feel guilty for living your life."

"And you shouldn't feel like you're not enough for your son. You're more than enough. You're a better dad than I ever…"

She bit her lip and looked down, obviously about to cry.

"Hey, hey." I tilted her chin up so she'd look at me. There were no tears, but her eyes were glassy with emotion. "You know your father worries and pushes you because he loves you too. That's what dads do. Sometimes we show it the wrong way or do things because we want what's best for our kids."

She nodded, her bottom lip still trapped between her teeth. Finally, she cleared her throat. "The difference is that Jake is only seven. You're a young dad and allowed to make a few mistakes, even though I haven't seen any that you've made. Everything you do is because you want what's best for him. But—"

She tried to avoid eye contact again. I dragged her chin back in my direction. "But?"

"I'm pushing thirty, and my father hasn't once, not *once*, supported what I wanted for myself. I'm no longer a child, and he still thinks he knows better. The problem is he doesn't know better because he doesn't even know *me*."

She grabbed my hand cupping her face and pulled it into her lap, her slender shoulders hunched forward, as if in defeat. Blowing out a breath that lifted the wispy strands of hair hanging by her cheeks, she stared down at my hand while playing with my fingers.

"I'm so happy for Jake." She lifted her somber gaze back to mine, slicing across my heart with sadness there in those clear blue eyes. "Because he has a father who cares about him, about his dreams, his hopes, his genuine happiness." She tucked some hair behind her ear. "Not everyone has a father like that."

I couldn't stand that look on her face any longer. Reaching for her, I hauled her back to the bed and rolled on top of her, our legs tangled.

"Do I need to go beat your dad up for you?"

She burst out laughing. Instantly, that fizzy feeling of joy bubbled inside me. I needed her smiles or my world just wasn't right.

"You, Mr. Follow-all-the-rules is going to go beat up my father for hurting my feelings."

I traced her smiling lips with one finger then along her jaw, unable to stop touching.

"I'll go after anyone who hurts someone I care about."

There I went admitting too much again. I couldn't help myself. I was unraveling quickly here.

"What did that growl mean?" she asked, smiling wider while I continued to map her face with the pad of my index finger.

"I growled?"

"Yep. That noise you make in your chest when you're mad or annoyed about something."

"I'm not mad at all, but I am frustrated."

"Why?"

"Because I think you've got a magical pussy." She belted out another laugh. I slid my finger down her nose then around her mouth to her chin, holding it there. "She's making me say way too much."

And the pretty girl who owns her is making me *feel* way too much.

"Is she now?" She opened her legs and bent her knees, allowing me to settle between her warm thighs. "Well, then. Why don't we put her magic to work so I can learn all your secrets?"

She clasped my nape and pulled me down. I wasn't a fool. I didn't resist kissing her soft lips or the invitation to sink inside her one more time before it was time to head back down the mountain. No matter how senseless she made me, I wanted more.

The following Wednesday, I was still flying high on the sex-fest with Wade up at the cabin. I'd had him and Jake over for dinner twice since then. Jake was highly impressed with my spaghetti and meatballs and my tacos. When he'd said I had the best tacos in town, I'd asked Wade if he also thought that I had the best tacos in town. He only scowled at me per usual, but I caught the quirk of his mouth before he bit into his taco.

We'd enjoyed a night of Battleship and Uno. Jake almost beat me in Battleship. Then he beat us both soundly in Uno. He was merciless with the *take-four* cards. It had been the best week I could remember.

I'd moonshined on Saturday and had taken Monday off again for my second to last batch. So far, I thought they were all good except the batch from Saturday. I blamed it on my constant fixation of staring longingly at the empty bed where Wade and I had spent a marvelous afternoon last week. I kept hoping he'd come and see me. He didn't. But he did check on me twice through the walkie-talkie, which he was pleased to hear I actually had remembered to take out of my car and keep close by.

But today was the best batch yet. This was the winner. I was sure of it. That's why I was zooming straight to Wade's house. I'd brought a sample of each jar in a milk crate I'd swiped from Piggly Wiggly. I didn't steal it exactly, but I did borrow it without asking when I saw a stack sitting by the employee entrance at the side door. I'd taken a jar of each batch and was going to make Wade help me decide though I knew which one was the best. Still, my first instinct was to share it with him. To see him.

I pulled up into his driveway, quickly noting the shiny, gold Cadillac Escalade parked beside Wade's truck. Immediately, an icky wave of sweat swept over my body. Who was here?

Ignoring all instincts to back out of the driveway since he had company and call later rather than barge into his house, I put my truck in park and hopped out. Rounding to the passenger side, I lifted the milk crate of moonshine out and walked to the door, set them down at my feet, and knocked.

To my shock, the door was opened by a beautiful brunette with perfect matte makeup, curled wavy hair, and dressed in a black pencil skirt and emerald-green, silky blouse that matched her eyes. It took me about five seconds to realize this was Jake's mother. I recognized her from a few photos with him around the house. But I had no idea she was such a stunner in person.

Suddenly, I wished I wasn't makeup-less with a messy bun and wearing stained jeans with my well-used purple jacket.

"Um, hi," I said rather dumbly.

"Hi," she said, flashing me a perfect white smile. "You must be Marly."

"I am." I nodded in affirmation, wondering if she knew about me from Jake or Wade or both.

"Come on in." She stepped back and widened the door.

I lifted my milk crate of moonshine, feeling very out of my comfort zone at the moment. It was the middle of the week. Why was she here? Did she have an unexpected break in work and stopped in Green Valley to see Jake on the way to somewhere else? That seemed unlikely. Wade had said she lived in Nashville now. Green Valley isn't really on the way to anywhere but deeper into the mountains.

"What do you have there?" she asked curiously, still smiling pleasantly.

"Moonshine. Peach moonshine." What was wrong with me? I was nervous—so nervous—my heart pounding insanely fast.

"Oh," she answered, her friendly expression transforming to confusion. "Is it for Pop? I know he likes moonshine."

"You know Pop?" Then I scoffed and squeezed my eyes shut for a second. "Of course you know Pop. You and Wade were married. So you've met his grandparents. Many times, I'm sure."

Her brow rose, and now I was seeing a very familiar look. Most of the time, I didn't care what people thought of me. But for some reason, her look of puzzlement agitated me immensely.

"Marly!" Jake ran through the living room toward me.

I set the milk crate on the coffee table right before he launched himself into my arms. "Hey, little man. I didn't know you had company." I gave him a quick kiss on the top of the head and let him go.

"Mom is taking me to her house for five whole days."

"That's awesome, dude."

A semblance of relief bloomed inside my chest, but there was still a nasty thought in the back of my mind. Why hadn't Wade mentioned it? And did it mean something that he hadn't? I mean, he was once married to this statuesque goddess, her business attire making me feel rather frumpy. My work attire was jeans and a Green Valley Shine polo with my Converse shoes.

"Hey," came Wade's deep, soft greeting, his eyes on me, frown in place as he carried out a small suitcase with SpongeBob Square Pants characters all over it. "I didn't know you were coming over."

No, he did not know. Did I surprise him? Like in a bad way? Were they having some post-divorce tete-a-tete that could lead to reconciliation? What was happening to me? Was I about to vomit on Kristie's expensive looking stilettos?

"You okay?" asked Wade as he sidled up next to me and set Jake's suitcase down, coasting a hand to the center of my back.

"I brought moonshine." I gestured down at the coffee table. "To taste. I mean, for you to taste. To compare, you know what I mean. You know what?" I leaned down and lifted the milk crate. "I'm going to go. I didn't realize you had company. So rude of me to stop by unexpectedly. But you know me, I never think. Just silly Marly. Not thinking again."

By the time I shut up, the pitch of my voice was freakishly high and I was nervous-laughing like a hyena. I took one step toward the door when Wade grabbed the milk crate and firmly pulled it from my hands.

"You're staying," he told me. And I mean *told* me. He gave me that smirky smile, while I fidgeted, tucking my hair behind my ear.

"I should go," I told him.

"No, you shouldn't."

"I *can* go," I corrected. "If you want me to—"

"Marly." He tilted his head lower. "You're staying."

Fortunately during my diarrhea of the mouth episode, Jake was frantically pouring out his entire day of events to his mother who was listening and beaming, sparkling. She was very sparkly, I thought.

"So Ms. Harley said we could try building the DaVinci bridge when we got back," Jake explained. "She said we don't need glue or anything if we do it right. Isn't that cool?"

His mom laughed. "So cool, sweetie." She ruffled his hair the way I usually did.

That had me wondering, do I have the right to ruffle his hair? If it's a Jake/Mom thing, then I probably shouldn't. Standing there with the three of them, I felt completely like an intruder.

Who was I kidding? I was intruding.

Wade hadn't told me she was coming and that was for a reason. Did I think that phenomenal sex and a few weeks of bonding over moonshine meant we were exclusive?

Yes. I did. But did he?

He'd set the milk crate on the dining room table and was walking back, his gaze was on me, his expression unreadable. I hope he wasn't mad I came. But he wouldn't have insisted I stay if he was, right?

It didn't help that he was looking absolutely delicious in faded Levis and a gray t-shirt that showed off his biceps. How could this woman at the door let those biceps go? It was mind-boggling. She was likely having second thoughts. I would.

Not true. If Wade was mine, I'd never let him go. Those big biceps and big everything else would be mine and only mine.

"Wade, we'll call you tonight so you can say goodnight to Jake." She leaned down to pick up the suitcase.

"I've got it," he told her, brushing her hand away and picking it up then lifting Jake over his shoulder like a sack of potatoes with the other hand.

Jake giggled, looking back at me upside down. "Bye, Marly! See you next week!"

"Bye, little man. Lo—" I stopped myself before the *love you* spilled out of my mouth, quickly correcting, "Y'all have fun!"

"It was nice meeting you," said the paragon of perfection and sweetness and apparently success as she walked out the door, closing it behind her.

I sank to the coffee table, propping my butt on the end. "What the hell, Marly?"

Then I shot up and over to the window, peeking through the blinds. Wade was strapping Jake into the backseat then he leaned over and gave him a kiss. I saw Jake's little arms wrap around his dad's neck before he pecked him on the cheek. My heart liquefied.

But then he walked around to the driver's side where Kristie was still standing outside her fancy SUV. She looked up at him and said something, tilting her head sweetly. He nodded and said something, hands low on his hips. A stance I realized was very typical for him.

I could imagine what they were like when they were married. They were two beautiful human beings. Who'd made this adorable, sweet, smart, beautiful little human being. And I didn't belong.

That melty sensation I'd experienced a second ago when Wade had tucked his son safely in his mother's vehicle hardened to a stone that dropped to the pit of my stomach.

"This is what people look like when they speak to each other," I mumbled to myself. They look at each other and nod and smile. It didn't mean anything. I didn't have supersonic hearing, so I wasn't going to be able to tell what they were saying.

Kristie laughed because of course she did. Wade was funny and charming, even when he was scowling at the world. Somehow the man was a magnet. She reached up and patted him on his forearm.

Oh, hell. She wanted him back.

Wade gestured toward the house. She looked over. I gasped and dropped the blinds.

I was being irrational. But also, could they be considering getting back together? I would if I was Wade. Hell, I'd tap that now, and I wasn't even into women. She was *fine*.

I hurried toward the bathroom because I was definitely going to hurl.

~WADE~

"She's very pretty." Kristie smiled up at me.

"Yeah. She is," I agreed, nodding. "She's a lot more than that."

"I can tell."

"How can you tell?"

She tilted her head. "I haven't seen that look on your face for a long, long time, Wade. And from what you and Jake have mentioned about her, I think she's just what you need."

"We're complete opposites, Kristie."

I wasn't arguing with her because I was starting to feel the same. But I was also wondering what my ex saw that maybe I didn't.

"Exactly. You need someone fun and spontaneous to kick you out of your pragmatic world sometimes. That's why you and I didn't make it."

"Because I was too pragmatic?"

"Because we both were."

I grunted assent. She was right about that. We were attracted to each other in our wild college days, but when we left that world for one of marriage and parenthood, the only thing we had in common was Jake. We didn't have fun or enjoy each other. Not like I did with Marly.

"I'm glad you think so," I said, gesturing toward the house, "because I plan to keep her. If she'll have me."

Kristie looked toward the house then smiled. "Oh, I think she'll keep you." She climbed up into her Escalade, the door still open. "Have you told her yet?"

"Not yet."

"A little word of advice, Wade…you better let her know how you feel pretty damn soon."

"What do you mean?"

She shook her head. "Men." Then she shut the door.

I waved to Jake who was grinning and waving from the backseat. Rubbing my sternum from the sudden ache at watching him leave, I waited till they were out of sight before heading inside. I hated when he left even though I knew he deserved and needed time with his mother. I felt incomplete without my son at home.

When I closed the front door, Marly wasn't waiting in the living room. I heard water running in the bathroom from the hallway where I could see the door was open. I walked toward the bathroom.

"Marly?"

From the doorway, I watched her splashing water on her face leaning over the sink.

"You okay?"

She popped up, water dripping off her chin. She grabbed the towel she must've found in the cabinet and dried off her face, yelling, "Fine" from behind the terry cloth.

"You don't seem fine."

She didn't. She was acting jumpy from the second she stepped into my house. That's why I wanted her to stay, so I could find out what had happened to throw her off-kilter.

"Did something happen at the cabin?"

I had visions of her burning the place to the ground with some kind of accident with the still. My brain tended to think of the worst-case scenario first. I'd like to say it was caused from being a parent, but I'd always been that way.

"The cabin?" she squeaked, folding the towel. "Why would something happen at the cabin?"

If she had burned it down, I'd be upset for Pop. But buildings can be rebuilt. I'd be more upset she'd nearly hurt herself somehow. Then I'd have to set up rules that she could only go up there with me. I was working through possible scenarios when I realized her face was a dark shade of pink.

"Are you sick?" I stepped forward and pressed my hand to her forehead the way I would to see if Jake was feverish. I'd dealt with the flu and ear infections enough times to know the signs of a fever. "Your skin is clammy."

She huffed out a laugh and stepped back. "I thought I was going to be sick." She gestured toward the toilet. "But I'm fine. Needed to cool my face off."

"Did you eat something bad?"

I reached for her again but she evaded and ducked around me to head back to the living room. I followed her.

"I'd brought my batches to see which one you liked best," she said over her shoulder, walking away. She heaved out a sigh, looking down at the milk crate once she reached the dining room table, avoiding me.

Not going to happen.

I marched to her side and gripped her by the upper arms and firmly but gently turned her to me. "What's wrong?"

"Nothing. I just didn't realize your ex would be here. It threw me off."

"I forgot to tell you."

"Yeah." She snorted. "You did."

"It bothers you?"

Her flat expression was definitely a sign that it did. Marly always conveyed every emotion she was feeling through those bright blue eyes and expressive face. That's what had turned me on so much when I was inside her. Her obvious pleasure amplified my own. But she was definitely not feeling anything close to pleasure at the moment. Quite the opposite.

She cleared her throat, her arms at her sides while I held her still in case she tried to dart away from me again.

"Does it bother me that I showed up uninvited to your house to meet your Victoria Secret model look-alike ex-wife for the first time in my grubby jeans?" Her brow had risen almost to her hairline. "Yes, Wade. It does bother me. And does it bother me that you didn't even tell me that she was coming over?"

Hang on. Maybe I was a little slow, but it was finally dawning on me. "Do you think there are still feelings between me and my ex-wife?"

"I don't know. Are there? I'm not quite sure why you let her go, because she looks like a Greek goddess come to life but more couture and classy."

I couldn't help but laugh at that, which was the exact wrong thing to do. She wiggled away from me, but I caught her in two long strides, banding my arms around her from behind.

"You're jealous," I whispered into her ear.

"Stop it, Wade! Let me go!"

"Not a chance." I chuckled. "So this is what happens when Marly gets jealous about her man?"

"You're not my man, you big, giant Neanderthal!"

She was spitting mad, and my reaction to that was highly inappropriate, my jeans getting tighter the more she struggled in my arms.

"Calm down, hellcat." I carried her while she flailed and squirmed, one of her feet landing a kick on my shin. "Fuck."

"No, sir. You aren't getting any of this. No fucking," she hissed back, panting, while I lowered us both to the sofa and pressed her down gently beneath me.

Knowing how heavy I was, I leaned most my weight on my forearm. One of her arms was pinned beneath her chest. I caught her other wrist and restrained it above her head, pressing my torso into hers enough so that she couldn't move.

"Now then," I breathed close to her ear, her face in profile, cheek flat to the sofa, "let's talk about this calmly without you running away from me."

"I don't want to talk about it." She struggled again but it was useless. I was too strong for her.

She sounded almost…scared. The idea of her actually hurt or in any sort of pain, especially pain I caused, gutted me with a sharp sting. I lifted my weight so she could free her pinned arm.

"You're going to settle down and listen to me."

She huffed out a breath and rolled her eyes. "Do I have a choice?"

"No." I eased to one side so she could see me, still holding one wrist above her head so she couldn't wrestle free and run. "The only feelings I have for my ex-wife are that of respect because she is Jake's mother. And do you want to know what we were talking about out there?"

"No," she snapped, anger still simmering.

"You. She was telling me that you were good for me and Jake."

She stilled, examining me closely but didn't say a word. So I went on.

"And I was telling her that—" Shit, I hadn't thought exactly what I was going to say, so I didn't think about it. I took a note from Marly's book and just said what I was feeling without filtering it. "I was telling her that I cared about you. And I do. I care about you a lot, Marly."

The tension in her body relaxed partially beneath me. That wild-and-lost look vanished from her face for the first time since I'd found her standing in my living room with a milk crate of moonshine in her hands. She was quiet, not saying a word.

"What are you thinking?" I finally asked her, nervous that I'd said too much again.

"I was thinking I didn't have to call Lola now."

"Lola? Why were you going to call her?"

Guilt flashed across her face as she bit her lip.

"Marly. Why were you going to call Lola?"

"To tell her that I'd go out with the new guy over at Cage Erickson's gym she found for the next podcast date."

The fucking hell she would!

I flipped her over in a flash, pinning her down again, arms over her head.

"No, ma'am," I told her.

"Excuse me? You can't tell me what I can and can't do."

"Maybe not. But I can knock out any guy who tries to take you out on a date."

She scoffed. "That's really mature. It's not like I sleep with my podcast dates. Most the time I don't even kiss them. It's for the show."

I dipped my head lower till our faces were inches apart. "Marly. Listen to me and listen good. I don't want any guy taking you out, opening your car door, pulling out your chair, or looking at you across a table, thinking he's got a chance. Because he does *not* have a chance."

"Oh, yeah?" Fire sparked in her eyes as she squirmed beneath me. This time, it wasn't to get away. "And why's that?"

"Because you're fucking mine. And if you want me, I'm yours."

She whimpered and opened her legs wider so I settled right where I needed to be.

"I want you." Her voice was husky and sure.

I let go of her hands and lifted off of her. "Don't fucking move," I commanded.

I stripped my t-shirt as I strode to my bedroom to grab a condom. In the twenty seconds it took me to walk there and back, Marly had stripped down to nothing and had stretched out naked on my sofa.

"Holy fuck," I muttered, going for my belt buckle and zipper.

I was glad I'd paid extra for a soft rug in front of the sofa. I didn't want her knees to get rugburn.

"Come here," I told her.

She'd barely sat up when I lifted her bodily and maneuvered her onto her hands and knees on the rug.

"No foreplay?" she teased over her shoulder.

I slid a finger through her dripping slit, circling her entrance. "I don't think you need it. And I need inside you now."

Her answer was to bend her torso forward and down till her cheek was on the plush rug.

"Such a good girl," I crooned, gripping her hips and sliding my tip through her wetness.

She whimpered and rocked her hips back.

"Patience," I hissed, trying to ease myself inside her.

"No," she snapped, digging her nails into the carpet. "Get inside me, Wade."

"Fuck," I mumbled as I clasped her curvy hips with both hands and slammed home.

She cried out, pushing up onto her hands and arching her neck. The pleasure of being inside her was dizzyingly mind-blowing. My brain short-circuited, and all I wanted was to feel this intense pleasure over and over, forever.

If I thought she was in pain, I'd have stopped. But she was already rocking backward, trying to fuck herself onto me. I smacked her ass with a sharp thwack. She jumped then moaned.

"No topping from the bottom," I warned her.

"Then fuck me, Daddy Bear." She glanced back over her shoulder with a grin, knowing that stupid nickname riled me.

Couldn't get much more riled than this. Then she added, "And spank me again."

Guess I was wrong. Blood surged and pumped faster at her demand. Without a second's pause, I smacked her on the left cheek. Once, twice, three times. She dropped her torso back to the carpet, moaning while I pounded her from behind and smoothed a palm over her reddened flesh. I reached forward with one hand and wrapped my fist in her long hair, then tugged till her neck arched for me.

"You're soaking wet. You hear that?"

The slick sound of my dick sliding in and out of her was loud in the room. For once, she wasn't saying a word. She was nothing but whimpers and moans and sharp cries of ecstasy.

"You love being fucked hard, don't you, baby."

Another gasping moan. I fisted and pulled her hair tighter.

"Answer me." I spanked her ass again on the left cheek, knowing it would sting. "You love this, don't you." Not once did I slow my punishing pace, my own orgasm spiraling closer.

"Yes," she murmured.

"Louder. Tell me you love it."

"I love it, I fucking love it," she whimpered.

I hammered even harder, pushing her body up the carpet with each thrust. Growling, I let her hair go and scooped her torso off the rug, then pressed her back to my chest, upright. I mounded one of her breasts and cupped her pussy.

"I love it too," I growled into her ear before I licked her neck, groaning at the salty sweat I tasted. "I don't think I'll ever get enough of this sweet, tight cunt, Marly."

She latched her little claws behind her onto my ass, jutting out her perfect tits. I pinched and rolled her nipple with the fingers of one hand, while I slid my fingers through her slit, pinching her slick clit with the other.

"I can barely get a grip," I told her, feeling her flutter around my dick. "You're so slippery, so wet for me."

"Goddamn," she muttered. "That filthy mouth. I'm coming!"

"Yeah, you are. Mmmm." I licked her shoulder again, still thrusting as my cock swelled even more. "I'll never get enough, sweetheart."

Her head fell back against my shoulder on a cry as her sex squeezed and fluttered with her climax. I mounded her breast with a tight hold and cupped her again, spearing her deep as my own release came, opening my mouth onto her shoulder for a sucking bite.

As she fell limp in my arms, I smoothed my lips over her shoulder and up her slender throat. She angled to the side, offering me her neck. My cock pulsed inside her as I slowly came down from the most intense sex I think I've ever had.

Even so, my mind was clear as a bell. I coasted my mouth back up to her ear while I held her tight, cupping her intimately, still buried deep inside her.

I nuzzled her before I bit her lobe to be sure she was listening. She flinched, her hands sliding behind her, low over my hips. My head was buzzing, mind reeling, and yet I felt a certainty down to my bones. I'd never been the possessive type with women. Not until her. Not until now.

"I want you to be mine, Marly Rivers." I traced my nose and lips up and down the silken skin of her delicate throat. "I don't want other men looking at you and thinking they can have you." I scraped my teeth along the smooth slope to her shoulder then retraced the path with my tongue and lips. "Want you all to myself." I kissed her under her jaw, nuzzling my beard along her throat. "Tell me you're mine, baby."

An indescribable satisfaction swept through me when I saw her nod her head and heard the faint, breathless words I wanted so desperately to hear.

"I'm yours."

CHAPTER 16

~MARLY~

"Come on in, my friends! Come closer."

I waved my arms for the last tourist tasting party of the night, gathering them around the square bar at the back of Green Valley Shine. We worked with some of the local tour groups who hopped to three or four distilleries. Today, we had this last group scheduled for four o'clock, not long before I got off. I wasn't closing for once this week.

The other reason I was high on life was because Wade had texted me three times today. *Three* times. And it wasn't like he was responding back to some meme I'd sent. He was the instigator. On top of that, every one of them ended with something sweet.

The first ended with, ***I hope you have a wonderful day.*** That was after a good morning text. The second text began with ***I can't stop thinking about you*** and ended with ***I miss you***. The last one was about what time I got off of work, and he said he'd see me afterwards then. When I sent him a kissy face emoji, he replied with a red heart.

Are you kidding me right now? What planet was I living on that grumpy Wade Kelley was sending me heart emojis and pining about how much he missed me?

My insides were nothing but gelatinous goo from all his saccharine sweet texts all day that I'd reread at least a hundred times. I was well and truly gone for this guy.

"We're going to start you all off with something mild," I told the ten tourists who'd lined up in front of each row of mini shot glasses. "This one is called Red Hot Mama. If you like the red hots candy then you'll love this one."

One of the men—good-looking and in his forties with a roguish smirk—held up the shot. "This is starting off mild?" he asked, arching a brow down at a pretty woman with him.

"Oh, yeah," I assured him. "Y'all just wait till we get to Pink Panty Dropper."

The roguish guy got a wicked look on his face. "Does it work?"

"I don't know. But after she tries it," I pointed to the pretty lady with him, "you can call me later and let me know."

They all laughed then I went into my usual spiel about the Green Valley Shine company and how it started way back when, how you can only buy our moonshine right here in Tennessee. There were laws preventing the export of moonshine outside of the state, so if they wanted more they'd have to come back and visit.

While I talked a mile a minute, I kept smiling at the handsome couple giving each other moony looks as they tasted the different moonshine flavors. My thoughts repeatedly strayed to Wade and his swoony, possessiveness yesterday.

Ordinarily, I'd have bristled when a guy tried to pin me down with his domineering and territorial bullshit. Many times before when a guy got possessive, I'd walked right out the door with a few feisty words over my shoulder. I'd certainly never before let and welcomed a man to pin me down and fuck me senseless, bite and spank me then demand I agreed that I was *his*. And I sure as hell had never agreed to it. Or wanted to. Not once, not ever.

Until Wade.

He didn't exactly demand it though, did he? He kind of begged in that dark, throaty, sex-laced voice of his. I'd never been hypnotized, but I was pretty damn sure Wade had put me in a sex trance with his big dick and his soft mouth that seemed to kiss every inch of my skin last night.

Rather than want to run from the house and never look back, I'd wanted Wade to hold me like that forever, to whisper dirty things in my ear and tell me I was his woman. It was absolutely nuts and undeniably wonderful.

When my phone buzzed in my back pocket, I grinned and poured the last shot of 128 proof alongside a shot of pickle-back.

"I know, you're wondering how in the world a shot of pickle juice can be a good chaser for 128 proof alcohol. You're just gonna have to trust me, folks. Give it a shot." I winked. "See what I did there."

They laughed at my corny joke and started taking the last of their flight of moonshine shots. I took that second to pull my phone out, fully expecting another text from Wade. My stomach flopped sickeningly when I saw my dad's name light up.

I knew I couldn't avoid him forever, but I could sure as hell try. I already know what he had to say, and I had no interest in hearing it for the hundredth time. There truly was only so many times you could hear versions of *you're a failure* from your own father. Ignoring the second call and fourth text I'd gotten from him this week that we needed "to talk", I shoved it back in my pocket and wound up the moonshine tasting.

"Please feel free to take a look around the store and find your favorites. We appreciate you coming in to Green Valley Shine today."

I wondered if I'd ever say those exact words but with "Marly's Moonshine" at the end of that sentence. Maybe I was fooling myself that I could actually make a living off a one-woman moonshine distillery. I mean, I'd have employees and help with distilling, but most of the moonshine distilleries around here were made up of entire families and were generations' old.

I sure as hell wouldn't be a family operation. Flying solo had been my MO in life, and this would be no different.

Pushing all negative thoughts away, I checked the time on my phone and smiled wider, saying goodbye to the tourists as I popped into the breakroom where I'd hung my jacket then made my way to the front of the store where Kayla was working the register. She'd be closing up for the night.

"They're all yours, Kayla." I waved as I passed.

"You going out with that tall drink of water again?"

"He has a name." I grabbed my purse behind the register and headed for the door. "Stop objectifying him."

"You didn't have any problem objectifying him before," she sassed back.

"That was before he was mine."

"Oooweee." She smiled wide. "Now those are some feisty words I never thought I'd hear you say."

I pressed my back to the exit door. "First time for everything."

I laughed as I headed to my car and smiled like a lovesick goofball all the way home. My heart dropped into my stomach though when I pulled into my driveway. Parked in front of my house was a motorcycle, a fine one, with an equally fine man sitting on it with two helmets sitting in his lap.

Jumping out of my truck laughing, I hurried across the yard toward him in long strides.

"Are you Wade Kelley?" I called.

"Why do you ask?" He wore that sexiest smirk that did all the melty things to my insides.

"Because the grumbly, practical guy I know would never drive up to my house on a motorcycle looking like a delicious man-sickle."

He laughed, his eyes hidden behind some super, sexy shades. "A what?"

"You know?" I stopped right in front of him, panting with my hands on my hips. "Like a popsicle made of a man I really want to lick."

He curled his fingers into the front of my jeans and gave me a sharp tug till my legs were leaning against his thick thigh. Without ceremony, he angled his mouth over mine and gave me a sweet, lingering kiss. A touch of tongue and a little nip with teeth then he pulled gently away.

"You better be careful," I whispered against his lips, loving the feel of his whiskers tickling my chin. "People around town are gonna start talking."

"What are they gonna be saying?"

"That Wade Kelley is completely smitten with Mad Marly. That he's chasing her all over town."

"If they look close," his hazel eyes burned into mine, "they'll see he's caught her, and he's not planning on letting go."

Then he kissed me again, groaning into my mouth with a thorough, melty kiss before abruptly pulling away.

"Come on," he said, handing me one of the helmets. "I'm taking my girl for a ride."

"Say that again."

His smile widened. "My girl," he rumbled low.

"Good Lord, Wade. Lola should've warned me about this side of you."

"Which side is that?"

I laced my fingers at his nape, holding the helmet with the other hand. "The one that makes me wet with one grumbly word."

"Well, sweetheart, Lola couldn't tell you because she's never seen that side of me. And truth be told, I'm not sure any woman has put me in my current state but you."

I leaned closer, curling one arm all the way around his neck, the tops of my thighs pressing against his leg, helmet dangling at my side. "Define this current state."

He splayed one hand at the small of my back and pulled me tighter, his mouth coasting against mine but never landing. "Sick with want. Desperate to see you. Touch you. Kiss you. All the fucking time."

Then he really kissed me. Nothing gentle about the way he took my mouth, delving deep till I moaned. That had him clenching me tighter and nibbling at my lips before he broke away and slapped my ass.

"Get on the bike."

Blowing out a shaky breath that seemed to make him smile, I said, "Let me go let Scooter and Pooter out first."

Hurrying inside, I let my two babies out of their kennels and into the backyard. I put some food and fresh water down on the patio, making sure to unlock the doggie entry on the patio door. There were big hawks around here, and my babies were still little. Thankfully, they were smart, and spent more time sunning underneath the windows than running around outside.

"Mommy will be back soon."

Then I was tearing out the front door while putting the helmet on. Wade had started the bike and put his own helmet on while watching me cross the yard. He looked so fucking hot, his shades hiding his eyes. But I could feel them devouring me from head to toe, which was silly because I was just wearing my dark work jeans, polo work shirt, and puffy purple jacket. I was not looking sexy, but he made me feel like I was anyway.

Before I could get on, he stopped me and zipped up my jacket to the top.

I swung a leg over behind him and clasped my hands around his waist. "Let's go, hottie."

His laugh rumbled against my chest that I had pressed to his back. But before we took off, he unclasped my hands, pressed a kiss to one palm, then tucked them both into his leather jacket pockets. He was right. It was really cold. I sighed and lay my cheek against his back as he zoomed out of my neighborhood like he'd ridden a bike all his life.

A blooming sensation of warmth and affection and deep adoration opened inside of me. Then it gushed right out, pouring an endless waterfall of feelings out into the ether, amplified when he'd stop at a light and reach back to clasp my thigh protectively.

This was new and bright and beautiful. I'd never been in love, but I couldn't imagine that this was anything else. Strangely, it didn't terrify me. Some people described it as scary. But I think that's for people who aren't sure if the one they're falling for feels the same way.

Don't tell me how, but I knew Wade was falling for me too. We both had that same lingering look on each other when we were together now. It wasn't lust. Well, not all lust. It was something bigger, and I felt the binding between us growing tighter and drawing us closer every time we were together now.

That's why I wasn't freaking the hell out and hiding in my house. We were in this together, this lovely, risky, vulnerable path. I might be wearing rose-colored glasses, seeing only the good in Wade. I wasn't an idiot. We all had faults, but I was okay accepting his. I think that's where we were, falling deep and opening to the possibility of sharing our flawed selves with each other.

Now, *that* was fucking terrifying. I'd been told my entire adult life how flawed I was by the one man who should be simply accepting and loving me. My dad wasn't ever that man for me. And that was the only reason I found sharing those flaws with Wade so scary. Because maybe my father was right. Maybe I didn't know what was best for me. I shook those thoughts off and tried to stay in this blissful moment.

Wade wound us through Green Valley and out the other side, coasting past the turn-off for Bandit Lake and a little higher, but not up the highway to the cabin. Dammit. I could've gone for a romp in the cabin right about now. I wondered if Granny Mae had turned over in her grave, knowing what the hand-made quilt she'd made for me as a baby had witnessed.

Doubt it. Granny would've told me, "Go live your beautiful life, sweet girl."

That's what she'd always said to me. I know that was why I couldn't just sell her house after she died. I couldn't give up the love she'd sheltered me with all my life so easily. I wanted that shell of protection around me forever.

Wade pulled over at a lookout. The sun was sliding low beyond the highest peak of the Smoky Mountains, gilding the landscape in a rim of gold. This was a scenic spot to get a good view of the mountains and the valley below.

He cut the engine and pulled off his helmet. Reluctantly, I pulled my hands out of his pockets and took mine off too. Reaching back, he took my helmet out of my hand and propped them both on the handlebars. Then he took one hand and tugged.

"Come here. Let me keep you warm."

I slipped off and let him guide me closer beside him, then he lifted me to sit sideways on his lap facing the sunset, my bum settling on the bike between his legs. He wrapped one arm around my waist, another hand landing on my thigh as he tugged me close against him. I locked my arms around one of his, resting my chin on his bicep as I looked out. He rested his on the top of my head.

We sat there like that, wrapped up together, watching the sun go down and saying nothing for quite a while, simply holding onto each other. The only movement was his steady breaths going in and out, the warm feel of him around me a bone-deep comfort I wasn't sure I'd ever felt before. A feeling I could get used to very easily.

"It's so quiet here," I whispered. "So beautiful."

He grunted and hugged me tighter against him.

"I could stay here forever," I admitted on a sigh.

"We'd get pretty damn cold come nighttime."

Huffing out a laugh, I said, "Leave it to grumpy-pants to ruin the moment with logic and reasoning."

He nuzzled the hair at my temple and kissed me there. Softly. Sweetly. My breath caught at the intimate touch.

"Or we could stay right here, and I'd find a way to keep you warm," he rumbled.

My heart hammered faster, butterflies flitting every which way.

"That's highly impractical on a motorcycle."

"I think that you'll find my logical brain can reason through and manage just about any tough situation."

I chuckled lightly. Rather than try to maneuver me around to get sexy, which his words and husky voice implied, he simply pressed another kiss to my temple and tucked my head beneath his chin.

The sun slipped lower, casting the valley and rolling hills in deep purple and blues.

"I'm going deer hunting with Jed tomorrow."

"Is there a reason I need this information?" I asked.

"No. Just thought you'd want to know where I'll be."

"You didn't tell me exactly where you'd be though, did you?"

His body shook with a chuckle. "We'll be at Buck Rogers property. We've been going there for years now. Nice and flat land so we don't have to haul the deer out of valleys like on Pop's."

Buck Rogers was the son of the former governor of Tennessee. I wasn't sure how Wade was friends with him, but just about everyone in Green Valley knew everyone else or knew somebody who knew somebody who knew everyone else.

Buck Rogers was a nice guy. His family came from old Southern money, and Buck was the kind of guy who didn't mind sharing at all.

"I like that," I finally said.

"That I'm going deer hunting?"

I turned my face so I could see his. "That we're at that phase in our relationship. The telling each other our whereabouts phase."

That lop-sided smile made a reappearance. "I like that phase too."

I turned back to the sunset, which was sliding into darker, cooler hues.

"When does Jake come home?" I asked after a bit.

"Sunday. Would you like to pick him up with me?"

"You have to go to Nashville? To Kristie's?"

"No. She's got another meeting in Knoxville Monday. She said she'd come into town and drop him then go on and spend the night in Knoxville."

"You don't mind me coming?" My extremely rare shyness had just shown up.

"I want you to come. Jake will want to see you too."

"If you want me to."

He sat back and looked down at me. I pulled my gaze from the darkening valley and looked up at him. He was so handsome in this light it hurt.

"Marly, I wouldn't ask you if I didn't want you to. That's one thing you can be sure of when it comes to me. I'm not about to say anything or do anything unless I firmly believe in it. Do you not think Jake will want to see you or something?"

"Jake loves me, and the feeling is mutual." I glanced away from those piercing hazel eyes.

"But?" he asked, tugging my chin toward him again so I'd look at him.

"I'm just surprised you want me to see so much of Jake."

Last time they'd come over for dinner, Wade had given me a kiss at the door in front of Jake. It wasn't a barbarian-invader kiss but it was a definite, lingering press to my lips that said we were more than friends.

"I'm a little surprised too," he admitted.

"What?" I shouted on a laugh but also, I was offended.

His smile widened. "I just mean that at the beginning I was determined not to show Jake that we were dating. I've always been protective of him."

"As you should be. He's your son."

"I haven't brought one woman around since his mom officially moved out of the house two years ago."

I studied his serious expression. "So why me?"

He hauled me tighter against him again. "It feels right, Marly." He dipped his head down and swept his lips across mine. "You feel right."

"You're still moving impractically and illogically fast where he's concerned. You came to dinner several times already. He's now addicted to my spaghetti and my taco nights."

"If we break up, then I'll still bring him to visit for spaghetti night."

"Then of course, *you're* addicted to my taco too."

"I am," he agreed so easily. "Which is why we won't be breaking up."

I snorted. "If you think I'm going to keep dating you just to feed your addiction to my taco, Wade Kelley, then you have sadly misinterpreted my motivations for this relationship."

"What motivates you, sweetheart? My hotdog?"

I belted out a laugh because he said it so seriously. "Among other things."

"Like what?" His brow arched curiously.

"Well," I said softly, "I like this."

He squeezed my hip where his hand had been resting and holding onto me for quite some time. "We can't have a relationship based on hugs and sunset watching."

"Or taco and hotdog nights," I added.

"Agreed. So what else is keeping you in this relationship?" He coasted a hand up to wrap behind my nape beneath the collar of my jacket. His thumb brushed lightly over my collarbone.

"I like you," I found myself admitting easily, not wanting to admit that I was pretty damn sure this was the other four-letter l-word.

His mouth tilted into a smirky smile. "What do you like?"

"I like that you're a good father." He brushed his thumb up the side of my throat. "I like the way you're logical and careful about things."

"Why's that?"

"Because I'm not most the time. It makes me feel," I shrugged a shoulder, "comforted, I guess, that you're worrying about the things I never do. It makes me feel safe in a way I hadn't realized I kind of needed."

He hummed and stared at me with that intense, adoring expression.

"So you tell me." I squeezed his nape. "Why do you like me?"

"Who says I like you? Maybe it's just your taco I like."

I reached under his leather jacket till I found some flesh at his hip and pinched.

"Ow!" He laughed and caught my wrist, dragging it from under his shirt and jacket.

"Tell me right now."

He pressed a kiss to the inside of my wrist, the bristles of his beard making me shiver. He let go and wrapped his hand back around my thigh to keep me steady on the bike.

"I like the way you're so honest."

I blinked, not expecting that.

"You always say what you feel without a filter. And when you don't, it's written all over your face. And I like the way you see things differently than me. Though I don't always like to break out of my shell, I know I need to sometimes. I like that you push me, but you push gently. Softly."

I wrapped my arms around his neck and combed my fingers through his hair. "Keep going. Tell me more things about how wonderful I am."

He rumbled a laugh. "I like how good you are with Jake. How you get along so well and how he trusts you. How he cares about you and you care about him."

"He's easy to love," I admitted freely.

"So are you," he snapped right back, then his eyes rounded slightly at what he'd admitted.

Rather than torture him with that, though it was tempting, I asked, "What about my wild, crazy side? That doesn't bother you?"

Why I was asking this, I had no idea. I'd already tensed up for his answer, readying myself for ridicule. Which was why it was so surprising when he actually did criticize me.

"I love your wild side, sweetheart. Though sometimes you can let your responsibilities go for a whim."

"What do you mean?" My question was small and unassuming, but the answer held the power to annihilate me.

He didn't reply for a minute. I leaned back so I could see his face again, now mostly in shadows.

"Tell me," I urged him.

Clearing his throat, he said, "I was surprised you took work days off to use the time to moonshine when you're the manager."

"I can't go up there after work. It's too late then. And the contest is around the corner. I've got to get as many batches done as I can to be sure I've got the best one."

"I understand that."

"No, you don't," I snapped tartly, "You think I'm being ridiculous about this contest and that I'm wasting valuable time that should be spent at my job." I was stiff in his arms now, but I hadn't hopped off his lap though the urge was there. "It's more than a contest and a cash prize to me."

He eased his hands to my arms, since I was now leaning away from him. "I know. You want your own distillery."

"Yes. I mean obviously it won't be a giant commercial distillery like Green Valley Shine with multiple stores. Mine will be smaller, of course. But that's why winning the contest is so important. It would put my name on the moonshine map locally. It would give me a huge boost."

He nodded but didn't agree with me, which sent a twist of panic into my gut. *Was he doubting me like my father?*

"You don't think I could do it?"

"I never said that. But if you don't win? You're going to give up on your distillery then?"

"That's what you think? Or is that what you hope?" I wiggled out of his hold and stood up next to the bike.

"Marly, what are you talking about? I'm just asking."

"I know, I know. You're thinking it's a *crazy* idea, and why would I waste my life on things that will never happen?"

"That's not at all what I'm thinking."

"Well, if you can't accept that I've got plans of my own and I'm not changing them because maybe they're not the *logical* course of action or the safe path toward success, well then, I can't help you."

"Marly." His voice was calm while my brain and my mouth spun out of control. "You're getting worked up. That's not at all what I'm thinking."

"Please don't tell me I'm getting worked up. The next thing you know, you'll be calling me *hysterical*, and then I'll have to kick you in the balls just on principle's sake for all the women fighting the patriarchy."

He huffed out a sound of disbelief. "What are you talking about?"

I was spiraling. I knew it. But I couldn't think straight when my emotions took over like this. All I could do was let the shitshow play out. I could feel the anger like a living, breathing beast, and I didn't even know why I was getting so fucking angry at him.

I jerked my helmet off of the handlebars. "I can't talk about this anymore." I hurriedly snapped the strap in place. I needed to get away and not make this even worse. "It's getting late. You should take me home."

I hopped on the back of the bike and wrapped my arms around him. For a few seconds he didn't move at all then he heaved out a sigh and started it up.

Without another word, he pulled out of the lookout parking spot and turned the bike around to head back toward the valley. I blinked my eyes furiously, refusing to cry about this. Though I wasn't even sure why I was so upset.

Was it because Wade had come dangerously close to saying something my father was trying to drill into my skull with his paternal screwdriver? Or was it because I overreacted in a heartbeat, cutting him off so I wouldn't have to hear anything else he had to say. So I wouldn't have to know what he really thought of me. Or was it because I should've calmed the fuck down and let him explain himself rather than attack him with my overly emotional response?

The ride down wasn't nearly as pleasant because of the turmoil spinning my stomach into a nauseous soup. Such a different feeling than the ride up.

When Wade pulled into my driveway, he turned off the motorcycle as I hopped off and unstrapped the helmet.

"Marly, listen. I'm sorry if I offended you. I was just trying to figure out why—"

"I know, I know," I cut him off.

He was trying to figure out the method to my madness. Sometimes people just couldn't understand me. I was totally fine with that. But I wasn't ready to hear one iota of criticism from Wade. I couldn't take it. Not from him. His opinion meant too much, and if he dared to start talking along lines parallel to my father's then my heart would be crushed. I'd be left with no alternative than to break it off. I wasn't quite ready to tear my own heart out and watch it bleed.

"I'll talk to you later," I told him, handing over the helmet then fidgeting with my hair.

"Hey. Can we talk about this? I don't want you to walk away mad."

"I'd rather not. I just want to go to bed. I'm tired," I told him without once meeting his eyes. I turned and called over my shoulder, "Have fun deer hunting."

He didn't say anything else as I continued to take deep breaths so the tears wouldn't fall. I wouldn't let them. I unlocked my door, opened and shut it, then leaned back against it.

I waited, half expecting to hear a knock at the door behind me. But after about two minutes, the motorcycle engine started up. I peeked through the blinds and watched him back out and drive away.

Then I decided it was okay to cry. So I did for a long time.

CHAPTER 17
~WADE~

The gray light of early morning spread across the meadow below me. A light fog drifted over the grass and fallen leaves. There was no sound but a few larks twittering in the branches of the trees to my right.

Jed had moved on a quarter mile up the trail to his regular spot. We didn't hunt often like when we were younger, but we still liked to keep this childhood tradition going. Strange since hunting was really a solitary business. But there was something about the stillness of the woods and watching the world wake that settled me into peacefulness.

That was what I loved best about this sport. Simply being in this place of solitude in the woods. There were many times I'd had the chance to get a deer and let it pass on by. As a responsible hunter, I knew the importance of keeping the balance of the ecosystem. But sometimes, all I wanted was to be in this serene place with my thoughts without anyone needing anything from me.

Of course, my thoughts were anything but peaceful at the moment. They were a stormy mess spinning me into a deeper state of frustration. Jed had noticed right away, asking me what was wrong when I'd picked him up before dawn this morning, but I didn't want to talk about it.

The thing was, I'd never actually had an argument with a woman I was dating. Kristie and I were friends who started fooling around in college, always with easy temperaments. Then we were friends and married, never arguing over how or where to raise Jake. Even our separation was amicable. So was our divorce.

I didn't know how to handle this situation with Marly. I'd obviously hurt her feelings, but an apology didn't seem to be enough last night. And she wouldn't let me talk to her. I'd left the house at five a.m. this morning, so all I could do now till Jed and I were done was stew in the fact that we were officially in our first fight as a couple. It had my gut tied in knots.

Blowing out a breath, I removed my gloves and set them on the tiny shelf I'd built into this deer stand. I held my hands over the portable heater I'd brought as well. I'm sure I'd be excommunicated by the old-style hunters who basked in the misery of frigid pre-dawn temperatures as part of the true hunting experience, but I didn't care. That was completely illogical when I could bring my mini heater and be perfectly warm up here while watching the world wake.

The stand was two stories, built between two thick oak trees. The entrance was a hole in the bottom right corner that aligned with the trunk of one tree, which let in a lot of cold air. But I'd covered the front of the box-shaped stand with burlap for camouflage as well as to keep the bitter cold out of my little box.

Trying to think about something else besides upsetting Marly last night, I recalled my conversation with Ben earlier in the week. He'd gone to check that first trail where he'd spotted the truck and ATV tracks heading into the park and had noticed fresh ones. Buzzards were circling overhead, which led him to a pile of entrails not far into the woods. When I'd met him to check it, we determined it must've been an elk from the type of fur attached to some of the innards. Those damn poachers had killed an elk and dressed it right in the damn woods and gotten away with it in my territory, which really chapped my ass.

Irritated, I was debating whether to call this hunt off early so I could head straight to Marly's. I planned to demand that she fight with me properly so we could hurry and make up when I heard the sharp crack of a twig breaking off toward the left of the meadow.

Sound carried far and easy in these woods. I slid the burlap open a little wider to get a better view off to the left where the sound was coming from. More crunching leaves and heavy steps.

Damn. No way was that a deer. They didn't tromp that loud. Had to be a bear, I thought when a flash of orange crossed what I knew was the trail we usually took that curved in that direction.

Hmph. Must be another hunter. I wondered if Buck Rogers hadn't informed his family we were coming out. I'd sent him our dates a month ago, and he was good about letting his family know we'd be here so no one else would use our spots for that weekend.

The hunter-orange vest passed in and out of view again. Looked like he was wearing a camouflage cap. I clamped my jaw tight, wondering if this could possibly be the poachers who'd been evading us the whole season. Probably not since they'd always been spotted higher up in the mountains where they might avoid getting caught.

Then the hunter veered off the trail it seemed, tromping straight through the woods toward the meadow. Confused, I peered closer, wondering why in the hell he'd be making all that damn noise and then marching straight into the meadow where the game was supposed to be appearing. Then what I'd thought to be a hunter came fully into view, waltzing right out into the open.

"What in the hell?" I muttered as I watched Marly take a few more steps then stop and bend over.

She picked up something off the ground. A leaf? Then another and put them in the pocket of a camouflage jumpsuit she was wearing underneath her orange vest. She stood and looked out at the meadow, propping her hands on her hips then she turned back around and faced the woods. She took two steps in one direction then stopped and looked right, took one step in that direction then stopped again, looking around the tree line.

"What in the hell is she doing?"

Then I realized it, she was lost. Before she could take another step, I opened my burlap blind wide and whistled loud through my teeth. When she jumped and turned, I waved my neon orange cap out the deer stand window.

Her shocked expression instantly morphed into a giant, smiling one. A swell of relief and affection filled me at that face. She wasn't still mad at me if she was smiling like that.

I dropped my hat inside on the floor and watched her jog closer along the edge of the woods till I could see her clearly.

"Marly Rivers, what are you doing tromping through the woods where hunters are before the crack of dawn?"

She stopped below the deer stand and beamed up at me. "Looking for you." She glanced at the tree beneath the stand where the wooden ladder-steps were hammered into the trunk.

"How did you know where to find me?"

"You see, I have this best friend who happens to be engaged to your best friend. She gives real good directions."

I grinned at her sassy mouth.

"I'm coming up," she announced before disappearing underneath me.

Shaking my head, I set my rifle in the back corner and peered down the opening. She crawled through the top, and I hauled her the rest of the way inside.

"Ouch." She bumped her head on the roof when she tried to stand up fully.

"Sorry. Watch your head," I warned, though it was obviously too late.

The stand was built big enough for one man to move around with limited mobility. There was a bench seat where I was that had just enough room left over for her if I scooted all the way to the far side. So I did.

She was panting as she took the seat. I smiled at how cute she looked with her ponytail pulled through the back of her camo hat and her little camo jumper.

"You happened to have this tucked away in your closet?" I touched the sleeve of her jumpsuit.

"Yeah."

"You go hunting much?"

"Never been hunting," she stated matter-of-factly. "I had this from when Green Valley Shine launched their Hunter's Paradise line."

"Of moonshine?"

"Yep. We had three new flavors—*Sweet Sunrise, Mountain Mist*, and *Autumn Spice*." Her gaze kept darting all over my face. She was acting a little shy, letting her mouth run to cover it up.

I took her hand, which was cold. Frowning, I said, "Give me your hands."

She turned sideways, her knees hitting mine, and handed them over. I rubbed them between mine to warm them up. "I was just thinking about you when you came stomping through the woods."

"I was not stomping," she protested, head down, watching me warm her hands.

"Sounded like a baby bigfoot making all that racket."

She giggled and peered up at me with a soft expression. "You're not mad at me?"

"For what? Scaring all the deer away in a five-mile radius?"

"I mean about last night."

"Marly, you were the one angry at me."

"I'm still angry," she said evenly, which almost made me laugh, because she was so matter-of-fact about it. But I knew that would've been a mistake.

"You don't seem that angry."

"Well, I am." She pulled her hands from mine. "But I know I was mean and fussing at you and never even let you talk. I know you were trying to explain what you meant, and I wouldn't even let you."

"Contrary to what you believe, I can handle Mad Marly." I reached up and pulled her hat off then tucked a loose strand of hair behind her ears. "I like Mad Marly a whole lot."

"You do?" she looked completely shocked and ecstatic at the same time.

"I do." I held her gaze, enjoying the sweet, soft side she was showing me

She nodded and unzipped her hunter-orange vest. "I came out here for something else." She tossed it aside and then knelt between my knees, wrapping her slender fingers around my thighs.

"What was that?" My camo pants were getting awfully tight at the sight of her on her knees, those blue eyes sparkling up at me with mischief.

Then she gripped the zipper hanging between her breasts and pulled it all the way down to the crotch. When she tugged the sleeves off her shoulders, revealing that she was completely naked underneath, I lost my breath.

"I want to make it up to you." She shoved off her Converse shoes and then wiggled out of the jumpsuit, managing to pull it completely off somehow without letting her naked bum touch the wooden floor. "For being so mean."

She folded her jumpsuit on the floor of the deer stand between my legs, her thick socks still on, and knelt on top of it.

"Wait, wait, wait." I closed my eyes and cursed myself, but I had to make her understand something. I had to make this right.

Cupping her face, I leaned forward, keeping my eyes on hers and not on the tempting sight of her half naked body.

"I need you to know I'm really sorry for upsetting you. And whatever plans you have for your career or your future, I'm here to help you."

I stroked a thumb over her silken skin, mesmerized by how soft she was. She was so tough and strong all the time that discovering her softness always seemed to surprise me.

"I'll support you in whatever you need from me."

Her smile widened to something wicked. She pushed higher and kissed me in a way that was quickly weakening my resolve. Then she whispered, "I'm going to give you the best blow job of your life, Wade Kelley."

And all I could do was swallow against the strangled noise in the back of my throat. "You don't have to do that," I heard my lips saying even while my body burned at the mere thought of her mouth on me.

"Oh, I don't do anything I don't want to." She reached for my belt and started working it out of the buckle, blue eyes flicking up to mine. "Trust me, baby. I want to."

My heart hammered at the sound of her using an endearment while all the blood rushed to my dick. I was equal parts turned on and schoolboy smitten.

I watched her hands working, needing to talk so I wouldn't lose my mind at how aroused I was. "Is this how couples make-up after they fight?"

"Not sure," she answered, unzipping my pants. "I've never fought with a boyfriend before."

"Neither have I," I admitted, finding that coincidence funny. And heartwarming, somehow.

"But you know what," she whispered, tilting her face up to mine while she pulled my boxer briefs down with one hand and gripped my thickening dick with the other. I hissed in a breath as she scooted closer between my spread legs. "I think making up is going to feel really good."

"I think you're right," I agreed, because what else could I do with her slender fingers already working me into a frenzy.

She leaned forward, her gaze holding mine. "I know I am." Then she opened her mouth over the crown of my cock and I saw stars.

"Fuuuck," I breathed out heavily, leaning my back against the wall to give her more room and wedging my pants and boxers lower on my hips.

"Mmm." She dragged her tongue down the side then underneath, flicking the head where I was sensitive. "Sure am glad you've got this little heater. It's keeping my bum nice and warm so I can take my time sucking on your big dick."

I groaned and dropped my head to the wall, unable to keep my eyes off of her as I slid my fingers to the back of her nape and urged her further down.

"Take more," I groaned, begged.

She laughed with her mouth full of my cock then sucked me down more.

"Oh, fuck, sweetheart. Just like that."

I was overwhelmed by the erotic sensations and tender emotions spinning like mad through my body and brain. I wanted more of this, more of Marly.

I never liked messy or unpredictable. I sure as hell never liked spontaneous. A well-thought-out plan was what I'd always relied on in my life. Never once did I imagine a girl tracking me down at a deer stand and climbing up here so she could give me the best blow job of my life. Especially when she was mad at me. She baffled me completely, and it only made me want her more.

Marly would always surprise me. Rather than make me anxious, it soothed the tense edges of my psyche that always shied away from impulsiveness. That part of me that needed things clear and orderly didn't mind a little chaos in the form of the sexy, sweet girl on her knees in front of me. As a matter of fact, her recklessness seemed to fill a need I never knew I had. Somehow, she fit me just right.

"Marly," I whispered again but with reverence this time as I coasted my hand up to the back of her skull, cradling her as she took me into her mouth with deep strokes.

She hummed in her throat, one hand clutching my thigh, the other at the base of my dick, pumping in tempo with her mouth.

"Such a good girl," I murmured.

She moaned then dropped her hand from my thigh and between her legs.

"You all wet from sucking my dick?" I crooned, knowing my filthy words worked her up.

She made a humming noise. I gripped onto her ponytail and tugged her head back till my dick slipped free. Her beautiful mouth was puffy, her eyes hazy with lust, her fingers still working herself between her thighs. She pumped me slowly with one hand.

"Tell me. Does sucking me make you wet?"

"Yes," she answered emphatically on another whimper.

I loved her like this. Completely mindless and responsive to me. One thing I knew, my girl liked dirty talk.

Leaning down, I fisted her ponytail and urged her forward till I could kiss her with deep, drugging strokes of my tongue. She moaned again.

"Fuck, I wish I'd brought a condom," I told her. "Didn't expect this situation when I left this morning."

She was still stroking me, slower now, her thumb grazing over my crown. I had to clench my jaw so I wouldn't bellow in pleasure, her sweet touches driving me insane.

"I'm on the pill," she told me, nibbling my lip. "It's safe."

I'd never trusted a woman when it came to that. Not even my wife after we were married. But I realized something suddenly. A hard truth. I trusted Marly—deeply and sincerely.

"Why don't you come sit on my lap then," I suggested more than asked.

She made another one of those delicious little feminine sounds that thickened my cock as she crawled up between my legs. But when she started to try to straddle me, I gripped her waist.

"Turn around, sweetheart. This bench will hurt your knees."

"I don't have any control in reverse cowgirl," she whined even as she was turning herself around and easing back onto my lap.

"Then I guess you're going to have to give me all the control and let me take care of you."

Hands on her hips, I hauled her back just as she reached between us and guided my dick to her entrance. I slid her down on a feral groan till I was buried to the hilt.

"Fuck." I wrapped one hand around her breast and slid my other fingers to her clit, working the slick bud in a circle.

She had her hands on my spread thighs, trying to rock against me.

"Be still," I told her, tapping her clit with a light slap.

She flinched and mewled again. "Not this again. You're not holding me hostage without moving inside me again."

I chuckled in her ear and nipped her earlobe. "You feel so good, baby. I just want to feel you before I fuck you."

She gasped. "Feels like heaven," she agreed, circling her hips since I wouldn't let her move up at all.

"So fucking good." I kissed and nipped her bare shoulder, silken skin sliding under my lips. "Lean forward and grab the edge of the window."

She did, pressing her ass further up.

"Yes, like that," I praised as I gripped her hips again and pounded up inside her.

Stroking inside her with nothing between us was beyond pleasurable. It was almost paralyzing in its level of ecstasy.

"Ah!" she cried out as I felt the first flutters.

"Coming already?"

"Yes! I can't...oh, God..."

Then she was spasming around my dick and moaning loud. I hauled her back, pressing my chest close while I buried my face into her neck. I emptied inside her, my dick pulsing fiercely, the pleasure making me moan long and loud against the skin of her throat.

When she flinched at my touch on her clit, I steered away, still petting her slick folds, marveling at the fact that I wasn't terrified I'd had unprotected sex with someone. Quite the opposite, I was wallowing in a blissful feeling that felt a lot like peace, like the way I felt watching the sun rise in the woods. But deeper, more intimate, more special.

She reached back with a hand to slide into my hair and turned her head for a kiss. I obliged easily, lingering a long time on her sweet mouth, trying to press my feelings into that kiss.

"I truly am sorry for losing my shit last night," she whispered against my lips.

"It's okay. And I'm sorry I sounded critical. Now that I know your plan, I'll support you. I'm here for you, Marly."

She sighed with contentment. "Let's get in a fight at least once a month. Maybe once a week."

I smiled, grazing my nose along hers. "We don't need a fight to feel like this."

"We don't?" Her brow rose in question. "We can have wild deer stand sex all the time?"

"I think we can move the venue and have wild sex anywhere we want."

"Like where?" she pushed, nuzzling her nose along my beard and inhaling.

"Wherever you want, Mad Marly." I smoothed a soft kiss to her lips again before adding, "But this feeling isn't just about sex."

"It's not?" she asked in that mock-innocent voice and wearing that wide-eyed, oblivious expression that didn't fool me at all.

"No, ma'am. You know it's not. Don't you?"

She stared at my mouth then back up into my eyes, her face broadcasting all the tender emotions I'd been feeling for some time now.

"Yes, Wade Kelley. I know."

I helped her get dressed, both of us quiet. Then I pulled her back onto my lap, opening the flap of the burlap wider. The sun beamed orange rays across the meadow, the fog gone now. The morning was more beautiful than I'd ever seen it, and I knew it was because I was watching it with the incredible woman sitting on my lap.

"What were you doing walking out into the middle of the meadow? You could've gotten yourself killed parading right out onto hunting ground."

"Uh oh. The bear is back," she teased at my growled question. "I only paraded myself in front of one hunter. And he didn't shoot me." Her voice dropped. "Though he did stab me with his spear a couple times."

I tickled her ribs, and she squealed then turned her head to look at me. "You didn't seem to mind all that much."

Ignoring her sassy mouth, I asked, "What were you picking up off the ground?"

"Oh." She shifted on my lap and pulled out two leaves from her pocket. "Look. These leaves are so red and this one is shaped like a heart. But this one is shaped like an elephant with a big butt. I thought Jake would like it."

I looked at the leaf she twirled by the stem, which indeed looked like an elephant with a big butt. Chuckling at the fact she never stopped surprising me and that I enjoyed it way too much, I placed a kiss on her throat.

"Yeah. Jake will love that," I agreed, holding her close and never wanting to let her go.

CHAPTER 18
~MARLY~

"Marly!" screamed Jake as he ran across the parking lot of Daisy's Nut House. He launched into my arms and I swung him around.

"Hey, little man!" I laughed as I set him down, giving him one more tight squeeze.

Wade walked my way, Jake's suitcase in hand, smirky smile in place. Kristie looked over at me from her SUV behind him and waved with a big smile. I waved back, deciding that I really did like Wade's ex-wife, which was weird. But also quite nice. No drama on that end, which was rather wonderful.

"So how was your visit with Mom?" I asked Jake.

"We had so much fun, Marly. And guess what? Mom got a dog. His name is Rex, and he's giant. A big black Doberman, but he's also very nice. To me, anyway."

Wade made it to our side after setting Jake's suitcase in the truck.

"Your Mom's new dog is named Rex? Like T-rex?" I waggled my eyebrows at Wade who scowled and shook his head at me.

"That's right!" Jake added excitedly. "Mom said she named him that because I like dinosaurs so much. She said he doesn't usually like strangers but he liked me right away, and she called me a dog whisperer. But I didn't know what that was so she said it was someone who has like a natural way with dogs, you know, so I told her about Scooter and Pooter. And she laughed so hard at their names."

I laughed too. "She did?"

"Yeah. She said she liked the names though. She wasn't laughing to be mean."

"I didn't think so. Your mom seems really nice."

"She is. We went to the zoo too in Nashville. Did you know they have a rare species of Central American giant galliwasps? They're real name is *Dioploglossus monotropis*."

"And what is this gilly-wasp?"

"Galliwasp," he corrected me, giggling. "It's a lizard. And the Nashville Zoo is the only one to breed them and make babies. They're really pretty. They're so long and they've got yellow heads and white stripes and red bellies."

"They sound like the coolest lizards I've heard of."

"They are. Hey, Dad. Can we get a bearded dragon since I can't have a dog?"

"A what?" he asked as he held open the door.

"It's not a real dragon." He laughed and rolled his eyes at me as if we were in on a secret, like there was no such thing as dragons. "It's a lizard. They had those too at the zoo and the reptile lady there said you could even get them as pets. But you had to be really good at taking care of them."

"Can we talk about this after I've had something to eat?"

"Sure, Dad. I think I want to be a herpetologist when I grow up now. Not a paleontologist."

"And what's that exactly?" I asked, grinning at Wade's expression which was a mixture of confusion and adoration as he focused his attention on his son.

"That's what the reptile lady is. She takes care of reptiles and studies them and knows *everything* about reptiles."

I leaned into Wade and whispered, "I think someone fell in love while he was in Nashville."

Wade slid his hand around my nape and bent close as we stopped at an empty booth. "He isn't the only one."

I know I turned seven shades of pink at his easy declaration. I couldn't speak, and he didn't seem to expect me to. Neither of us had officially said I love you. But it was whispering and winding around us ever since the deer stand. Who would've known that sex in the outdoors could have that kind of effect? Still, I was waiting for the right moment to tell him I was crazy in love with him. So far, that moment hadn't appeared just yet.

Thankfully, I didn't need to say a thing. Jake was filling up every single second with his adventures in Nashville. Yes, Kristie was a good mom. The sight of seeing Jake so extraordinarily happy and excited filled me with a tender emotion.

That's when I realized I hadn't simply fallen for Wade, but I'd fallen for Jake too. Who wouldn't? The kid was beyond endearing. But also, when he looked at me very similarly to the way he looked at his beloved father, with pure, tender love in a way only a child could, I was smitten and completely wrapped around this little future-herpetologist's fingers.

Wade guided me onto one side of the booth and Jake in with me then took the opposite side, facing us, his contented smile fixed as his gaze soaked up his son, flicking to me here and there.

"But the Green Crested Basilisk was my favorite. Even more than the snakes."

"Basilisk?" I teased, giving him my quizzical look. "Like in *Harry Potter*?"

Jake's head tipped back as he howled with laughter. Wade and I both laughed with him, because apparently I'd said something so funny he was losing his mind over it.

"Marly," he finally managed to say, shaking his little head. "There's no such thing as giant basilisks like in *Harry Potter*."

"Oh. Right. Of course." I nodded seriously.

"No, these are green. A real pretty green. You know, some can run over water. They're native to Nicaragua and Costa Rica."

"Fascinating," I said, propping my chin in my hand and listened as he rambled. I wasn't lying. It was fascinating. This kid was like a walking dictionary of reptilian facts.

"Hi, there," said Rebecca, a long-time waitress of Daisy's. "Good gracious, Jake Kelley. If you keep growing, you're going to be bigger than your daddy."

Jake's eyes rounded. "Really?" He looked over at Wade with the widest smile. "Did you hear that, Dad?"

"I did," he answered laconically, mouth ticking up on one side.

"I bet you could pass him up easily," I added. "But only if you eat all your dinner."

"Can I have waffles for dinner?" he asked me.

It stunned me for a second, because he'd asked me, not his dad. I looked across the table where Wade wasn't mad at all, still smiling that little tilted smile of his.

"Um, I think you can have waffles for dinner if you get sausage or bacon on the side. You need a protein if you want to keep growing. And that is, if Daisy's kitchen doesn't mind making them."

"He can have whatever he wants. Tons of folks come in wanting breakfast for dinner."

Wade and I ordered some burgers and fries then went back to listening to Jake's dissertation on the thirteen new species of reptiles he'd seen with his own eyes and learned about.

Our meals were delivered and we had settled into eating when the door opened and Jackson James walked in. He headed to the counter and ordered a coffee. Since he was in his deputy uniform, I suppose he was stopping in for a pick-me-up. His head swiveled around the room and landed on us. Wade raised a hand to give him one of those male not-waves but sort of like a wave in greeting.

Jackson shoved off the counter and walked over. "Hey, Marly, Jake. Wade." He gave me and Jake that typical charming smile I was used to from Jackson James. He was known for being a charmer and a looker. But his smile faded, his eyes pinching with serious thoughts when he looked at Wade. "Can I talk to you for a second?"

He immediately set his napkin on the table. "Just a second, guys," he said to us.

Jake was devouring his syrup-soaked waffles and telling me how Rex liked to catch the frisbee. For the first time since we'd picked Jake up, I couldn't pay full attention. My focus was on the two men talking close enough that I could still hear most of their conversation.

"Stopped at Donner Bakery, if you can believe that," Jackson was saying.

"Seriously?" Wade asked in disbelief. "Are you sure?"

"Tempest said they ordered coffees and banana cake to go. Since she knew they weren't locals, she checked out their plates. North Carolina. Two big men in their thirties. Definitely hunters pulling a trailer with an ATV in the back. And stranger still, a tarp strapped with bungie cords and covering the bed of the truck. Like they didn't want anyone seeing what was in the back. She couldn't tell if they had anything, but it seemed suspicious to her."

"Damn. And that was yesterday?"

"Yeah. Unfortunately, she didn't think anything of it until her man, Cage mentioned that we were on the lookout for poachers. I'd run into him last week and spread the word to anyone I could."

"Right under our damn noses, and we can't get these fuckers."

"Wade, we need to catch them in the act or coming out of the park. With or without dead game."

Uh-oh. I recognized that stern, hard look on Wade more times than I could count.

"I know," he said emphatically. "Even if we get them outside the park, all I need to do is stop them long enough to compare the tracks we found. I'll bet they don't even have Tennessee gaming licenses."

"Probably not," agreed Jackson. "They wouldn't want to be on our radar at all if they were poaching."

"Exactly."

"Seems odd though if you and Ben were right that it was them who dressed that elk right outside the park in the woods. Why would they take the chance to come back again if they'd gotten some game?"

Wade paused, glancing out the window, his voice downright cold when he answered. "Because they're not after deer. They're likely after a black bear. Cocky hunters like that want the biggest and baddest game as a trophy. And if they succeed and we catch them, that's definite prison time. Not just a fine."

"Got that right," added Jackson. "Our judges don't play."

Wade glanced over at the table, catching me watching and listening. I didn't pretend I wasn't. I gave him a comforting smile, even though I hated this part of his job that stressed him out. His jaw clenched tighter, then Jackson said something else in parting, and Wade returned to the table.

"Everything okay?" I asked, though I could tell that it wasn't.

"It will be when we catch these bastards," he said, knowing I'd heard enough to know what was up.

"Dad, you said a bad word," commented Jake as he shoveled the last piece of sausage in his mouth.

"Sorry, son."

"Look, a clean plate." He lifted it up to show me.

"Awesome, little man. You're definitely going to be bigger than your daddy if you keep this up."

We settled into lighter conversation and talked about Pop's upcoming birthday party next Saturday. I was excited about my present which was a basket of my best batch of moonshine so far. I'd created labels with pretty filigree and the name of the moonshine: *Pop's Peaches and Dreams*. I hadn't told Wade yet because I wanted the name to be a surprise. I couldn't wait to show him and Pop.

CHAPTER 19

~MARLY~

I t had been the perfect Saturday. Too perfect. I should've known something was coming to ruin it all.

We had two tour groups and both of them were big spenders and big tippers. Bekah and Kayla were on duty with me, but Bekah was closing up. I had a hot date with an eighty-one-year-old man, and I wasn't going to miss a minute of it. Okay, so maybe my date was his grandson, but I was more excited to see Pop's face when he opened my present which was tucked away in my truck and ready to go.

I was actually preparing to leave—double-checking the inventory that had come in, counting boxes against the order and the shipping slip—when I heard a voice that made my heart sink with dread.

"She's in the back," Bekah said cheerily, but I didn't wait for her to fetch me.

Always best to hold your head high when facing imminent doom. So I waltzed out and handed the clipboard to Bekah along the way to meeting the tall, lean figure of my father near the door. His dark blonde hair was combed back, receding more around the hairlines I noticed, and he was wearing a dark business suit like he'd just stepped out of court.

Of course, he always looked like that. Dress for success. That was one of his many mottos he'd tried to hammer into my stubborn brain over the years. Some-times I thought the harder he'd tried, the more I wanted to rebel.

I'd even talked to a therapist once, questioning whether my behavior was simply my rebellious nature or whatever. But when we'd delved deeper, we'd both come to the conclusion that no, it wasn't what she'd labeled opposition defiant disorder, it was simply that my life viewpoint and goals were vastly different than my father's. I was fine with that. The problem was, he wasn't.

"Hi, Dad."

"Hello, Marleen." He gave me one of his tight, semi-good-to-see-you smiles.

Even though he wasn't the huggy kind, I still reached up and pressed a kiss to his cheek. He always endured my affectionate ways. When I settled back onto my heels, I was pleased to see the tightness around his eyes had softened a little. He liked my hugs whether he admitted it to himself or not. But then he ruined our somewhat cordial greeting right away.

"I've been trying to reach you," he added with a little bite. "Though I'm sure you know that."

"Of course, I do. I just already knew what you were going to say, and I didn't want to hear it."

His hands were tucked in his pockets. He sighed and glanced upward. Not in a full eye-roll, but my father's version of one, all the feelings of exasperation leaking out of his pores.

"Can we talk outside? Just for a minute." He glanced around. "I have something important to tell you. Since you won't answer my calls, I had to come all the way out here."

Dad doesn't waste time, so he must actually have something to say besides *get a real job*. Or so I thought.

I followed him into the parking lot, the air already chilly in the early afternoon. It was going to be a cold one tonight. My weather app had the cute little snowflakes on it this morning when I checked, but so far, no snow.

"What's up?" I asked, crossing my arms against the cold, my jacket still in the breakroom.

"Honey, listen."

Oh, boy. He was pulling out his sweet-talking voice. This wasn't good.

"I know that you don't think I understand you."

He didn't.

"But I do. I get it. You don't want to work under the thumb of your father. I wouldn't either if I were you."

I laughed. He even smiled back. For a second, I saw the father who'd spent Saturday afternoons watching Law and Order reruns with me through my teen years.

"I'm glad I didn't have to tell you for the hundredth time," I said lightly though I spoke the truth.

The thing was, I was interested in law for a while. It was intriguing when I watched the dramatic courtroom displays on television. But after a few pre-law classes in undergrad school, my romantic views of being a high-powered attorney in a badass but sexy business suit withered and died. I didn't even tell dad when I changed my major to business, since I'd decided I really wanted to be my own boss someday.

But even then it was a subconscious dream. I tried to pretend I was planning on going to law school while I worked as his paralegal. It wasn't until Granny Mae died that I realized life was too short to waste. That was the beginning of this war between Dad and me. The one where he kept thinking if he laid siege forever, I'd eventually run out of resources and willpower and then surrender. Maybe he'd finally caught on, and he was the one who was about to yield.

"I understand it took me awhile to understand that," he added, "but stubbornness does run in the family. So I have a solution." His blue eyes, the same as mine, brightened with actual joy. "Do you remember my old partner Morgan Danvers? He has an opening for a paralegal, and he said in about four years he'll actually have a spot open in his law firm. His father is retiring and he'll need someone. With our family connections, he'd be more than willing to give you the spot. If you prove yourself, which I know you will."

The entire time he was talking, my heart was shrinking with every word he said. The light in his eyes, the hope he had for me, it was beyond shattering. Because once again, I had to be the one to take my bat of truth and smash his hope to pieces. It wasn't fucking fair.

"Dad," I started, my voice cracking already. "I don't want to be a lawyer. Not now, not ever. I know you keep holding onto this idea that I'll change my mind, but it's never going to happen." I straightened, my spine already stiffening with resolve. "Never," I snapped.

He winced at my uncharacteristically angry demeanor. That was another problem I had. I'd always tried to let my father down gently. I was afraid that it was my fault that he still had this impression that I'd come around and see the error of my ways. I was going to make damn sure he heard the truth loud and clear this time.

Crossing his own arms in a mirror of my position, he clenched his jaw, his gaze turning icy before it slid to the door of Green Valley Shine.

"And what is it exactly that you plan to do with your life, Marleen? You do have a plan, don't you?"

"Yes. I have a plan."

"Please don't tell me it's to work here for the rest of your life." He nodded at the shop with obvious disdain.

"No."

I held my breath while he waited for me to spill it. This was so much harder than I ever thought possible, because I knew what his reaction would be. Still, a sliver of hope propelled me forward. Wade was as pragmatic as my father, and he supported me. He believed in me. Maybe it wasn't crazy to think Dad would too.

"I plan to open my own distillery," I said bluntly. "I've been studying and learning everything I need to know since I've been working here. My business degree has helped me come up with a logistical plan to start small and ways I can market, so I—"

"You've got to be kidding me."

A slicing sensation slithered down my spine. I blinked quickly, unable to respond, willing the sudden stinging in my nose to go away.

"This is worse than I thought. And how in the hell do you plan to open up this shop of yours? If you plan to tell me that you're going to use the inheritance my mother gave you, then I'm going to lose my mind, Marleen."

I stood frozen under his furious gaze and spiteful words, begging myself internally not to burst into tears in front of him. Showing him any weakness, and my father deplored what he considered the feminine weakness of tears, was tantamount to surrender. And I was not going to. Not fucking ever. Not even if he disowned me right here on the spot, which I was starting to think he was going to do.

"You are, aren't you?" His voice was cool and detached now, the scariest voice my father had. "You're going to take the money my mother carefully saved over her lifetime, the money she decided to give to you above everyone else, even your sister."

Ouch. That stung the worst. I knew Granny Mae had chosen to give me the majority of the nest egg she'd never spent because my sister had her life together and had a successful career. But I also knew that Granny Mae believed in me.

I didn't know what I wanted when she was alive, but she always told me I'd figure it out. *You'll be damn good at whatever it is, Marly Mae*, she'd said. My middle name was Marie, but she always liked to use her own name with mine as a nickname. I loved that. I loved her. And I wasn't going to let my father bully me into ignoring what I wanted and forget that others had and did believe in me.

My father scoffed. "And you're going to waste it all on some stupid scheme of running a moonshine distillery?"

His words were like tiny knives, slashing and piercing my flesh. Still, I remained upright and unmoving and unspeaking. He uncrossed his arms and turned away muttering something, then turned so sharply back to me that I flinched.

"You're out of your mind, Marleen. You are truly *crazy* if you think you're going to succeed in this. And I'm telling you right now, I will not pick you back up when you lose everything." He was pointing in my face now, while I remained a stone statue. "You're on your own when it fails."

He stormed away, marching toward his Audi. I remained in place until he backed up and sped out of the parking lot, not once looking back at me. Then I promptly burst into a sob.

Not even thinking, I hurled myself back into the shop and toward the register, reaching for my phone and purse beneath the counter.

"Hey," said Bekah softly as I sobbed. "Marly, you okay?"

"I need to leave."

"Fine, fine. You go. It's almost end of your shift anyway. Can I do something for you?"

I shook my head, lifting the strap of my purse to my shoulder. "I just need to go."

"No problem. You go take care of yourself."

Nodding and swiping at the tears with the back of my hand, I hurried back out to my truck. I revved it quick and tore out of there, driving fast though I didn't know where I was going. I hiccupped because I was crying so hard, and flicked on my heater since it was freezing in here.

Realizing I forgot my jacket, I started crying harder, because I didn't want to turn around and face anyone right now. I needed to get my sobbing out of the way so I could even think straight. So I kept driving and crying, which made me laugh remembering that was kind of a cool, old indie band from the eighties that my dad loved to listen to when he was younger and cool.

"Not some cold dickish dictator like he is now," I mumbled, then burst into fresh tears.

I didn't even realize where I was driving till I was halfway up the mountain and turning off the main highway toward Pop's cabin. I needed my sanctuary, my safe place. Once I was up there and curled up with Granny Mae's quilt, I'd walkie-talkie Wade and he could come meet me. It was still several hours till the party. He'd be getting off work soon. I didn't want to make him leave work early to tend to my meltdown. By the time he got off, I'd be calmer anyway.

I'd managed to stop leaking like a sieve and blew out a heavy, jagged breath, the hiccups finally gone as I wound off the main highway. Y-tree Road would be coming up soon, my body easing at the thought of the comfort at Pop's cabin right around the corner.

That's when I saw the big Dodge truck on the side of the road up ahead. It was one of those Ram 3500 Heavy Duty trucks that were wide as a Mack truck. A man stood in front of the hood, hands on his hips and looking down. Looked like he might've hit an animal or something. If so, he might've done some damage and need help. Looked like he had a cell phone in his hand but that wouldn't work up here.

Slowing in the road, he turned at the sound of my approach. I didn't recognize him. Maybe in his thirties, built big, scruff on his face like he hadn't shaved in a day or two.

I rolled down my window. "Hey, there. You have some trouble? I have a—"

His expression when he locked eyes with me was nothing but mean. Immediately, I stopped talking. Something was wrong. That's when I realized what he was staring down at. It was at the four-wheeler stopped on a partial incline. I couldn't see it as I drove up because his giant truck was blocking it.

Sitting on the four-wheeler was another man looking equally menacing. My heart rate tripled at the sudden fear and instinct that I'd stumbled on something I shouldn't have, which was exactly when I saw the bloody carcass of a giant black bear half hanging off the rack on the back of the four-wheeler.

The four-wheeler guy stared at me, his expression shifting as he gave me a dangerous, sinister smile that was straight out of a movie like a super-villain. He snapped to the other man, "Get her!"

"Fuck," I mumbled as I floored it.

Glancing back in my rearview, my pulse pounded even faster as I saw both men had jumped into their truck and were coming after me.

"Shit, shit, shit!"

I punched my truck faster and didn't turn at Y-tree Road toward Pop's cabin because I knew that road lead to dead-ends, and they could see where I turned. They'd just follow and block me in. I reached for the walkie-talkie in my console. As soon as I got it in my hand, I had to take a sharper curve, the walkie-talkie flying to the floor on the passenger side. The basket of Pop's present toppled on its side, a jar of moonshine rolling onto the floor but not breaking.

"Goddammit!"

I grabbed my phone but couldn't look down to text or I'd run off the road. I had no idea where I was now, heading deeper into the woods. Their truck came into view again in my rearview, coming up on me fast. I accelerated even faster, taking the turns tight and quick as I could without wrecking. When I rounded another bend, I saw a turn-off that must've been for the Pruitt property, the ones Wade had mentioned owned the land up here next to his Pop's. The very property these poachers had come wandering out of with an illegally shot black bear.

I turned off and sped fast, making it about a half a mile till I saw them fly by on the main road in my rearview mirror.

"Thank you, thank you," I muttered, easing up a little and turning onto another gravel road off the main one. I could hide back here and call Wade. I'd made it nearly to another bend in the road when I saw that big black truck appear in my rearview again.

"No!" I screamed, my heart rate catapulting and my foot laying my acceleration pedal flat in fear.

I was going so fast that when I had to make another sharp turn, I hit the brakes and slid on the gravel right off the road, banging my head on the steering wheel, the distinct sound of glass breaking when the basket completely-upended on its side on the passenger window. The smell of peach moonshine filled my truck which was now mostly on its side in a ditch.

Survival mode had kicked in, my fight-or-flight instincts screaming at me to *run*, so I shoved open the door and crawled out, my cell phone still clutched in my hand. With the driver's side tilted toward the sky I knew I couldn't reach the ground, so I let myself fall. At least there was a pile of dead leaves to soften my hard landing. The sky was quickly darkening and without a thought, adrenaline driving me now, I sprinted into the woods.

I fell and slid down a hill on my ass, the fallen leaves helping me slide down quickly. Then I was in a dried-out ravine, running in the opposite direction of the road. The crunch of my footsteps sounded so loud in my ears that I was sure they'd hear me, so I leaped over a fallen tree and lay flat on the ground on my belly.

Their engine died and the ominous sound of two truck doors slamming had me near tears again. These fuckers were going to come hunt me down in the woods? And then what? Threaten me? Hurt me? Worse?

Assault and murder would give them much harder prison terms than poaching. But who the hell knew? If you were brazen enough to be a poacher and a hunter, maybe they were shameless enough to hurt people too. The very thought had my blood running cold. Not to mention I was actually fucking freezing. I was still in my polo shirt with short sleeves and the sun was setting, the temperature dropping.

Pulling my phone in front of me, I opened my texts, but there were no bars. Still, I could go back up after they left and get my walkie-talkie.

"You see her?" I heard one of them bellow.

"Nah."

Woods carried sound easily, so they could still be far away. Very carefully, I peeked up over the log. Movement through the trees on the ridge showed the silhouette of one of them up there. I didn't see the other then I heard a truck door slam. It sounded distinctly like mine, not as heavy as theirs.

"Look what I found."

Then one of the men chuckled. "She can't call nobody now. Let's go get her."

Those motherfuckers had my walkie talkie. I lifted up quietly onto my feet, staying crouched low to the ground. The sound of twigs snapping as they grabbed small trees on the hillside to help them down the incline had my heart hammering even faster. They were truly coming after me!

As soundlessly as I could, I followed the dry ravine in the other direction. It had more rocks than leaves so they wouldn't hear my footsteps. I made sure to avoid as many leaves as possible and ran and ran like my life depended on it. Because it looked like it did.

CHAPTER 20

~WADE~

"I made a vanilla cake too just in case your girl Marly doesn't like chocolate. Your grandfather has to have chocolate." Nana was fussing around the birthday table in her living room.

"I promise you she will probably eat both. She isn't particular from what I've seen."

My parents had come in too and were chatting with Pop in the living room as I walked back to join them. I checked my watch again then pulled out my phone, wondering where Marly was. It wasn't like her to be late. I'd texted with her at lunch, and she'd promised she'd get off early and meet me here on time, which was fifteen minutes ago.

"Here are the late-comers," said Dad.

My stomach flipped with excitement at seeing her. *Finally.*

We'd been busy this week, meeting up only on Wednesday for dinner at my place where I'd grilled some steaks. I smiled at the memory when Jake informed her I made the best steaks in the world and she'd replied that she was aware I was the best man at handling meat.

But when I rounded the corner into my grandparents' living room, it was just Jed and Lola walking through the door. No one else.

"Hey," said Lola with a smile, glancing around while Jed was hugging my mother. "Where's Marly?"

"I don't know," I said, starting to get annoyed. "You haven't heard from her?"

"Well, yeah. I talked to her around two. She said she just had to run home and shower and change after work then she'd be here."

"What's up?" asked Jed, sidling over.

"Nothing," assured Lola. "It's just that Marly's late. And I know she wouldn't be late for this. Not to meet Wade's parents and she'd told me about a surprise she had for Pop that she was excited about."

My annoyance immediately morphed into concern. This wasn't like Marly. I pulled out my phone and called her. It went straight to voicemail.

"Let me text Bekah." Jed had his phone out and was texting as he said it.

Five seconds later, his phone rang. I saw Bekah's name right before he answered.

"Hey," said Jed. "Is she still working?"

Jed listened, a frown forming between his brow. "And that was what time?" He glanced down at his watch, concern etched on every line of his face.

My gut had clenched and locked up. "What is it?"

He hung up and said, "Bekah said her dad came by the store. They went outside to talk about something. About ten minutes later, her dad drove off and Marly ran back inside crying and left so fast she forgot her jacket."

"Oh, no." Lola grabbed hold of Jed's arm. "I bet she's still upset at her house. I should go—"

"I'll go." I was already moving toward the door.

"But it's your Pop's birthday," argued Jed.

"Pop!" I shouted over to where he was reclining in his chair. "Marly's upset because her dad is an asshole, and I'm going to get her."

"Fine, son. We'll save some cake."

Then I was out the door. I knew my grandfather, and he wouldn't care if I left to fetch Marly. He loved her. He wouldn't shut up about her ever since that one visit to the house and then her sending her moonshine to him through me. He thought the sun rose and set with Marly Rivers.

And so did I. Which was why I couldn't just sit there and pretend I wasn't dying inside because my girl was crying her eyes out at home all alone.

It took me about eight minutes to get to her house. But when I pulled up, her truck wasn't there.

"What the hell?"

I hopped out and jogged up to the porch, peering in the window. Not sure what I was expecting to find, but I looked around anyway, hearing her dogs barking. However, they weren't coming to the door, which meant they were still in their kennels inside the house. She wouldn't have left them this long without taking them out.

That worry quickly morphed into terror. Something was definitely wrong.

I shot a text to Jed, telling him she wasn't here. And hadn't been here.

My phone rang suddenly. I was expecting it to be Jed, but I frowned down at Jackson James's name.

"Hey," I growled, heading back to my truck. "I'm glad you called. Marly's missing."

There was a pause.

"I was actually calling because I found something that I'm pretty sure could be yours."

"What are you talking about?"

"I've got a walkie-talkie that's the same brand you and Ben and the rangers use."

"Look on the back. I mark ours in metallic Sharpie. Does it have letters and numbers?"

"Yeah, it does."

"What does it say?"

I was breathing heavy as dread sank like a dagger into my heart, because I knew what he was going to say before he said it."

"WR-M1."

"That's Marly's. Where'd you find it, Jackson?" My knuckles cracked as my grip tightened on the steering wheel, adrenaline racing.

Another pause. "Wade, I need you to meet me at the junction near Bandit Lake."

"Where'd you find it?" My brain was spiraling, and my heart was ready to pound through my rib cage and right out of my body. "Tell me," I growled. "Tell me now or I'm going to lose my mind here."

He sighed. "I found it on the poachers. We got 'em."

I was backing out and tearing down the road before he could finish those two sentences.

"Don't move. I'm coming."

I raced in a blind madness, breaking every speed limit, as I tore across town and back out the other side to the junction Jackson was talking about. It was the one where the road split, one heading straight to the interstate. That meant Jackson caught them as they were almost out of town and likely heading home.

Why the fuck would these assholes have Marly's walkie-talkie? She kept it in her fucking truck. Scenarios that had me about to vomit in my cab pulsed furiously through my mind.

"No," I muttered, my knuckles white on the steering wheel. "Please let her be okay," I prayed, begging someone to hear me.

The darkness of the road lit up with the blinking blue lights of Jackson's police car. His deputy, Boone, was there too, standing outside Jackson's car. Ben was too. They must've called him before calling me.

Slamming the brakes on my truck as I raced up behind Ben's, I shoved it into park and stormed across the street.

"Hold on, Wade," Boone was telling me, but I didn't hear fucking anything.

All my focus was on the two men in the back of his vehicle, watching me come for them.

"Wade," Jackson warned.

They'd have to have superhuman strength to keep me from them. Jerking open the door to the backseat, I gripped the first guy by his jacket, hauled him out and practically carried him to the hood where I slammed him backwards and punched him twice—one near his eye, the other across the jaw—a desperate madness sweeping over me. I'm pretty sure I broke a knuckle.

"Where is she?!"

I was in a frenzy, fear and fury driving me with senseless rage. I barely registered the others shouting at me as I drew my fist back but someone caught my arm.

"Who, man?" the guy gurgled, gripping my wrist and trying to push me off. He wasn't handcuffed. "What are you talking about?"

"Wade!" shouted Jackson, holding my arm before I could land another one. "We'll do this down at the station."

"No," I growled down at the motherfucker beneath me, my free hand now around his throat. "He's going to tell me where she is right now." I leaned closer, knowing Jackson could hear me but really not giving a shit. "If you hurt her," I warned with cold menace, "I'll fucking kill you. No jail cell will hold me back."

The man who was easily near my size suddenly looked at me with true fear in his eyes, the left one starting to swell. He saw the truth. I wasn't playing around, wasn't making an empty threat. I clamped my fingers tighter around his throat.

"We didn't touch her!" he yelled, eyes round.

I eased up on his throat. "Where is she? How'd you get her radio?"

"She ran her truck off the road then took off into the woods."

My stomach fell with both relief and fear. These fuckers had scared her, so she'd ran. My fingers itched to close around his throat tighter, to make him hurt for that.

"I swear, I swear!" he yelled.

Apparently, my hand had tightened on its own.

I gripped him by the jacket with my one free hand since Jackson, smart man that he was, wasn't letting me go. I picked up the poacher and shoved him back down.

"Where?" I yelled.

"I don't know, man. I don't know the names of these fucking roads. Up the mountain."

"Jackson!" I yelled, fear spiking my nerves higher.

"Yeah." He was standing right behind me, still holding one of my arms to make sure I didn't actually kill a man in his custody but also giving me some leeway in my "questioning."

"You got a map?"

"I've got one," Ben volunteered.

Though I didn't want to, I hauled the asshole off of Jackson's hood, keeping one fist in his jacket. I glanced through the windshield to the backseat where the other poacher was watching with wide eyes. When he caught my gaze, he quickly looked away out the window.

Yeah, he better be fucking scared. This prick better not be lying either. If I find out they hurt her, I'd lose my mind for sure. I was terrified by the level of violence that coursed through me at the mere thought of it.

Ben quickly spread out the map. Boone shined a flashlight down onto it. I shoved the guy forward, finally letting him go.

"We're here," I pointed on the map. "The mountain highway is here. Show me where she got out."

The poacher leaned forward, rubbing his jaw where I'd punched him. "I'm pretty sure it was right in this area."

I stared down at the map to where he pointed, knowing he was telling the truth. That was the road that led to Pop's cabin.

"When you followed her and scared her," I said, looking him in the eye, watching the truth shine back at me that I was right, "which way did she turn off the main road. Left or right?"

He simply blinked at me, his breaths coming out in white puffs, obviously shocked that I'd figured out what had happened, what they'd done. But I didn't have time to mess with him anymore. I needed to find her.

"Left," I demanded coldly. "Or right."

"Left, left." He nodded shakily. "Definitely left."

I shoved off the hood. "Thank you, Jackson," was all I managed to say as I marched to my truck.

"We'll get them in custody and meet you up there," said Jackson. "Call me on the radio when you find her vehicle."

I turned to him and nodded, no longer able to speak.

"I'm coming with you," said Ben, jogging to his truck.

I didn't argue. We'd likely need a lot more to find her, depending where she was and how far she'd run.

I started my truck and did a U-turn, heading back up the mountain. The poacher had said she'd taken a left so that meant she'd turned onto one of the roads leading into the Pruitt property.

Passing up Y-tree Road leading to Pop's cabin, my gut clenched. I could imagine what had happened. She'd gotten in a fight with her dad, and she'd come up here to cry it out most likely. She loved that cabin. It made me both happy and sad because she wouldn't be in trouble if she hadn't loved the place so damn much.

Turning onto the first road that led to the Pruitt property, Ben right behind me, I slowed so that I didn't miss anything. Though I was pretty sure that I wouldn't miss her truck off in the ditch. My gut clenched at the thought that maybe she'd gone off and right down one of these hills to the bottom.

After three miles, I realized this wasn't the road. I slowed to a stop and used my radio to tell Ben, "This must not be the one. Let's turn around and go up to the next turn-off."

"Got it," he called back.

We turned back around, this time he was leading since he'd been behind me on the turn-around. When we headed down the second road, I was sure we might be on the wrong track again. Then Ben turned on his high-beams, and I saw it. A sliding gouge in the muddy gravel where a truck had turned onto a smaller gravel road.

Speeding up, I followed it. I didn't have to go far before that familiar white

F-150 appeared up ahead nearly flipped on its side in the ditch. My gut clenched with alarm for the tenth time tonight.

Quickly pulling over, I grabbed my big flashlight out the back and slid down into the ditch to peer in through the front windshield. I could smell peach moonshine before I saw the broken jars. Nothing else inside.

Swiveling my flashlight to the woods, I shouted, "Marly!"

Nothing. Only silence and darkness.

I rushed back to my truck, passing Ben who had his own flashlight pointed toward the woods. After grabbing a backpack from my truck which I kept a first-aid kit in and water—the basic survival kit—I slipped my arms through and walked back to Ben.

"Call the sheriff's office and tell them where we found Marly's truck and wait for them. There are flares in my truck to light up the road."

"What are you doing?"

I didn't even answer as I buckled the strap of the backpack across my chest.

"Wade, you should wait for them so we can get a plan together. You're the biggest planner I know, and this definitely needs a plan so we can do the search methodically."

"Ben." I finally looked up at him. "Marly is out there all alone in the cold, dark woods. No way in hell am I standing here and waiting." I lifted my radio to show him I had it then slid it in the holster on my belt. "Contact me when you get started and I'll tell you where I'm at." I glanced down at my compass watch, noting the road where I stood was northeast of the woods. "I'm going to get my girl."

Then I headed out into the darkness to find her.

CHAPTER 21

~MARLY~

Why didn't I pay more attention while watching all those episodes of *Survivor*? The drama was what kept me riveted, not the fire-making struggle. I wouldn't even know where to start to make a fire with a bow drill. Not that I could if I did. My fingers were curled into balls and aching with the frigid cold.

I now had the whole-body shivers as I curled up in my makeshift shelter. Well, if you could call a blanket of dry leaves a shelter.

I'd run a good long ways from those men before I finally stopped. When I did, I crouched and hid, waiting to hear them tromping closer. I never did. I never heard anything at all, not a shout from one to the other, no truck doors slamming, no engine revving. That's when I realized that in my adrenaline-fed flight, I'd wandered *far* away from the road.

I tried to backtrack, returning in the same direction I'd come. I used the light from my phone, which still had no cell service. Then I came upon a fork in the ravine I'd been following. I didn't remember a fork. I didn't remember much of anything besides blinding fear driving me farther and deeper into the woods.

I took one path till it dead-ended at a giant tree that had fallen across it, nearly giving me a heart attack because it looked like a giant bear in the dark, arms raised, which turned out to be branches jutting toward the night sky. I definitely didn't remember that being there.

When I backtracked again, my phone suddenly died. Without the light, I continued on a little farther, tripped and then slid down another hill, breaking my fall on a sharp branch or something and scratching up my bare forearm.

That's when I got really scared. I was well and truly lost. If I kept trying to stumble through the dark, I could possibly trip and break my neck. There were long falls out here, and I could stumble right off one and truly hurt myself. No telling how long it would take for someone to find me. *If* they found me.

I decided the best thing to do was to stay put and wait until daybreak. Then I'd set out again to try and find my way back.

I huddled myself against a giant oak tree trunk and scooped more dead leaves on top of me. My mind wandered back to those men, the poachers.

"What total assholes," I muttered, my chin shaking as I shivered violently, my voice sounding funny.

It wasn't enough that they were breaking the law, illegally killing a bear out on private property, but they chased me down to do who knows what and left me stranded out here. They had to know how potentially dangerous this was for me. Maybe that was the whole point. If I got well and truly lost and no one found me then…

Squeezing my eyes shut, I willed that horrific thought away. No way was I going to die out here. I'd wait till the sun started to rise then I'd walk till I found a road and find my way back down the mountain. If I didn't freeze to death.

Opening my eyes, I tilted my chin up, focusing on the stars straight up above me in the sky, the only light I had. They were so beautiful and bright. More so than the view from down in the valley with lights from the town dimming their luster. I focused on that, this little piece of beauty I got to see because I was out here in the dark by myself.

I'd never have seen how pretty the night sky is if I was safe and warm back home. Had to look on the bright side, no matter how teeny tiny the bright side was.

My teeth started clicking together again. I wondered if anyone travelled these roads and might happen to see my truck in the ditch.

"No," I mumbled.

I knew they didn't. Wade had said that the Pruitts never came out here anymore and this was their property. No one would find me. Definitely not tonight anyway.

"Not a problem," I told myself shakily. I'd find my own way out. This was not going to be the end of Marly Rivers.

My hands were turning numb. I pulled them inside my shirt and tucked them under my arms, hoping the skin-to-skin contact would help. But then my nose itched, so I shoved one back out so I could scratch it. Dried dirt came away under my fingernail.

I laughed at myself. My nose itched from the mud I'd caked on my face. I managed to find a semi-wet spot of mud in the ravine in my wanderings before I fell down this other hill. Then I'd put the mud on my face to prevent the mosquitos. That's what Jake said to do, and he was a smart kid. It was the only survival skill I had to keep my brain from spiraling into the terror of being alone in these very dark woods all by myself. That, and don't pee near your campsite.

Not that I had a campsite exactly, but I did have a leafy nest against this thick tree trunk. I sure as hell wasn't going to pee anywhere near it to attract a bear or mountain lion or something. I'm not sure I had any liquid left in me. The crying jag on my way up the mountain and the run through the woods had sweated out the last of any liquid I had left from my water at lunch today.

I scratched my chin, another glob of dirt crumbling away.

"There are no damn mosquitos." They'd freeze their wings off out here.

I shifted to pull my legs to my chest but an ache slowed my movements. My whole body felt sluggish. I was getting awfully cold. And sleepy.

"Sunrise might be too far away," I told myself, the fire and determination from earlier wilting.

I never was one to talk to myself but the quiet stillness in the dark was overwhelming. Terrifying. Hearing my own voice helped me feel not so alone even though I whispered so no animals would hear me. I was losing my voice anyway.

My mind drifted. I remembered that my gift for Pop was ruined

"Assholes," I muttered again.

Then I thought of the party. Wade would be upset when he saw that I was missing. So would Jed and Lola.

I sniffed, a stinging coming to my nose and eyes. Wade would come looking for me in the morning. I knew that he would.

That big, strong grumpy man wouldn't let me freeze to death out here. Then my mind really decided to torture me, dragging up the memory of him cradling me close against his chest on his motorcycle. The day I had a conniption fit about him thinking my plan for my own distillery was crazy.

He liked to call me Mad Marly. But when he said it, I didn't get any of the bad feelings I sometimes did when someone else said it with sarcasm or meanness. Wade said it with endearment and affection. With love. A tightening in my chest made my breath hitch. He loved me.

"I love him," I confessed to the dark. A tear slipped free, and I sucked in a jagged breath.

I loved him so much. I'd never been in love before. I didn't want to die out here before I told him. What if I did? What if he never knew that he was the best thing that ever happened to me? He and Jake. Their faces appeared in my mind, Jake laughing at me around the campfire in their backyard. Wade's mouth tilted with that lopsided smile that was filled with tender affection.

Then the tears really started to fall. Pitiful feelings of helplessness and grief swept through me at the thought of Wade finally finding my body curled up in a ball in a pile of dead leaves.

"No ma'am, Marly. Get your ass up," I ordered myself, sniffing.

Pain shot through my legs as I forced my body into a standing position. I couldn't feel my feet or my hands anymore, but I was still shivering. That was a good sign. It meant my body was trying to raise its core temperature. I learned that watching *Naked and Afraid*. Maybe I had learned something from watching those crazy shows.

I might be afraid but at least I'm not naked. And I sure as hell wasn't going to curl up in a ball and die on the side of a mountain.

Once standing, I marched in place a minute, the needle-like pinpricks filling my feet as I did. Good sign, though painful.

Marching felt stupid, so I decided to dance. But I needed music. My phone in my back pocket had been dead for hours. So I started to sing. Yeah, that would also scare away any critters out here nosy enough to come check out the human woman in the vicinity. Then I started dancing. My body felt warmer. It was working! I kept dancing and singing and thinking about Wade and Jake and getting back home to them.

~WADE~

WHEN I'D TREKKED down the incline of the road, I turned left at the bottom of the hill where a dried-up creek-bed was the only path to use with steep hills on both sides. After about a quarter mile though, I saw no signs of her having gone this way. No leaves disturbed, no tracks in the mud. If she'd been running in this direction to get away from the poachers, I'd have seen some sign of her. This ravine was the only path to take to move quickly.

Turning back the other direction, I retraced my steps and kept going. Then I saw it. My heart leaped into my throat as I knelt in the packed mud and river rock where a definite partial track of a Converse shoe I knew all too well had impacted. My pulse raced with hope.

"Hold on, sweetheart."

Moving more quickly, I kept my flashlight on the rocky creek-bed, thanking heaven and all the angels for the dry fall season we'd had, except for the one or two snows so far. It had allowed this creek to go dry so my girl had an even path to run and get away from those fuckers. The snows had melted, leaving just enough moisture for me to see that beautiful imprint of her foot in the mud.

In my other hand, I carried one of the battery-operated lanterns I'd bought for our at-home camping night. She'd be able to see the light easier from far away than the beam of my flashlight and could call to me if she spotted me from wherever she was in this darkness. The thought of her curled up and scared out here made my blood run cold.

Shaking that off because I couldn't focus otherwise, I thought about that night of camping in the backyard—our first date. Warmth spread inside me as I remembered how she'd talked and laughed and listened to Jake, how I didn't mind one bit that he'd taken all of her attention. And how she'd kissed me when she left. That was the night I knew she was meant for me, for both me and Jake.

That wild girl with the brightest smile in the world stole my heart. The strangest thing was when I realized it, I wasn't afraid at all. In fact, I was elated. It felt more right than any decision I'd made next to being the best father I could be for my son.

She was it for me, and there was no way in hell I was leaving these woods till I found her. I'd hiked at least a mile down the dry rock-bed. I'd seen one more track of her shoe, but that was a half a mile back. I paused, heaving white breaths into the air.

Looking up through the bare tops of trees to the starry night, I whispered "Where are you, Marly?"

Jackson, Boone, and Ben had organized a search party which included Jed and the firefighters and other deputies of Green Valley. They were making their way through the woods as well, but I'd only heard them once. They'd gone west, southwest, and northeast while I'd gone directly east. I wondered if they'd had any luck, but they'd radio me first thing if they had. She was still out here, and it had been hours. It was close to midnight now.

Maybe if I called out, she'd hear me. I was about to do just that when I heard something. A voice singing. Not just any voice. I followed it, back in the other direction. I left the creek-bed and caught myself at the edge of a drop-off before I walked right off of it.

Sliding the hook of the lantern over my forearm, I grabbed the trunks of slender trees to ease my way down to the bottom of the hill. Her voice was closer, my heart thumping so hard I felt it in my throat.

"Marly!" I called into the dark, but she kept singing.

Was I imagining this? Why would she be singing? I'd heard of strange things happening to people lost in the woods. The mind can conjure up all manner of fantasies and hallucinations to appease the psyche. I remember a hunter had gotten lost a few years ago. When we'd found him after he'd been alone for six days in the national park, he'd told us he'd managed to make it because the night fairies had come out and kept him company.

We'd gotten him to a hospital, but I remember how he'd looked so peaceful even after being near death from malnutrition. Was my brain forcing me to imagine what I was longing for? The sound of the woman I loved?

Then the song belted louder, off-key, and I nearly sobbed with relief because only Marly would be singing Meghan Trainor's "Dear Future Husband" in the woods all by herself.

I walked faster and made it to level ground again then strode fast toward the beautiful sound of Marly's horrible singing.

"Marly!" I called again, but she still didn't hear me, continuing to sing.

Rounding some thick brush, I finally saw her. I froze for a few seconds, making sure my eyes weren't playing tricks on me. Her hair was a god-awful mess, leaves sticking out and clinging to her short-sleeved shirt, even out of her collar. Her face and arms were caked in dried mud. And she was dancing with an invisible partner, eyes closed, moving this way and that, singing to her heart's delight like she was at a club and not near-frozen and lost in the middle of nowhere.

"Marly!"

She jumped and stopped, her eyes wide and terrified as she stared in my direction. I held up the lantern and hurried toward her. She stared in shock blinking quickly then whispered in the softest, saddest voice, "Wade?"

"Oh, baby." I dropped the lantern and flashlight and lunged the last step, scooping her up into my arms, lifting her feet off the ground. She shook with sobs as I rocked her against me. "I've got you, sweetheart. It's okay."

"You came for me?" she managed after a full minute, her voice breaking.

"Marly." I eased her down onto her feet and cupped the sides of her head, so happy to see her face even if it was in the dim lantern-light and apparently covered in dried mud for some reason. "I'll always come for you. Always."

"But how'd you find me? With that compass watch?"

Her gaze was bleary and confused and lost.

"That's not how a compass works, sweetheart." I was combing her hair back with one hand. It looked terrible, and I loved it. I didn't bother to explain that compasses can't guide you to a specific person if she wasn't aware of that. She seemed confused, in shock, possibly.

"Then how'd you find me?" She hiccupped.

"I don't know." I pressed a kiss to her forehead, not caring that it was caked with dirt. "You're my true north, Marly Rivers. I'll always find you."

Her shoulders shook and tears streaked through the dried mud on her face. "I was so scared."

"I know. I know. I'm here now."

"I thought I might die."

"No, baby. I'd never let that happen."

"I should've paid more attention watching *Naked and Afraid*."

"What?"

"I wanted to tell you something."

"I'm listening."

"I love you."

I stared down at her, face covered in mud, hair a horrific mess. She was the most beautiful sight I'd ever seen.

"I love you too, sweetheart. So much."

I pulled her into another tight hug. Her next sob turned into laughter, her face pressed to my chest. "Thought I was hallucinating when I heard you call my name."

"Why were you singing and dancing?"

"I was thinking about you." My heart sank then expanded in the same second. "And I didn't want to freeze to death before I could *tell* you I love you, so I had to move around."

"Oh, shit." I jerked back and pulled off my jacket, guiding her arms into the sleeves. I pulled off my gloves and forced her shaking fingers into them. "Come on. Let's get you home." I radioed first, holding her against me with one arm. "Jackson. I've got Marly. I found her."

A click of the radio on the other end and a sigh then, "Thank the Lord. We'll meet you back at the road. Calling paramedics now."

"It'll take me about forty-five minutes, I think, to make it to the main road," I said, checking my watch and the compass to see which direction to take. "I'll likely come out a mile farther down."

"We'll be waiting for you."

Marly didn't say a word, just shivered against me. I lifted her into my arms, another wave of deep, earth-shaking relief passing through me that I'd found her and she was going to be okay. We were going to be okay. She trembled, and so did I, but her arms came around my neck, and I laughed as I carried her back the way I'd come.

"Why're you laughing?" she asked, her voice soft and hoarse, but the sweetest sound I'd ever heard.

"Because I thought I'd stumbled up on baby bigfoot in the middle of the woods, singing about her future husband. Why are you covered in mud, Marly?"

"Jake told me it helped with the mosquitos."

"There are no mosquitos out this time of year."

"I know that now. But I'd already covered myself in mud by then. I wasn't thinking clearly."

I pressed a kiss to her temple and hugged her closer, basking in the feel of her body warming up next to mine.

"I was singing about you," she told me, again in that soft voice.

"Your future husband?" My heart galloped away.

"If you'll have me. One day."

"Future husband," I murmured against her ratty hair. "I like the sound of that."

I tromped on in silence, except for the sound of my boots carrying us out of here, knowing down to my bones that Marly Rivers was without a doubt my future wife. I'd found her and no way was I letting her get away.

"Thank you for coming and finding me," she said on another soft sniffle. She was crying again.

I squeezed her close and pressed my mouth to the crown of her head. "I would've looked forever, love. I'd never leave you alone out here."

That made her cry harder. "I love you, Wade."

"I love you too, sweetheart."

Then I carried my girl out of the dark woods and back home with me where she belonged.

EPILOGUE
~WADE~

One Year Later...

Smiling, I walked under the sign reading *Mad Marly's Moonshine* and opened the door to a sweet sight—a bustling Saturday at the newest moonshine distillery in Green Valley. Taking a look around, my heart burst with pride.

She did it. Not that I ever truly doubted her because when that woman gets something into her head, it's going to happen one way or another. For a second, I simply soaked it all in.

Customers ambled from one shelf and display to another. Jed's dad and Lola's Aunt Polly, who were hinting there would be a wedding soon, meandered around the pyramid display of Pop's Peaches and Dreams, the first-place winner of the Green Valley Shine Amateur Moonshine Contest last year. Chase was there, chatting with them, seemingly proud that his peaches were a key ingredient.

Then there was the postal worker who delivered in Marly's neighborhood, Gwen, and her new man, Sebastian, a paramedic from the fire station at another display. He'd helped the night we all searched for Marly in the woods. Though I was happy to be the one who'd found her, I was so grateful to every single man and woman who'd helped that night. It reminded me yet again how quickly our community came together to help a friend in need, yet another reason I loved this town and planned to raise Jake in it. I planned to raise our future children here too.

Gwen and Sebastian were checking out the wall of Marly's newest flavor, Coffee Caramel Swirl, which she said I'd inspired that one night I'd made her coffee moonshine as a nightcap. It was before we'd started dating but it was also the night when I was positive that my interest in her was more than friendly.

Bekah and Kayla had both left Green Valley Shine to work for Marly, her only two employees at the moment. Marly knew already, but starting your own business had nearly worn her out. There had been more than one night where I'd had to come to the store and make her leave with me when she'd missed dinner at my house.

She was expected over for dinner every night now. Sometimes she happened to sleep over, and that was fine by me. The first time she had and wandered into the kitchen in one of my t-shirts and boxers—yes, she'd swiped them both from my dresser without asking—Jake had asked excitedly, "You're sleeping over at our house now?"

She'd gotten that shy, unsure look and replied, "If that's okay with you."

Of course, Jake had smiled wide and said, "That's great by me."

And so it was settled. Marly was permanent in our lives, and I couldn't be happier. Neither could Jake, because that meant Scooter and Pooter had also become his dogs too.

Well, I could actually be happier. Once I got a ring on her finger and she moved in for good, then my world would be complete. That day was coming soon with Christmas around the corner.

Nana was leading Pop toward the back of the store where I could see Marly talking to a small group, but Pop pulled her to a stop to swipe a jar of his namesake peach moonshine as he passed, grinning like the proud grandpa he was.

Knowing they were waiting on me, I headed to the back corner where the tasting bar had been constructed. Jake was talking to Jed who nodded and appeared interested in whatever he was saying. Or pretended to be anyway. Lola and Kayla were helping Marly behind the bar, setting tiny glass mugs on the counter.

That was different. Moonshine was only tasted in shot glasses at most distilleries, and today she was revealing her newest flavor to the family and whoever else happened to be in the store.

Glancing around, I wished Marly's family had come. Her parents and sister and her family had come to the ribbon-cutting three weeks ago. Her mother and sister seemed genuinely happy, but it was obvious her father still had reservations even though he had given her a hug and congratulated her. She'd told me she knew he was waiting for it to fail so he could say he told her so.

I don't know what it was about some parents. They only saw their own path of success for their children. Eventually, when she was opening up her second store, he might finally admit she was doing alright with her little dream. Because whether Marly knew it or not, her store was a huge hit in town. She'd expand eventually. Probably sooner than she imagined.

Everywhere I went, someone told me they'd stopped in and bought one of her moonshines and how good it was. I suppose everyone thought I was her keeper and they needed to inform me of how well she was doing.

They didn't need to tell me. Marly was amazing, and I was hoping that come Christmas I could officially call myself her keeper. Or, her future keeper anyway. Maybe she and Lola could plan their weddings together since Lola and Jed had finally set a date for next fall. Took them long enough.

Lola's Aunt Polly and Mr. Lawson wandered into the tasting area behind me.

"It's good to see you, Wade."

"You too, Mr. Lawson. Ms. Polly."

Mr. Lawson clapped me on the shoulder. "So when are you going to take care of business and put a ring on that girl's finger." He nodded toward Marly who hadn't noticed me yet.

I laughed. Seemed everyone had the same idea as me. "Soon, I hope."

Christmas morning was my plan, but I wasn't telling anybody. She would be the first to know, except for Jake. I wanted his blessing, but I had absolutely zero worries that he would give it gladly.

At that moment, Marly looked up from the counter where she had a sign on an easel covered in a towel and a stack of moonshine along the bar also covered in towels. My girl liked to do a big reveal for new flavors. She was a bit dramatic, and that was fine by me. I needed a little dramatic. I needed Marly.

For this reveal, she'd asked me to make sure Jake was here so he had come with Pop and Nana since I was needed at the office a few hours this morning.

Marly rounded the tasting bar and hurried into my arms. "Hey," she pecked me on the lips. "I was wondering when you'd get here."

"I'm not late."

"Yeah, but I'm excited and you know when I'm excited about a new flavor I can barely hold onto the secret."

"Well, let's get to the reveal." I turned her and swatted her behind.

"Wade," chastised Nana, frowning at me.

Pop barely cracked a smile but he gave me a wink before turning his attention back to the front.

"Thank you for coming, everyone," she called to the room, needing no microphone to get her voice to reach the back. "Today is a special reveal for Mad Marly's Moonshine because it isn't a moonshine at all."

I frowned, because I had no idea what she was revealing. This was one she'd kept secret even from me.

"Jake, can I have my favorite little man come up to the front."

My son was not shy, but being called front and center of everyone's attention, he blushed pink all the way to the tips of his ears as he wandered up to her.

"Jake," Marly put her arm over his shoulder while she had him face us, "I made this flavor especially for you. And because you can't drink moonshine, this one is non-alcoholic."

"Um, Marly?" Jake mumbled hesitantly.

"Yes?"

"If it doesn't have alcohol then it isn't actually moonshine."

A wave of light laughter filled the back of the store as other customers gathered.

"You're right, little man." She ruffled his hair. "But I'm making this exception for you."

His smile reappeared, big and wide.

Marly turned toward her small audience, gaze lingering on me. "Without further ado, I'd like to reveal our first non-alcoholic drink that is not actually moonshine as Jake Kelley so gracefully announced," she whipped off the towel from the easel while Lola and Zoe lifted the towels from the jars on the back bar, "Christmas Campout!" She put her arm back around Jake. "And it tastes like s'mores. Also, a big thank you to my bestie Lola who helped with the packaging on this one."

There was a smattering of applause and an *oooo* from my Nana who bustled up front before anyone else. My Nana loved chocolate.

I stood there while everyone chatted and moved close to the bar for samples while Lola and Kayla poured them. The jars were topped with red and white gingham with a sprig of holly, and the labels had an icon of a campfire on one side and a s'more on the other. As I moved closer, I could see the printed "Kid Friendly" below the scripted title of the drink.

I watched as Marly beamed under the praise from our family and her customers who were now all tasting the chocolatey drink. And how smart to sell a non-alcoholic drink that was perfect for the holidays. Mad Marly's was already expanding to create for the underage customers. Great idea, since families and tourists liked to browse the downtown area of Green Valley.

"It's delicious!" shouted Jake, a chocolate mustache on his upper lip.

She cupped his cheeks and leaned down, planting a kiss on his forehead. "I'm so glad you like it, Jake."

Then she wandered to the back of the crowd to me. "What do you think?"

Pulling her into me, I said, "I think you're amazing."

Her blue eyes crinkled with joy. "I think you're pretty amazing, too."

"Then it's official. Move in with me."

She laughed, used to this demand from me. She answered in her usual way. "Not a chance, Daddy Bear. Not until we're engaged at least."

"Fine then," I grumbled, like that was far away. It wasn't though. Christmas was around the corner.

"Oh, look! Dad, Marly, look!" Jake ran by us and straight to the window overlooking downtown Green Valley. "It's snowing!"

"Our first snow," said Lola, taking Jed by the hand and dragging him outside to follow Jake who'd fled out the door with his jug of Christmas Campout.

I took Marly's hand and pulled her outside too. A few others had wandered out to see. Green Valley was beautiful on any day, but with the snow falling and blanketing it in white fluffy flakes, it was even more lovely.

We stood under the awning of her store and watched Jake do circles in the parking lot, having set his mug on the ground. He stared up, arms and mouth open wide, catching snowflakes.

I set my chin on Marly's head as we watched him. "Reminds me of the first snow last year up at Pop's cabin."

Her arms were under my jacket I was still wearing and clasped around my waist. "You remember that?"

I peered down at her and lifted her chin up so she'd look at me. "Do I remember the day I fell in love with you? Yeah. I remember it."

Her smile widened, eyes blinking rapidly at the moisture gathering. "I love it when you're like this."

"Like what?"

"All uncharacteristically sweet."

"I'm sweet," I argued.

"Oh, I know. I've tasted you."

"Marly," I hissed a warning.

"Kinda salty actually." She waggled her eyebrows. "But you're my favorite flavor."

"Stop right now or we're going to have a problem."

"A *big* problem? You promise?"

"Hell, woman." I exhaled a heavy sigh, fighting back a smile and losing.

"If I'd known that underneath all this grumpy bear was a soft, sexy one I'd have come after you a long time ago."

"Nah." I eased my face closer to hers, taking in those pretty eyes that I loved having fixed on me. "We found each other right when we were supposed to."

"As long as we found each other."

"We did." I pressed a tender kiss to her sweet mouth. "And I'm not letting you go, Mad Marly."

Her smile widened, blue eyes glinting with happiness. "If that's the truth, then one day I'm going to give you some wild and crazy kids. You okay with that?"

"Jake and I both are more than okay with that."

I thought she couldn't smile any bigger, but she did anyway, burrowing deeper into my heart and warming my soul.

"What did you say the first snow was like that day?"

Her brow pinched in concentration then she said, "It's like hope and happiness floating down. Like a blessing."

I grunted. "Well, I definitely feel blessed, *darlin'*."

She got that mischievous feline look on her face. "Say that again."

I'd said it in the first place because I knew it got her all hot and bothered. Dipping my head, I whispered in her ear, "I love you, darlin'."

Then I kissed her again, and we simply held each other and watched our little man dance and twirl in the first snow of the season, truly content in knowing that there were many more to come.

ACKNOWLEDGMENTS

A special thank you goes to *Penelope Reid*, for giving me the opportunity and the gift of writing in her beautiful world, Green Valley. It has been an honor, a privilege, and a pleasure.

To *Brooke Nowiski* and *Fiona Fischer*, the dynamic duo who run Smartypants Romance like a well-oiled machine. Thank you for being my guides and my friends as an SPR author.

And to all of the Smartypants Romance readers, thank you for spending time with and giving love to my characters. Lola, Jed, Wade, and Marly will forever be near and dear to my heart.

And take my advice, sex nachos for the win, y'all! 😉

ABOUT THE AUTHOR

JULIETTE CROSS is a multi-published author of paranormal and fantasy romance & the co-host of the podcast, Smart Women Read Romance. As a native of Louisiana, she lives in the heart of Cajun land with her husband, four kids, her labs, Kona and Jeaux, and kitty, Betty. When she isn't working on her next project, she enjoys binge-watching her favorite shows with her husband and a glass (or two) of red wine.

Find Juliette Cross online:
Website: https://www.juliettecross.com/
Newsletter: https://bit.ly/3HwQgXb
Facebook: https://www.facebook.com/juliettecrossauthor
Goodreads: https://www.goodreads.com/author/show/7795664.Juliette_Cross
Twitter: https://twitter.com/Juliette__Cross
Instagram: https://www.instagram.com/juliettecrossauthor/
Amazon: http://www.amazon.com/Juliette-Cross/e/B00MQ18Z1W/

Find Smartypants Romance online:
Website: www.smartypantsromance.com
Facebook: www.facebook.com/smartypantsromance/
Goodreads: www.goodreads.com/smartypantsromance
Twitter: @smartypantsrom
Instagram: @smartypantsromance

ALSO BY JULIETTE CROSS

BEAUVILLE SERIES:

• *Bright Like Wildfire*

STAY A SPELL SERIES:

• *Wolf Gone Wild*

• *Don't Hex and Drive*

• *Witches Get Stitches*

• *Always Practice Safe Hex*

• *Walking in a Witchy Wonderland: Holiday Anthology*

• *Resting Witch Face*

• *Grim and Bear It*

NIGHTWING SERIES:

• *Soulfire*

• *Windburn*

• *Nightbloom*

VALE OF STARS SERIES:

• *Dragon Heartstring: Prequel*

• *Waking the Dragon*

• *Dragon in the Blood*

• *Dragon Fire*

• *Hunt of the Dragon*

THE VESSEL TRILOGY:

• *Forged in Fire*

• *Sealed in Sin*

• *Bound in Black*

ALSO BY SMARTYPANTS ROMANCE

<u>Green Valley Chronicles</u>

<u>The Love at First Sight Series</u>

Baking Me Crazy by Karla Sorensen (#1)

Batter of Wits by Karla Sorensen (#2)

Steal My Magnolia by Karla Sorensen (#3)

Worth the Wait by Karla Sorensen (#4)

<u>Fighting For Love Series</u>

Stud Muffin by Jiffy Kate (#1)

Beef Cake by Jiffy Kate (#2)

Eye Candy by Jiffy Kate (#3)

Knock Out by Jiffy Kate (#4)

<u>The Donner Bakery Series</u>

No Whisk, No Reward by Ellie Kay (#1)

Dough You Love Me? By Stacy Travis (#2)

Tough Cookie by Talia Hunter (#3)

<u>The Green Valley Library Series</u>

Love in Due Time by L.B. Dunbar (#1)

Crime and Periodicals by Nora Everly (#2)

Prose Before Bros by Cathy Yardley (#3)

Shelf Awareness by Katie Ashley (#4)

Carpentry and Cocktails by Nora Everly (#5)

Love in Deed by L.B. Dunbar (#6)

Dewey Belong Together by Ann Whynot (#7)

Hotshot and Hospitality by Nora Everly (#8)

Love in a Pickle by L.B. Dunbar (#9)

Not Fooling Anyone by Allie Winters (#2)

Can't Fight It by Allie Winters (#3)

The Vinyl Frontier by Lola West (#4)

Out of this World

London Ladies Embroidery Series

Neanderthal Seeks Duchess by Laney Hatcher (#1)

Well Acquainted by Laney Hatcher (#2)

Love Matched by Laney Hatcher (#3)